Murder To Go
A University Mystery

Brenda Donelan

Murder To Go

This book is dedicated to everyone who read my first two books.

Thanks for sticking with me!

Table of Contents

It's better to have loved and lost than never to have loved at all.

Or is it?

Chapter 1

She didn't mean to hit him with her car. Really, she didn't.

As she drove her mud-caked SUV through the historical district in Elmwood, South Dakota, she heard a distinctive thud on the front passenger side of her vehicle. She was so busy looking at the stately home in need of repairs that she never saw the jogger crossing the street in front of her. The jogger never saw her either; because it was dark and she was cruising by with her lights off so as not to draw the attention of those in the older home.

Marlee McCabe was on her usual stalking run, checking for any sign of Vince Chipperton at the home he shared with his brother. The thirty-eight-year-old professor was interested in the handsome probation officer, and drove by his home several nights per week. She had known Vince for a few years, starting when she worked at the Federal Probation Office in Elmwood. At that time, he was employed with the state probation

BRENDA DONELAN

agency in town, so their paths crossed once in a while. After a few years, Marlee left her job at probation and eventually started teaching at Midwestern State

University. Vince applied to be a federal probation officer and was hired there, essentially filling the position Marlee once held.

Marlee was taken with the tall, dark haired man the first time she met him. He was quiet, mysterious, and did not pay much attention to Marlee, so she was immediately intrigued. Over the years, he was in a relationship while Marlee was single, and then when he broke up with his girlfriend, Marlee had a boyfriend. Neither of them were in a relationship now and Marlee thought if she had a bit more intel on Vince, she might be able to capture his interest. Thus, the drive-bys at his home and the frequent stops at his office.

After hearing the thud and seeing a hint of an orange glove from the glow of a distant street light, Marlee screeched to a halt. She sprang from the SUV, leaving the engine running, and crossed in front of her vehicle to determine the damage.

"Oh my god!" Marlee exclaimed as she saw a body slumped on the street beside her Honda CR-V. The person splayed on the ground was dressed in a dark jacket and sweatpants. As she knelt down beside the person, she heard a groan and saw the movement of a leg.

"Are you okay? I'm calling an ambulance right now," Marlee stammered as she fished around in her coat pocket for her cell phone.

"No. No, don't do that," croaked a male voice. "I'll be alright." As he struggled to prop himself into an upright sitting position, Marlee saw that it was none other than Vince Chipperton.

8

"Vince, is that you?" Marlee asked, grabbing his elbow and helping him sit against the front passenger side tire of the vehicle.

"Yeah?" Vince said, not knowing who she was, nor quite comprehending that he had just been hit by a moving vehicle.

"Vince, it's me. Marlee McCabe. From Midwestern State University. A friend of Aleece Jorgenson, your co-worker at probation. Remember?" Marlee asked, alarmed and embarrassed, but also a little exhilarated since she was talking to the guy she'd been stalking. And she was touching his elbow!

"Oh. Yeah," Vince mumbled, touching his left ankle and then wincing. "Why are you driving with your lights off?"

Marlee was not going to tell him why she drove with her lights off when she passed his house in hopes that she could see him, yet not wanting him or his neighbors to become suspicious with her frequent drive-bys. "Uh, guess I forgot to turn them on when I got in my car," she lied.

Vince struggled, with Marlee's help, to get to his feet. His left ankle was either broken or severely sprained and Marlee insisted on driving him to the emergency room. With a degree of reluctance, he finally agreed and she assisted him into her SUV.

Two hours later, Marlee took Vince back to his house. The X-rays indicated he had a badly sprained ankle that happened when he fell to the ground after being struck with Marlee's car. He also had some bumps and bruises along his ribcage from the impact of the vehicle. Vince, with the aid of crutches, was able to navigate his way from the car to the sidewalk, up the short flight of stairs, and into the large house. Marlee followed him, insisting she wanted to make sure he got inside without any problems.

Spud Chipperton, Vince's older brother, reclined before the enormous television in their living room. "Jeez, Vince. What happened to you? And who's this lovely lady?"

"I was out for a run and she hit me with her car. This is Mary McDonald," Vince said easing himself into the green matching Lay-Z-Boy next to his brother.

"Um, it's Marlee McCabe," Marlee corrected. "And I don't know that I *hit* you, so much as you ran into my vehicle."

"She was driving with her lights off and her SUV is gray," Vince focused his dreamy blue eyes on Marlee as he talked. His tone was not accusatory. He was merely stating the facts as they happened, which were wildly different from Marlee's account of the incident.

"Marlee McCabe." Spud looked at her with a creepy yearning in his eyes. As much as she was attracted to Vince Chipperton, she was equally repulsed by his brother. Spud was true to his nickname; he had the physical characteristics of a potato and the personality to match. He wore stained jeans, a red flannel work shirt, and light gray socks that were originally white. The house reeked of the sauce from buffalo wings, and a paper plate loaded with wing bones was balanced on a stand next to Spud.

"I like your red hair. You must be Irish. Or Scottish." Spud leered at Marlee like a wolf eyeing a lamb.

"Irish," Marlee said, wishing she had put a baseball cap on over her wavy auburn hair before she left home. She always tried to fix herself up a bit before she drove by Vince's house, just in case he saw her driving by or there was some opportunity for her to stop. Although her efforts in grooming did not make much of an impression on Vince, Spud sure seemed to be taking the bait.

Marlee recognized Spud, as he frequented one of the drinking establishments where she and her friends gathered. He lurked around the bar, repeatedly asking women to dance until the bouncer took notice and forced Spud to leave them alone. Marlee and her friends had been on the receiving end of this unwanted attention on two separate occasions. As much as she wanted to stay at the house and tend to Vince, the professor knew she needed to leave before his creepy brother propositioned her.

"Well, it looks like you're all settled in, Vince. I'll check on you later to make sure you're doing okay." Marlee inched her way toward the door. Vince was already slouched in the chair with his leg elevated on the built-in footstool. He was given a pain pill at the emergency room and it appeared he was only minutes away from falling asleep. Spud, on the other hand, was wide awake and ready to chat.

"When do you think you'll be back?" Spud asked. He worked as a machinist at a factory and although his work schedule was not that flexible, he could trade shifts with a co-worker when necessary. Marlee suspected if she pinpointed a day and time she would return, Spud would be there waiting to greet her.

"Um, I don't know for sure. I'll just play it by ear. Bye." Marlee was at the front door and left before Spud could engage her in further conversation. She jumped into the small SUV and sped off, this time with her lights in the on position.

Now Marlee no longer needed to stalk Vince from afar. She had a bona fide reason to go to his house and his place of employment. As his ankle healed, he was eventually able to laugh about the whole incident, although he maintained Marlee struck him with her vehicle. Marlee argued that he ran right into her car because he didn't look where he was running. Vince finally learned Marlee's name and after two weeks of stopping by his home and work, he asked her out on a date. One date led to another, and within the month they were exclusive.

Marlee was on top of the world and she paraded her new beau around campus like a trophy. The only real problem she found with the relationship was Spud Chipperton. He tried to insert himself into their dates whenever he could manage it. She tired of Spud going with them to movies and out to supper. Three was a crowd. Part of it was loneliness on Spud's part, but Marlee had the feeling he secretly wished for the demise of her relationship with his brother. Marlee stopped going over to the Chipperton house and just had Vince come to her place as a way of avoiding Spud. She didn't know how to tell Vince of her dislike of his brother, so she kept it to herself.

Spud, on the other hand, made his feelings about Marlee very clear when Vince was out of earshot. On several occasions, he brought up the names of Vince's past girlfriends and how beautiful they all were. Spud more than insinuated Marlee would be better off with him than Vince. If Spud couldn't have her, then he'd make damn sure that Vince couldn't either.

Karma will bite you in the ass.
Every. Damn.
Time.

Chapter 2

The spring 2006 semester ended with a bang. Ira Green, the Dean of the College of Arts and Sciences and Marlee's boss, had threatened Marlee with non-renewal of her teaching contract the previous fall because she had failed to comply with his directives. He instructed her not to become involved in the Shane Seaboy murder investigation on campus, an instruction which she promptly disregarded. Marlee also engaged in some questionable behavior, such as asking students to help her with her own personal investigation into Seaboy's death. The matter went before the disciplinary board and Marlee was allowed to remain teaching until May of 2006. After that, it was to be determined if she would be offered a contract for the upcoming year.

The spring semester ended and Marlee had one class left to teach. It was held during the two-week break between the end of the spring semester and the start of summer school. The class was called Criminal Justice To

Go and involved Marlee taking students on a tour of prisons, jails, treatment centers, and juvenile homes in South Dakota. The class was developed by her predecessor and was popular with traditional-aged students and non-trads alike.

As much as she detested dealing with Dean Green, Marlee knew she needed to approach him for signatures on paperwork authorizing Criminal Justice To Go. Without his authorization, she wouldn't get paid for the class, and getting paid was something Marlee had become accustomed to. She hiked the stairs in Scobey Hall to the dean's office and knocked on the door. There was no answer and Louise, the department secretary, was nowhere to be found. Marlee thumbed through the stacks of papers and letters in her mailbox in the outer office while she waited for either Louise or the dean to appear.

"Hey, *girrrrl*," drawled Della Halter as she marched into the department office. Della was from Georgia and fancied herself hip on the lingo of the day— that day being about ten years earlier. "If you're lookin' for the dean, you won't find him."

"Why? Where's he at?" Marlee wondered how Della always managed to find out so much campus information. She didn't have close friends at the university and wasn't aligned with any individual or group. Yet, Della knew what was happening to whom and why. When questioned about the gossip she reported, Della never named her sources.

"Last I heard he was over at the president's office, answering some questions about his behavior," Della said, waiting for Marlee to ask for details.

"Oh, I figured his rough language would get him into trouble sooner or later. He really needs to watch his mouth when he's talking to certain people." Marlee had been the recipient of Dean Green's various rants, many of which involved the F word and other choice words. She guessed Mean Dean Ira Green used his foul, tactless language when addressing President Ross, and the president was calling him to task for it.

"Nope. Not even close. Green was accused of sexual harassment by somebody at the library," Della said, standing just a bit taller with pride that she had information and was able to share it. After all, knowledge was power and that was something Della sought.

"What? When? Who? At the MSU library?" Marlee could not ask her questions quickly enough.

"You bet your ass! It was Roxie Harper. You know her, she's a criminal justice major and she's also a work-study student at the campus library. Roxie's a non-trad, probably in her early thirties. She said good morning to the dean when he walked in, and he grabbed her, and gave her a big bear-hug and a kiss on the lips. No one else was around to see it, so we only know what Roxie had to say about it. Here's the funny thing: Dean Green doesn't deny it. He said he hugged her, but denies it was sexual harassment. Said he was just being friendly and she's taking it all wrong."

"Sure, I know Roxie. She took my Intro to Criminal Justice class last fall and she's taking Criminal Justice To Go with me starting next week. When did this incident happen?" Marlee asked.

"A week ago, from what I heard. Today Green is meeting with President Ross, the VP, and Human Resources to figure out what's going on," Della reported.

"Where did you find this out?" Marlee asked.

Della raised her eyebrows, sporting a cagey grin.

"What do you think will happen with Dean Green?" Marlee asked. She had not heard of this type of behavior on campus since she'd been there and had no idea what the outcome would be.

"Probably a slap on the wrist. He's not real well-liked by Administration, but he gets things done so they tolerate him. Plus, everybody knows how slutty the campus librarians and work-study students over there are, so I doubt anyone will take it very seriously that Dean Green put the moves on one of them. My guess is that he'll try to say it was mutual, or she encouraged him."

Marlee shook her head, knowing all too well how the dean's behavior would be handled. Nothing would be done to him personally while all faculty, staff, and some administrators would have to undergo sexual harassment training during in-service at the beginning of the fall semester—and probably every in-service after that for the foreseeable future.

"Well, I have to finish up grading finals for one last class and then I'm done," Marlee eased her way toward the doorway. Della was not the easiest person from which to escape. If Della wanted to continue a conversation, then it would carry on until she was bored or had to tend to a teaching responsibility.

"I have all of my finals left to grade. I have the worst fucking gas I've ever had in my life." No topic was off limits for Della. "Not only gas, but I've been on the pot all morning. Think I might just go home. The grading can wait."

Marlee exited the department secretary's office, but not before catching wind of Della's aforementioned flatulence. Holding her breath until she rounded the corner, Marlee hurried back to her office. Her door was locked and she searched for the keys in her jacket pocket. Unattended grades and tests in open offices had a way of becoming compromised, so most profs were cautious about leaving their offices unattended for very long, especially around test times or when grading was taking place.

As Marlee sat in her office, she reflected on her conversation with Della. The dean had gotten himself into some hot water and, even though he would probably have little in the way of consequences for his actions, he was still being asked to explain his behavior to the university president. A small smile crept to the female professor's lips as she thought about the stress and troubles Mean Dean Green had caused her over the past three years and how he was now getting a taste of his own medicine. She would have to remind herself not to gloat the next time she saw that evil bastard!

Later that day, Marlee did indeed have a conversation with Dean Ira Green. She stopped by his office again and his door was ajar. He was sitting at a round wooden table piled with maps and atlases. Dean Green held his head in one hand as he slumped over the table, peering at the bevy of maps. For the first time since Marlee had known him, the dean looked defeated. Had he not been such a horse's ass to her since she started at MSU, she might have felt sorry for him.

The knock on the door frame brought Dean Green into an upright sitting position. He glared at Marlee with his usual level of disdain. "What do you want, McCabe?"

"I need to get your signatures on some papers for my Criminal Justice To Go class. Since it's a class offered during the May interim, I need to complete special paperwork in order to get paid," Marlee said, pushing two documents toward him on the table.

"So you leave on Monday and you take students to these prisons, and jails, and whatnot. What do you require of them other than just touring?" Dean Green's voice was accusatory. This was not the first time Marlee taught the class, so she was puzzled by the dean's questions. Had he not read the documentation she submitted in previous years concerning the class?

"In addition to participating in all the tours and asking questions, students have to write two papers. One is based on a book I selected dealing with the correctional system. The second requirement is a reaction paper based on the tours. I provide them with a list of things I want them to respond to in their reaction paper. Plus, each night after we've finished with our tours, we have a group meeting to process what they observed and experienced."

"The vice-president is requiring all of the deans to provide more accountability for the classes in each of our colleges. For your Criminal Justice To Go class, I'll need a list of every town you'll be staying in and the motels you'll be at each night along with an estimated time that you and the students will check in." The dean looked Marlee square in the eye, not blinking even once as he rattled off his list of demands.

"That's shouldn't be too hard to provide. I already have a list of the towns we're staying on a previous document I submitted to you. I can email you the names of the hotels. The times we arrive might be a bit harder to get to you, but I can give you an estimate," Marlee said. The last thing she needed was a hiccup in the paperwork portion of developing the class, especially since it was starting in three days.

"Fine. I need it right now!" Dean Green growled as he returned to his study of maps on the round table. He looked up when Marlee did not leave. "What else do you need?" The old Mean Dean Green was back. He was surly as ever, which made Marlee feel like a fool for feeling a twinge of empathy for him when she entered his office.

"I just wanted to say that I'm sorry for all your troubles going on right now." Marlee could not help herself. Dean Green already had a knife stuck in him and the professor could not resist giving it a little twist.

"Sorry, my ass! Get the fuck out!" Dean Green shouted as he waved her away from his door and resumed looking at the pile of maps.

Marlee rounded the corner to her office with a smile on her face. She normally did not take pleasure in the suffering of other people, but Dean Ira Green hardly counted as a human being.

When it comes to old buildings, there's nothing to be afraid of. They're creaky and rickety, but rarely dangerous. The same can be said about old people. Well, most old people.

Chapter 3

The sun was shining, the birds were chirping, and it was a perfect day to be outside, enjoying one of the first nice spring days Elmwood had seen this year. Marlee was in her office with the harsh fluorescent lighting, staring at a pile of exams that needed grading. It would not be that difficult, she just wasn't motivated to do the work. Especially on such a nice day.

Marlee turned away from her grading and turned toward her computer. She emailed Dean Green the requested list of towns the Criminal Justice To Go students would be visiting, the hotels where they were staying, and their estimated time they would finish each day. Every time she taught the class, she had one more hoop to jump through. As she pushed the send button, she hoped this was the last of the extra paperwork requirements the dean had for this class. She would stop down to his office later to pick up the signed documents she needed to begin on Monday.

After looking at the pile of exams one more time, Marlee decided to take them home. The final grades were not due in the registrar's office until the following Wednesday, but by that time, she would be on the road with her Criminal Justice To Go class and didn't want to be hampered by grading responsibilities. Gathering up the exams and shoving them in her book bag, Marlee locked her office door and proceeded to the parking lot. After realizing she parked in the back lot that morning and not the front lot, she walked the opposite direction to the correct location of her car. This was not the first time Marlee parked on campus and then forgot where she parked. With over three thousand students and a few hundred employees, locating a specific vehicle was not easy if the driver forgot where she parked.

It was only 1:00 p.m., but Marlee grabbed a Bud Light bottle from her fridge and took the bag of exams out to the patio table with the huge unopened umbrella. She sat in one chair and propped up her feet on another, her pale calves exposed to the bright sun as her capris pants rode up almost to her knees. As she looked at her sandal-clad feet, Marlee noted that it was indeed time for a pedicure.

Marlee unwrapped the sandwich she bought on her way home. After finishing the meatball sub and the Bud Light, she unpacked the exams and began grading. After three exams, her red pen ran out of ink and she rummaged around in her book bag until she found another. Noting the heat of the day, Marlee went inside and fetched another Bud Light bottle and brought it back to the patio.

It was Marlee's next door neighbor, Sofie, who woke her up. The heavy sandwich along with two beers and the warm sun had put the professor to sleep. A breeze had come up and ruffled a few of the exams from the patio table to Marlee's back yard.

"Whoa! Guess I dozed for a bit. Thanks for waking me up, Sofie. Don't want these tests blowing all over the neighborhood," Marlee said as she jumped out of her chair to retrieve them.

"Looks like you got some sun," Sofie commented as she walked from her detached garage to her house.

"I've just been out here since one o'clock, so not much," Marlee said.

"It's four o'clock now," Sofie stated. "You might want to put something on your face to cool down that burn." With that bit of advice, Sofie walked in the unlocked back door to her house and shut the door behind her.

After gathering up all of the papers, Marlee walked inside to take a look at her burn. Three hours was a long time to be in the sun, especially with her fair complexion, but it was the beginning of spring and the sun probably was not all that strong yet. She gasped when she peered in the bathroom mirror at the tomato-red face staring back at her.

"Oh my god!" Marlee glanced away from the mirror to look at her legs and feet, which had also been exposed to the sun for three hours. They were even redder than her face. Her feet were beginning to swell from the sun damage and her sandals cut into the seared flesh atop her feet. She rummaged around in the linen closet and found a large bottle of aloe which had expired only a year ago. She poured a giant dollop into her right hand and rubbed it all over her face. Then she repeated the action on her lower legs and feet. Even though she looked terrible, she was not in any pain.

The next morning was an entirely different story. Marlee's face, neck, arms, lower legs, and feet burned with an intensity she had not felt since the mid-1980s when she coated herself with baby oil, put lemon juice in her hair, and laid out in the summer sun for six hours in an attempt to have the beach babe look she'd always longed for. That was her freshman year in college. She was now thirty-eight years old. Old enough to know better.

Marlee was feeling many things on Saturday morning, but a beach babe was not one of them. Her legs and feet were swollen and it hurt to walk, since every step pulled at the already-tightened skin on top of her feet. Peering in the bathroom mirror, she was dismayed that her right eye was swollen nearly shut from the sunburn. Her face remained tomato red and the beginning of a fever blister were forming on her upper lip. She found cold sore gel and gingerly applied a generous amount to her upper lip. With any luck, early application of the medication would reduce both the pain intensity and healing time of the fever blister.

After shuffling around the house, lamenting the time she spent in the sun the previous afternoon, Marlee remembered that she still needed to pick up some signed papers from Dean Green. He was not known to come to campus on the weekends, but he should have put the documents in Marlee's mailbox in the secretary's office. She had a key to that office, as did all faculty members in the department. Marlee put on a baggy T-shirt and a pair of loose-fitting plaid shorts and drove to campus.

An eerie silence hung over Scobey Hall as Marlee used her key to enter the locked building. A professor had been found dead right outside that very building a year and half ago and Marlee still had the creeps whenever she had to go there during weekends and evenings, when no one else was around.

Scobey Hall was rumored to be haunted. This rumor was in full effect when Marlee started teaching at

Midwestern State University a few years ago and persisted, in part, due to the death of Logan LeCroix, a professor of French, in the fall of 2004. *Get a grip*, Marlee thought as she entered the stairwell. It was an old building and would be demolished soon. The faculty and staff were being relocated to a new building within the next year because Scobey Hall did not comply with the Americans with Disabilities Act and it would not be cost effective to bring it up to code. The building was known as The Maze because of the narrow, winding stairways and the propensity of students to get lost when looking for their professors' offices.

The stairs creaked as Marlee walked up to the second floor. She also heard other sounds coming from behind the stairway door to the second floor. It made no sense that anyone else would be on campus early on a Saturday morning, right after finals week. There were no cars in the lot and there was no sign of activity in the dilapidated old building. Still, she could not shake the feeling that someone besides herself was in the building. Of course, Marlee always had this feeling when she entered Scobey Hall during non-business hours.

Probably just the old pipes and the deteriorating heating system making noise, she thought as she approached the door to the secretary's office.

Marlee swung open the door and turned on the lights. Nothing was out of sorts and she soon found the signed documents in a pile of papers in her mailbox. She grabbed the papers and backed out of the office, pulling the door behind her and preparing to lock it.

Just then, she was hit in the back of the knees and she fell to the floor, writhing in agony.

Information comes from the most unexpected sources.

Chapter 4

    Marlee's fall to the tiled floor was a painful one. After being hit behind the knees, she stumbled a couple steps to the side and lost her balance. She landed face down, slapping her burnt legs, face, and arms on the hard floor. A daze swept over her as she struggled to make sense of what had just happened. Marlee believed she was blacking out, because the next thing she felt after the intense pain was a wet tongue licking her ear. She shuddered and tried to move her head away from the offending person without much luck.

    "Rusty! Rusty! Get away from there! Rusty!" yelled out a voice in a familiar drawl. Della Halter did a slow jog toward Marlee, who was still splayed on the floor before the office door. She was wearing one of her typical outfits; a light blue prairie skirt with a lace ruffle underneath, reminiscent of the early 1980s, bright blue socks, scuffed brown clogs, and a tie dyed t-shirt with the word FREEDOM boldly printed on the front, highlighting the fact that she was not wearing a bra. Her short, dark hair was matted on one side and fluffy on the other, suggesting Della just rolled out of bed, threw on whatever conglomeration of clothes were in reach, and came to campus.

"Marlee! What are you doing?" Della Halter yelled in an accusing voice as her enormous red furred dog continued to lick Marlee's ear and neck.

"What am I doing?" Marlee shrieked as she turned her head to see Della and the large, overly-friendly dog. "Your dog just knocked me down!"

"Oh, she's just so friendly and wants attention all the time. She won't hurt anybody," Della said affectionately as she reached over to scratch behind Rusty's ears. At that moment, another large red dog bounded around the corner, ran up to Marlee, and began sniffing her undercarriage.

"Look who wants attention!" Della called out with pride. "Shep, you want in on all the fun too, don't you?"

"Della, get these animals off me right fucking now!"

"They don't mean any harm. They just really like people and want to be friends." Della couldn't comprehend Marlee's hostility toward her dogs and reluctantly pulled them both back so Marlee could rise to her feet.

"Girrrrl, what did you do to yourself? You're bright red!" Della stated the obvious.

"I was grading papers on my patio yesterday afternoon and fell asleep for a few hours," Marlee said, grimacing as she stood upright and gathered her signed papers. "Why are you here? And why do you have your dogs in the building?"

"I had massive gas yesterday and couldn't do any work, so I went home. Nearly farted myself to death.

Thought I'd ripped a hole in my sheets last night. So I needed to come up here today to get some work done and I brought the dogs along. They come up here with me sometimes and I take them to my night classes. The students love it when Rusty and Shep run right up and greet them in class."

Marlee doubted that everyone was as enamored with Della's dogs, but kept the thought to herself. She was not a dog person at all, and hated the intrusive sniffing and jumping of untrained dogs.

"Did you hear the big news about Dean Green?" Della asked, itching to tell a story.

"You told me yesterday. Remember?"

"There's more. A lot more. Yesterday he was fired and they escorted him off campus!" Della, like most of the profs in the department, was not a fan of the dean's and was taking pleasure in the announcement.

"What? I just talked to him, around noon yesterday."

"Yep. They shit-canned him, took his keys, and marched him off campus grounds. I heard he didn't even get to come back to his office to collect his things. Administration disabled his computer passwords and they cancelled his university credit card."

"Whoa! I never expected he would be punished at all for the sexual harassment claim, let alone be terminated," Marlee said.

"Apparently there's something else. I don't know what it is yet, but I'll do some digging," Della said as she motioned her dogs to follow her back to her office. "I'll let you know what I find out."

"Okay, thanks," Marlee muttered, attempting to make sense of Della's bombshell.

"Oh, and Marlee," Della called over her shoulder as she and her dogs noisily wrestled down the hallway, "don't forget to put something on that sunburn. You look terrible!"

Marlee was not offended by Della's comment on her looks. She didn't put much stock in fashion advice from Train Wreck Barbie. Still hobbling, due to both the sunburn and the recent dog assault, Marlee made her way to her office. She hadn't intended to stick around campus, but now wanted more information about Mean Dean Ira Green and his expulsion from campus. She checked to ensure the documents she asked him to approve indeed carried his signature and was relieved when she noted he finished that before being ousted. Marlee checked her campus email and didn't see any information on Dean Green or his forced exit. She did, however, see an email from Stella DeVry, who had invited her to a picnic that day at her home. It was an end-of-the-semester bash, and several of the professors in the College of Arts and Sciences, along with people from the other colleges at the university, were invited to attend. Marlee was not feeling in much of a party mood, but knew the backyard picnic would be the best way to find out more news about the dean's firing. She tended to the papers she retrieved from the secretary's office and sent them through campus mail to the office that oversaw special interim classes like Marlee's Criminal Justice To Go.

"Less than enthused" was an understatement. Marlee dreaded going to Stella DeVry's party that afternoon. She was physically and emotionally exhausted and had no desire to hang out with some of the stuffed shirts she spent much of her time avoiding on campus. Still, some of her friends would probably be there. And it was the best way to find out the dirt on Mean Dean Green and what he was up to besides sexually harassing nontraditional-aged students.

After showering, Marlee tried an old sunburn treatment her mother used when she was a child and suffering from too much sun exposure. She lightly dabbed vinegar on the sunburned parts of her body and let it dry before dressing in a different baggy t-shirt and shorts combo. The vinegar treatment worked and she hardly felt the sting of the sunburn at all.

The party invitation requested that each guest bring a dish to share. Marlee was not feeling very Betty Crockerish at the moment and purchased a cherry pie from a local grocery store. She took the pie home, removed the wrapping with the store's name and price, and rewrapped the pie with her own plastic wrap. Some of the academics could be such food snobs and proclaimed they only ate home-cooked meals and desserts. Little did they know Marlee had been passing off prepared foods from the grocery store bakery and deli for years. Professors and students alike had raved about her chicken tortilla soup at the department holiday party in December. Her recipe was to purchase it from the local restaurant supply company, heat it up in her own crockpot, serve, and wait for the compliments to come rolling in. When asked for her recipe, Marlee rattled off a list of ingredients she guessed were in the dish, intentionally failing to account for amounts. Marlee actually loved cooking, but who had the time?

Marlee balanced her "homemade" pie in one hand and held a bottle of water in the other. The invitation had requested that everyone BYOB, bring their own bottle. Typically that referred to alcohol, but Marlee knew drinking today was out of the question, given her serious sunburn, the fact that she would be on the road with her Criminal Justice To Go class in two days, and her mission to get the dirt on Mean Dean Green.

As Marlee let herself in the gate to Stella's backyard, she observed one of her least favorite people from campus: Asshat. Professor Bob Ashman was a long time academic at Midwestern State University and an expert on all topics. His nickname, Asshat, was derived from a bastardization of his surname and the fact that he liked to wear all kinds of hats. Today, Asshat sported a sea-captain's hat and looked very nautical in his blue and white striped t-shirt and khaki shorts.

Observing Asshat talking to a new professor with glazed-over eyes, she moved around them and greeted the host. Stella DeVry was dressed in sporty jean capris and a white blouse. She gave Marlee a warm welcome and placed her pie on the table along with the salads, casseroles, chips, dips, and desserts brought by the other party goers.

"Thanks so much for coming!" Stella exclaimed. Where she found the enthusiasm at the end of the spring semester, Marlee had no idea. Stella, in her late fifties, taught chemistry and was only a few years from retirement, so that explained the upbeat mood. Then Marlee observed a clear plastic glass with a red substance within. She guessed it was some sort of vodka cranberry concoction, thus giving further explanation of Stella's effervescent attitude.

"Sure. Thanks for inviting me." Marlee looked around the backyard to see who she wanted to talk with and who she wanted to avoid.

"You sure have a bad sunburn," Stella stated, as she reached for her class of red liquid and took a mighty slug. How she managed to keep her scarlet colored drink from dribbling on her white shirt was a mystery to Marlee.

"Yep, fell asleep outside grading exams yesterday." Marlee was already losing interest in the conversation and surveying the crowd to see who she could talk to once she broke away from her hostess. She knew Stella probably had less information than she did about Dean Green. Marlee had a limited amount of energy and patience that afternoon and decided to maximize her time by only associating with those who would know the scoop.

"That's too bad..." Stella's voice trailed off as soon as she realized she no longer had an audience. Marlee walked over to Amos Sharp a professor from the English Department. Amos was a long-time fixture in the MSU English Department and taught creative writing. He was also an incurable gossip. With him was his student muse, Grayson, which most people suspected was the undergraduate the professor was sleeping with that semester. Amos always called them his muses, but they were really nothing more for him than the flavor of the week. Grayson would be gone soon and replaced by another new, shiny, adoring student.

"Marlee, you survived the end of the semester," called out Amos as she approached him. He wrinkled his nose as she came closer. "Do you smell pickles?"

"Nope." Marlee knew he caught a whiff of her vinegar sunburn tonic but was not going to get into that discussion with him.

"I don't suppose you've heard the big news?" Amos was ready to dish, as were most faculty members, but Amos took it to a higher degree. In addition to digging for information and passing it on to whoever would listen, Marlee suspected he added his own juicy details, just to add some creative flair to the story.

"Are you talking about our illustrious dean?"

"Ah, you have heard." Amos was disappointed and it showed on his face. He immediately perked up, however, when Marlee began to ask questions.

"Amos, why was Dean Green terminated? I heard it was for something other than the sexual harassment of somebody at the library."

"Yes, it was for something much more scandalous than that. He lied on his application," the gossipy prof said with smug satisfaction.

Marlee was puzzled. *What could the dean have lied about that would result in immediate suspension?* "Did he kill someone?"

"Puh-lease," Amos said with a flourish of his hand. "This is South Dakota. You don't lose your job just for killing someone. It was much more devious."

Knowing Amos was waiting for more questions before he would continue, Marlee asked, "Well, what was it? What did he lie about?"

"Several things. First, his name is not Ira Green, it's Reuben Ira Green. He went by his middle name here so his background could not be traced as easily. Reuben Green was not just a professor of biochemistry and then an associate dean before he came to MSU, he was the president of Keystone State University in Pennsylvania for three years before he was charged with sexual harassment and demoted back to professor status. When Green interviewed here, he told us he was interviewing because he wanted to move to a smaller school where he could make a bigger impact on the faculty and students. I was on the search committee and talked to him myself. What he failed to mention was that he had been terminated at Keystone State due to several separate instances of sexual harassment. He's being sued by at least three different women right now."

"What the hell! How did this all come to light?"

"Somebody who knew Green from his tenure as president at Keystone State notified the MSU president and it took off from there," Amos said.

"How was this not discovered during the interview process? Didn't anybody check his references before he was hired?" Marlee couldn't believe someone with this type of a past could just waltz into Elmwood, South Dakota, and begin a career as a university administrator.

"We dropped the ball on that," Amos said, taking partial ownership of the debacle. "The members of the search committee contacted his references, but as you know, supervisors cannot tell the whole story for fear of being sued by the applicant. Everyone we talked to gave him a glowing reference. There was no hint of impropriety on Green's part."

"Didn't anyone on the search committee know someone at Keystone State that they could unofficially ask about him?"

Amos shook his head. "Like I said, we dropped the ball. We were trying to fill the position in a limited amount of time. When Green came to campus, he made a great first impression. We thought we'd be lucky to have him here. Of course, that all changed once he revealed his true vulgar personality."

"How about an internet search? Did anybody do that?" Marlee continued, gob-smacked at how Green was able to slip into a deanship at MSU.

"Look, I don't know why that wasn't checked." Amos was becoming defensive, assuming Marlee was judging him for the failures of the whole search committee.

"It could've happened to any of us on a search committee," Marlee lied to smooth Amos' ruffled feathers. She had a background in criminal justice, both educationally and professionally, so this type of boondoggle would not have occurred had she been on the committee.

Amos nodded at her concession and Grayson nodded as well, ready to mimic the English professor's every thought and action.

"Where's Dean Green—um, I mean former-Dean Green—at now?" Marlee asked. After all the trouble Green had caused her over the years, she was secretly enjoying his fall from grace.

"I heard he was going to Florida. He and his wife already vacated their apartment and left town," Amos reported.

That must have been why he had all those maps on his desk when I met with him yesterday to get my papers signed. He knew the cat was out of the bag and he was planning his departure to Florida, Marlee thought as she finished up the conversation with Amos Sharp and his adoring student, Grayson. The sun was peeking through the clouds now and it was causing Marlee's skin to sting. After chatting with a few more people and not uncovering any additional information, she thanked the hostess and went home to think about all she learned about Dean Reuben Ira Green that day.

Brenda Donelan

*Education and knowledge are not the same thing.
One can be purchased.*

Chapter 5

The remainder of the weekend was without drama. Marlee finished her grading and submitted the final grades to the registrar's office. *Let the bitching begin*, she thought, as this was typically the time when a student with a low final grade would contact her to express utter shock that they failed the class. Then Marlee would need to launch into a detailed email explanation of how the grades were calculated and that no matter how the test scores were added up, the student still failed the course.

Vince Chipperton called twice, both times suggesting he come over to her house. Marlee lied and told him she needed to rest before she embarked on her week long Criminal Justice To Go class. The real truth was that she did not want him to see her looking as she did. What started as a small fever blister had fortunately been stopped with the aid of generous applications of some leftover prescription cold sore gel found in the back of a bathroom drawer. That, however; was the end of Marlee's good luck.

Her face was still bright red and swollen. The skin was pulled tight from the sunburn, giving her the appearance of someone who had just underwent an aggressive facelift. Marlee's arms, neck, lower legs, and feet were tomato red and still felt hot to the touch. The last thing she wanted was hunky Vince Chipperton getting an eyeful of her sunburned self. She wouldn't see him all week while she was on the road, and her sunburn would be healed up by the time she returned to Elmwood.

By the time the sun came up on Monday morning, Marlee had her bags packed for the week-long Criminal Justice To Go. Pippa, her gray Persian kitty, would be cared for by her friend, Diane Frasier. Marlee would return Friday evening, ready to have absolutely no contact with any students until the start of the fall semester. One week on the road with students became tiring after about three hours. There were constant student questions, behavioral issues to address, timing snafus, and a host of other unexpected and unpredictable problems.

Stopping by the donut shop before her initial meeting with the students on campus, Marlee procured a selection of rolls and donuts for the students. By Wednesday, she would hate most of them, but today she was full of energy and good will toward those she taught.

Ten students were enrolled in the course and Marlee was allowed an assistant to help her control the herd. Marlee's assistant was Marcus Johansen, a criminal justice major who just graduated the week prior. He had taken Criminal Justice To Go two years earlier, so he knew what to expect. Marcus already had full-time professional employment lined up, but he would not begin until mid-June; thus, he had some free time, and was willing to help Marlee with her class. Plus, he knew it would look good on his résumé when he applied for other jobs in the criminal justice field. Marcus was mature and Marlee knew she could count on him to assist her with the class while they were on the road.

The ten students in the class were comprised of six traditional aged students from MSU, one non-trad from MSU, and three students from the University of South Dakota in Vermillion, who were interested in the class but had nothing similar at their home institution. Marlee was familiar, to some degree, with all seven of the MSU students. The six students in their early twenties were all criminal justice majors and had taken two or more classes with Marlee in the past few years. Some had taken every single class she taught up to that point. The non-trad was none other than Roxie Harper, the work-study student from the library who was sexually harassed by Mean Dean Green. This would be only the second class Roxie had taken with Marlee. The three students from USD were unknown, but they all appeared to be in their early twenties.

"Okay, I think we'll get started. We have a lot to do," Marlee said as she moved to the front of the classroom to talk to the students. She passed the box of rolls around the room, encouraging students to partake. Marlee had already been over the rules, obligations, and expectations of the class with each student, either in person or through email, yet she knew the importance of reiterating them.

"So everyone has their rooming situation figured out, right?" No one spoke to the contrary, so Marlee took that as an affirmation. The class would be on the road for five days, thus they would be staying in motels in various towns for four nights. Most students preferred to share a room with one or more students to cut costs, although there were some who insisted on single rooms. The rooming situation for each town had been figured out ahead of time and reservations made at the motels. Luckily, Marlee was able to secure her own room since she was the professor. She had no intention of sharing a room with students only to find that she drooled, snored, and talked in her sleep.

"And everyone knows how they're getting from point A to point B, right?" Again, no answers from the students, so Marlee assumed it meant everything was under control. The class operated with students taking their own transportation since accessing a university bus was out of the question. Marlee and her student assistant would ride together in Marlee's vehicle while the other students made arrangements regarding who would drive and who would be a passenger.

"Okay, with those two things out of the way, I just want to go over a few ground rules which will make the whole week a lot easier on everybody. First, be on time. We are on a strict schedule and don't have time to wait for someone to get breakfast because they overslept. You can get wake up calls to your motel rooms if you think getting up on time might be a problem. We are scheduled at specific times for the tours at each of the facilities we will be visiting. The people there have taken time out of their schedules to give us the tours and answer our questions. Let's do our best to get to our locations on time. If someone is late then they may miss the tour of a particular facility, which will negatively impact their grade."

With no interruption for clarification, Marlee continued. "Second, be respectful to the people working at the facilities. You don't have to agree with everything you see and hear while on the tours, but you do need to show respect. Again, the people working there are under no obligation to show us around and answer your questions. If you make rude comments or act disrespectfully, then they probably won't let us do tours next year. You'll have ruined the experience for future classes."

The donut box was picked up from a desk top in the back of the classroom and began to circulate again as some students were making their second selections. Marlee was starting to wish she had taken one before they were all gone.

"And finally," she continued, "be respectful of the people who are held at the facilities. Yes, I know they have committed crimes and done some terrible things, but they are still people and deserve respect. They are not animals in a zoo just to be stared at and mocked. If any of them try to talk to you or harass you, don't say anything. Just ignore them or move away. No good will come of you shouting back insults if they're rude to you. Most will just watch you walk by and you'll be safe, but there may be some catcalling, especially at the State Penitentiary."

"Are there guards around to protect us?" asked one of the USD students.

"We aren't taken into dangerous areas. If there's a problem, then the warden will cancel the tour or reschedule it. If a problem does arise, follow the directions given by myself, my student assistant Marcus Johansen, and the staff at the facility. I've never had a situation arise before and I don't believe the man who taught this class before me did either. The worst that's ever happened were some lewd comments." Marlee wanted the students to be aware that there was always a possibility of danger, but not to be so consumed with it that they forgot to observe and ask questions.

The student who asked the question nodded her head and Marlee continued. "The last thing to keep in mind is that this is the time to ask questions about employment and internships. You might make a connection now with a staff member that can help you get an internship or even a job later on." Marlee had several former students working at the prisons, jails, treatment centers, and juvenile facilities throughout the state. Many of them found the career they loved, while some used the job as a means of gaining experience so they would be seen as more valuable when applying for the job they really wanted, like probation officer or FBI agent.

After a few more directives and responding to questions, Marlee passed out the syllabus which detailed the class's schedule for the next week. Students had specific directions, so there should be no chance of one or more student cars getting lost. The class drove nearly a thousand miles during the week, so it was essential that everyone knew how to get to the facilities in the shortest amount of time.

"Our first stop today is in Huron, to visit juvenile inpatient treatment programs, then we go to Pierre to tour the women's prison. We'll leave Pierre when we're finished at the women's prison and stay overnight in Chamberlain," Marlee reported. "Let's go. We have to be in Huron at 1:00 to start the tours. You're on your own for lunch before the tour. We'll be eating supper at the women's prison tonight. And by the way, the food at some of the facilities is pretty bad. You don't have to eat it, but just don't make rude comments. We can always hit a Burger King drive-thru when we're done with the tours if you don't want to eat the food that's served." Marlee knew food was of utmost importance to the students. They weren't so much concerned with quality as they were with volume. She did her best to keep them informed of tours that included meals.

As they walked out of the building, Marlee noticed the t-shirt worn by the male from USD. "Um, you'll have to change before you go into any of the facilities today."

He looked at her blankly. "Why?"

"Look at the picture. It's not appropriate to wear that in any of the facilities, but especially not to the program that helps kids with sexual adjustment issues," Marlee said pointing to his shirt which featured a cartoon depiction of a man having sex with a horse.

Before you can trust the message, you have to trust the messenger.

Chapter 6

The class was on the road. As Marlee drove her vehicle out of town, Marcus talked about his student experiences in taking Criminal Justice To Go a previous year. They were both excited about what the students would learn during this week, as most of them had never toured a prison or treatment facility. The prisons completed a criminal background check on all the students in the class to ensure no one had a prior record. A student with a criminal history was probably not going to be employable in the criminal justice field; plus, officials at the facilities did not want "past customers" touring the facilities and learning about the security measures.

Marlee handed Marcus three folders which laid on the dash of her vehicle. They contained background information on the students she did not know. All three came from the University of South Dakota in Vermillion and were majoring in criminal justice there. Marlee's files did not contain any sensitive information on the trio, so she felt comfortable in sharing it with Marcus.

As they drove, Marcus read from the files. "Bart Lamont, age twenty-three, in the National Guard, a brief tour in Iraq with the Army, which ended after a few weeks due to unspecified reasons. He's in his second year at USD. Uh, he's the one who had the wardrobe problem." Marlee nodded, and Marcus continued. "I don't know for sure, but I think he's dating Katie Daniels, the dark haired girl who sat next to him this morning. She's twenty-one and in the National Guard, but there's no military service overseas. She's double majoring in criminal justice and psychology. Becca Troutman is the third student from USD. She's twenty and in her third year there, although she just recently changed her major from chemistry to criminal justice."

"Thanks for reading through the files. I've had them for a while now, but never got around to familiarizing myself with their backgrounds. The other seven students are all from MSU and I know most of them fairly well. Donnie Stacks, Dominic Schmidt, and Jasper Evans I know really well. They're all good kids and we won't have any trouble from any of them. Of the other four students, there are Paula Stone and Violet Stone, who are sisters. They're the ones with the light brown curly hair and they're laughing and smiling most of the time. They're both a lot of fun and will probably be the ones who keep the morale up on the trip."

"Yeah, I know them. We had some classes together and I worked on a group project with Paula for a class," Marcus recalled.

"Johnny Marble is a really good friend of theirs from their home town. I know him fairly well, as he's been in my classes. He doesn't talk much, but seems like an okay kid," Marlee stated.

"Yeah, I was in a couple classes with him but he never really talked in them either. I don't know much about him."

"And finally, we have our one non-traditional student, Roxie Harper. I know her from being in one of my classes, but I don't really know much about her," Marlee said.

"I don't know anything about her. We had a couple classes together, but I never talked to her even though we were both CJ majors," Marcus said.

"Sometimes non-trad students in this class are a stabilizing influence. They can be sort of like a surrogate mother to the younger students and help keep the drama to a minimum. On the other hand, sometimes they can be the worst behaved of anyone on the trip." Marlee knew this from the first year she taught Criminal Justice To Go. A straight-A-earning non-trad took Marlee's class and managed to piss off all of the students, Marlee, and the student assistant before they were even halfway through the trip. She was a control freak and wanted to be in charge of the class. Marlee had to assert her authority with the troublesome non-trad more than once during the class, to the delight of the other students.

"Besides us, we have four cars of students; the USD students are all riding together; the Stone sisters and Johnny Marble are riding together; Dom, Jasper, and Donnie are riding together, and Roxie is driving herself. Those are also the same room arrangements. Roxie wanted to drive alone and room alone," Marlee said. "Nothing wrong with that. She must just like her space. Plus, she's probably afraid rooming with the younger students would be like living in a frat house. I don't blame her for carving out her own space on this trip. A week is a long time to be stuck with roommates you don't know."

"Yeah, I've had some bad roommate situations over the years," the assistant said. Marlee nodded and the two commiserated over the seemingly normal people they roomed with who, over the course of one semester, turned into complete psychopaths.

After a short lunch stop at McDonald's, Marlee and Marcus drove four miles out into the countryside to the juvenile treatment facilities. The Home Away From Home program comprised two large, unattached buildings. Both had rooms for sleeping, dining, and general recreation and meetings. A third large building contained the on-site school, which was divided into several classrooms. Attached to the school was a full sized gymnasium with a basketball court, weight lifting room, and area for treadmills and other exercise machines.

There were two treatment programs at Home Away From Home; one was for kids who were chemically dependent and the other treated juveniles with sexual adjustment issues. Many of the kids had both problems and once they finished with one program, they moved to the other.

Prior to entering the buildings, Marlee noted that Bart Lamont had changed out of his pornographic yellow t-shirt and into a red button down shirt without logos. The tour went as planned and ended a few minutes ahead of schedule. Gathering in the parking lot by their cars, the students were anxious to process what they had learned. Most of them were shocked by the offenses and unacceptable behavior engaged in by the kids in the sexual adjustment program.

"Dr. M., I had no idea things like this happened around here. And with such young kids," Jasper Evans said. "What makes a kid sexually abuse other kids or animals?"

"This happens everywhere all the time, Jasper. Some of the kids we saw today are not just perpetrators, but victims themselves. Somebody else, maybe a parent, older sibling, or family friend, sexually abused or exploited them and now they've done the same to another child."

"I couldn't believe the level of violence the kids carried out against other kids," Donnie Stacks said.

"Some of the kids aren't violent at all, while others will do whatever it takes to get their sexual desires met. That's why the bedrooms and bathrooms are monitored. If left alone for any length of time, some of the kids will coerce other kids into having sex. The counselors and staff here really have to be on their toes to make sure that doesn't happen." Marlee had been to the Home Away From Home programs several times before, mostly when she worked as a probation officer and placed kids there with sexual adjustment or chemical dependency issues. She had several stories she could tell about these juvenile sex offenders, but knew it would do little good other than to scare the students out of the criminal justice field.

"Let's go. We've got a couple of hours to get to our next tour," Marlee advised as she and Marcus got into her SUV.

When Marlee and her student assistant arrived at the Women's Prison in Pierre two hours later, all of the students were present in the parking lot. Marlee did a quick reminder that everyone needed to leave everything in their cars except for some form of identification and a pen and notebook. Cell phones, tobacco, knives, and any other type of contraband had to be left behind in the cars. "Attempting to smuggle in anything for whatever reason can get you charged in court and possibly a prison sentence, so be sure not to take anything inside other than your driver's license and something to take notes on." To speed up the process, Marlee collected all of the driver's licenses.

The students, following Marlee and Marcus, proceeded inside the front door of the prison and stood in an entryway while Marlee stated their reason for the visit and provided the stack of driver's licenses to the humorless uniformed woman behind the plexiglass enclosed desk. She looked at each license individually and then called out the person's name. When they stepped to the glass front desk, she peered out at them to see that the photo matched the person who stood before her. Fifteen minutes passed by the time everyone had successfully passed the initial inspection and were allowed through the locked door into the prison.

Once inside, the group was led to a dark, windowless room which contained a magnetometer; the device used to screen individuals to ensure they were not bringing in contraband or carrying weapons. Donnie Stacks was the first student in line and passed through the screening system without incident. "This is just like the machine at the airport," Donnie proclaimed to the students in line behind her.

"Oh, no. I didn't know we'd have to go through one of these," whispered Becca to Katie. She gently tapped Marlee on the shoulder and said, "Does this detect all metal?"

"Most of it. Why? What do you have on you that you're worried about?" Marlee was becoming agitated. She'd clearly stated that everything had to be left in the cars and now Becca was carrying some sort of metal.

"Well," Becca said, somewhat self-consciously, "there's a metal chain that goes around the waist band of my underwear."

Marlee was dumbfounded. Not only did she not know what to say to this comment, but she had no idea where someone would even buy underwear with a metal chain. "Uh, I guess you'll just have to go through the magnetometer and see what happens. If it detects metal then you'll have to tell the guard what it is."

"Well, I don't want to have to take off my underwear!" Becca was indignant.

"Why did you choose to wear metal underwear on a tour through prisons?" Marlee shot back.

"I don't know. I guess I thought it would be bad ass," Becca said. "Um, what about nipple rings? Can the detector sense them too? I just got my nipples pierced last week."

Marlee rolled her eyes. "Get in line and if the detector goes off, then tell the guard the scoop. It's up to the prison officials what they will want you to do with all your metal." It was only the first day and there were already two wardrobe issues. Policing student fashion choices was not what Marlee signed on for when she agreed to lead this class.

The stars aligned in Becca's favor, as the magnetometer sensed neither her metal underwear band nor her nipple rings. Marlee was not as fortunate. When the under wires in her bra set off the magnetometer, Marlee had to pull the guard aside and explain the issue. The guard insisted that Marlee be further screened and he ran a hand-held device all around her body. When the beeping started around her chest area, the guard loudly proclaimed the metal sensing devices were indeed picking up the under wires in her bra rather than knives, guns, or other contraband. The only good thing about a sunburn is that it conceals intense blushing.

Without any further ado, the group processed through the detector and was brought to the visitation room where the women prisoners met with their family and friends. The room was well-lit with windows allowing a southern exposure. The tables and chairs were hard plastic, reminiscent of middle school classrooms across America. There were also child-sized chairs and tables in a corner of the room. Stuffed animals, story books, and cartoon paintings on the wall were clustered into the small corner area. Most of the women at the prison had children, many of them very young kids. One of the goals of the prison was to maintain a connection between mothers and their children, so accommodations were made to allow the moms to play with the children.

After a welcome and introduction to the goals of the prison, Deputy Warden Liza McCall introduced Major Tim Borden, a high-ranking correctional officer who would be showing them around the institution.

"To get started," Major Borden said with military precision, "I will lead you on a tour through all security levels of the prison. Since there's only one prison for women in South Dakota, all women receiving a sentence of incarceration are sent here. We have women serving life sentences and women who will be released this week. There are murderers, rapists, drug dealers, thieves, embezzlers, and others involved in any type of crime you can imagine. These women are mothers, daughters, wives, friends, neighbors, co-workers, and most of all; manipulators. Nobody does anything in prison unless they see some potential gain for themselves. Do not give anything to the prisoners or take anything from them. Sometimes they will attempt to get a note outside to someone and will use a sympathetic visitor to do it."

After taking a deep breath and assessing that the students were paying attention, Major Borden said, "After the tour, you'll be taken to the chow hall for supper. The first group of inmates eats at 5:00 pm and other groups follow. Don't talk to anyone at supper either. After supper, we have an inmate panel discussion. A few women have agreed to talk to this class about themselves, their crimes, and what they hope to do when released. You are free to ask questions to the women on the inmate panel after they have each finished their presentations."

Major Borden marched toward a locked door with Marlee and the students following. After unlocking the door, the major stood back and did a head count as everyone passed through the door. He explained as he did this that there would be many times today they would be counted to ensure no one wandered off or was left behind. The women's prison consisted of four security levels; high, medium, low, and work release. Security level was determined by the offense committed, the individual's propensity toward violence, the length of the sentence, and behavior while in prison. One could be moved to higher or lower security in the prison based on accomplishments and rule infractions.

The tours of the differing security areas were of interest and students asked a variety of questions. What yielded the most interest was the house separate from the prison which was used for mothers and children to spend weekends together. The house was furnished like a normal home with a television, DVD player, a variety of G-rated movies, books, and toys. One inmate had access to the house for a given weekend and it was a privilege that had to be earned. She could keep her children in the house, cook meals for them, and act as an intact family; at least for a weekend. The children's rooms were painted with cartoon characters, a service provided by an artistically gifted inmate.

"Why would a mother want her children to see her in prison?" asked Dom.

"This house is meant to look as little like a prison as possible. We want families to maintain contact while the mother is in prison and this is one step toward keeping that family bond intact. For some women, this is all they have to look forward to. It's an incentive to maintain good behavior and work toward bettering themselves," said Major Borden.

"Do they have a house like this at the men's prison?" Jasper asked.

"No, they don't. Almost all of the women in here are mothers and most were the primary parent for their children. Although many of the men in prison are also fathers, they were not the parent who provided most of the care for the children. Some don't have any involvement in their kids' lives at all," said the major.

Following the tour, the group made their way to the dining area. They lined up and went through the line with the rest of the inmates. Spaghetti and meatballs were on the menu that night, along with mushy green beans and a slice of yeasty-tasting homemade bread. As Marlee and the students walked by tables filled with inmates, one was overheard grumbling to another, "Look, they got five meatballs. We only get three. They're trying to make it look good for the people who come here to visit." As Marlee glanced around the dining hall, she noticed that the women who had not yet started eating did indeed only have three meatballs while she and the students all had five.

The meal was bland, but Marlee didn't have the students dine at the prison because of the food quality. It was for them to understand the prison dynamics. Students could see that seating designated status, just like in high school. The dominant group sat with others in their clique at the center of the chow hall, while other inmates with less power were relegated to other seating areas on the far end of the dining room.

Nearly everyone working in the kitchen was an inmate and it was a trusted status. It was possible to sneak out food from the kitchen to their cells to eat later. Sometimes inmates took utensils and other items that could be used as weapons. Even if the inmate did not intend to use the weapon, she could trade it for something else she wanted.

Students were herded back into the visitation room where they had their orientation at the start of the tour. Now a long table with four chairs all on one side was pulled to the front of the room. As soon as everyone from Criminal Justice To Go was seated, the major used his walkie-talkie to summon a correctional officer. A door opened and in filed four women dressed in various colors of cotton tops and bottoms, similar to the smock type uniforms worn by nurses. Major Borden had explained earlier that tan meant low security, red meant high security, blue stood for medium security, orange signified those who were on work release in the Pierre area, and green indicated that the woman was pregnant, regardless of her security level.

The women sat down and the major introduced each of them starting from the left side of the table. "Arlys here in the blue is serving a ten year sentence for drugs. Echo in the red is doing a life sentence for murder. In the tan is Stephanie and she's serving two years for grand theft. And finally, Luverne is in orange and is serving twenty years for voluntary manslaughter. She's up for parole next week."

Marlee raised her hand. "Before we get started, I'd want to ask the women if it was their choice to talk to us." Each of the women on the panel nodded and a chorus of "yeah" was heard.

"Arlys, you can start now," advised Major Borden.

"Hi, everybody. I'm Arlys," said the large white woman with a long, straggly gray pony tail. She had a haggard appearance and looked to be in her early fifties.

"To answer your question," she said with a nod toward Marlee, "a lot of us want to talk to people from outside the prison. It's the only time some of us ever get to talk to someone who isn't a prisoner or a guard." Marlee gave Arlys a quick smile, glad that the students now knew the inmates were not being forced to participate.

With a nod back at Marlee, Arlys continued, "I'm serving a ten year sentence for drugs. I was always a good kid, but got involved with a drug dealer and he got me started using drugs. He's in the men's prison now doing fifteen years. We were dealing marijuana, heroin, meth, you name it. I was using too. He wasn't using, just dealing. I think I started abusing drugs because he was beating me up. I couldn't leave him. I didn't have anyone else or anywhere to go. My parents are dead and my sisters gave up on me years ago. I don't have any kids or anyone else to turn to. Drugs became my escape." Arlys continued to tell her story to the students including her plans upon release.

Next to speak was Echo, a diminutive Native American girl in her early twenties. "Hey. I'm Echo and I'm a lifer. This is my home for the rest of my life and it's what I deserve. I killed my baby. I don't even remember it because I was so drunk. I was back home on the rez and my boyfriend and I had a party at our house. We were all drinking and having a good time. After a while, I notice he's not around anymore. That's when I find him in our bedroom with my cousin. After that, everything went black. I don't remember anything till I woke up in jail the next morning. My sister was at the party and she said I came out of the bedroom screaming and grabbed my baby and...." Echo stammered, her voice rich with emotion and tears streaming down her cheeks. "And I picked him up and slammed him against the wall." Echo discontinued her story as she began sobbing to the point that she could no longer speak. She waved her hand toward the woman who sat next to her.

"My name's Stephanie and I'm doing time for grand theft," said the white woman with the blonde bob-cut. She appeared to be in her early thirties and carried herself as if she came from money. "I've always liked nice things and affording them wasn't a problem. My husband is a respiratory therapist and I worked part-time at a bank. We have two daughters, a nice home, took vacations, and didn't want for anything. Even though I could've bought the things I stole, I didn't. I got a thrill from it. My favorite things to take were clothes and makeup, not just for me but for the girls too. I gave really nice gifts to my family and friends and everything was taken from stores in malls. When I was finally caught, I was putting a thousand dollars-worth of jewelry in the trunk of my car. As soon as I was confronted, I admitted it and told the police about the stuff I had at home too. I wasn't abused as a child or in my marriage. I wasn't addicted to anything and I don't have mental health issues. Basically, I guess I'm a thrill seeker and used shoplifting to get a rush." With that, Stephanie ended her spiel and looked toward the last person on the panel.

"I'm Luverne, and I think I'm getting out of here pretty soon," said a woman in her forties with thinning grayish brown hair and dark brown eyes. "I've been in for twenty years now. My charge was killing my husband. I killed him because he was going to kill me. At least that's what I thought at the time. I was later diagnosed with paranoid schizophrenia, and the doctors tell me that he was most likely never a threat to me. It seemed so real, and I feared for my life. I've been on medication since coming here and they tell me I'll have to stay on it the rest of my life. My kids are grown and haven't visited me even once since I've been here. I heard that I have grandkids now, but I've never seen them. When I get out, I hope to stay at a halfway house for a bit until I can get a job and earn enough money to get an apartment. I never finished high school, so it'll be tough to get a job." Luverne looked at the major to signal that she was finished talking.

Major Borden cleared his throat and said, "Let's open it up for questions. You can ask whatever you like, but the women don't have to answer if they don't want to."

The students were all sitting wide eyed with their mouths agape, still in shock at the gravity of the stories they just heard. Marlee sensed the students had many questions, but just needed a start. "Thank you all for sharing your stories. That's very brave of you to do. Besides family, what do you miss most now that you're in prison?"

Echo, now composed, spoke first. "I miss going to the fridge and grabbing a Coke anytime I want. We're not allowed to have food in our cells and pop isn't served in the chow hall. When I get enough money for a Coke I have to pay a high price for it at the commissary."

Arlys nodded and said, "Besides my family, the thing I miss most is being able to put my bare feet on carpet. There's no carpet in here. Anywhere."

"I miss shopping," said Stephanie. "Just walking by stores and seeing the new clothes and makeup, walking in and touching the clothes and getting a makeover. I really miss all of that."

Luverne spoke last. "I've been in here so long I don't even know what I miss anymore. When I first came here nearly twenty years ago, I really missed the burgers and fries at this little diner my husband and I would go to. Guess it closed a few years back. Now I really don't miss anything anymore."

"What do you think will be your biggest obstacles when you get out?" asked Donnie Stacks, always one to ask well-thought out questions.

Luverne was the first to speak. "I don't have any education and I have a conviction for murder. I've been out of the workforce for twenty years. I was a stay at home mom and my husband worked, so I don't have much work experience. At least not the kind employers are looking for. I've been working in the kitchen here for over ten years, so that might help me get a job in a kitchen at a restaurant. I've been on work release for a few months and have been washing dishes at a diner downtown. I have no idea how technology works on the outside, other than what I've seen on TV shows. We can take classes here on computers, but I don't understand it." At this point, Marlee realized that Luverne probably had some learning disabilities, thus offering an explanation as to why she didn't finish high school and struggled with learning new things. A learning or a mental disability would add more obstacles to her reentry into society. It would not be an easy road for Luverne and the odds were stacked against her.

"Well, I'm never getting out, so you can skip me," Echo said with a little laugh that displayed anything but humor.

"You know, I just don't feel like there will be that many obstacles," said Stephanie. "My husband and kids are supportive of me. Probably the biggest thing is finding work in my field with a felony." Stephanie remained unaware of the issues that propelled her to shoplift in the first place. Marlee felt concern for this woman. Until she recognized that her problem was not stealing itself, but why she did it, Stephanie would be doomed to repeat her crimes.

Arlys had been looking down at the floor while the others spoke, almost as if she was not listening. When her turn came to talk she said, "I hear a lot about how everything will be all rosy when we get out, but I doubt that'll be the case. Very few people will hire convicted felons. Even if your family and friends have supported you so far, it doesn't mean they will continue to stand behind you. Some people will be hoping for your failure and will even try to get you to take a drink or smoke a joint. I think there will be pitfalls every day, some I haven't even thought of, that I'll have to watch for. So, my answer to the question is: everything. I think everything and everyone will be an obstacle in one way or another." Arlys' fatalistic attitude was not well received, judging by the looks on the faces of the other inmates and the students. Marlee knew all too well from her work with felons that Arlys was on target with society's perception of convicts, and how family and friends can hinder progress.

Roxie Harper, the non-traditional student in the Criminal Justice To Go class, had been silent on the tours up to this point. Now she chose to make her thoughts heard. "I'm hearing a lot of blame placed on society, family, boyfriends, husbands, and everyone else. I'm not hearing any of you taking much responsibility for your actions. One minute you cry when you talk about killing your baby," Roxie said as she pointed at Echo, "then the next minute you're whining because you can't have a Coke anytime you want. That doesn't seem very remorseful to me!"

"And you," Roxie pointed at Stephanie without taking a breath, "I bet you're back shoplifting within a month after you get out. You're a rich lady and had everything handed to you, but that just wasn't enough. But the one that pisses me off the most is Arlys because she's been in one abusive situation after another and wouldn't leave. Why stay? You could've left your boyfriend at any time and went to a shelter, but you didn't because you didn't want to. You were having fun with the drugs and getting money..."

"Roxie, that's enough!" Marlee shouted. "We aren't here to pass judgment on these women, just hear their stories so we can better understand why people get involved in crime."

Turning toward the inmate panel Marlee said, "I'm sorry, ladies. That was definitely uncalled for." She leveled a stern look at Roxie who had her lips pursed as if she were trying to hold back further comments. The rest of the students were stunned by Roxie's outburst and Marlee's chastisement of her. The women on the inmate panel shot Roxie daggers with their eyes, knowing that they could not respond to her criticisms lest they be punished.

"Ah, I think that wraps it up for the questions," said the major, sensing the whole climate of the room had changed since Roxie vocalized her judgments. He motioned the women at the table to stand up and he called on his walkie-talkie for the locked door to be opened. As the women were waiting to be escorted back to their cells, Luverne shouted at Roxie, "What makes you so perfect, bitch? You've probably done some things that would land you in here. You just didn't get caught!"

Roxie was now on her feet, ready to respond to Luverne's parting shot. "I've never killed anyone! And I've never dealt drugs! And I've never stolen anything other than a CD from a store when I was a teenager, so no, I don't think I'm just like you and that I should be in prison! And fuck you!" Roxie yelled, pointing at Luverne. "If you think you're gonna make it on the outside, you're delusional. Oh wait, I guess you're already delusional, according to your psychiatric diagnosis."

Marlee ran to the table where Roxie now stood. She grabbed the student's arm and hissed, "Shut up! Right now! I mean it!"

The door unlocked and the four inmates were led out of the room. Marlee looked at Major Borden, still dumfounded by what just occurred. "I am so sorry." The major did not even look at Marlee and ushered the class out to the main lobby and then through the locked doors to the outside.

The students and Marlee's assistant waited on the sidewalk, wondering what would be the next step. Roxie, driving alone, had already proceeded toward her car. "Wait here," Marlee directed as she walked past the students and caught up to Roxie.

"Roxie, I want to talk to you." Marlee made it to Roxie's car before she was able to unlock it and get in. "Why in the hell did you do that? I told you at the start of class today that we were to keep our judgments to ourselves and that we could talk about them later after we left the prisons."

"I couldn't stand hearing their BS any more. No one owned up to what they did. It was just 'poor me, poor me' and I thought somebody should say something," Roxie said, oblivious to the damage her words caused.

"Do you realize how inappropriate that was? It's not your job to confront people when we're on tours. You've jeopardized the chance that future Criminal Justice To Go classes will be able to tour the women's prison. At this point, I'm ready to kick you out of the class!"

Roxie's tone and demeanor changed immediately. "No, don't do that. I just got a bit emotional. It won't happen again," Roxie begged. Marlee was afraid Roxie would do the same thing on tours of other facilities that week. This was only the first day of the class and it would be a long stressful week. If Roxie was acting up on the first day, how would she react later in the week?

"Look, lack of insight is why many people are in prison. You actually made some good points, but that was not the time, nor the place to say them. It was completely out of line and put our class in a bad light with the administration of the women's prison. Some of your remarks were downright rude. You had no right to belittle Luverne because of her mental health diagnosis. I'm not sure I can trust you to go into other facilities and keep your comments to yourself," Marlee stated. She hated kicking someone out of class for one mistake, but this was a doozy.

"I promise you, I won't say one word while we're in the other places. I'll keep my mouth shut and just listen. Please, Dr. McCabe, I really need this class," Roxie pleaded, tears in her eyes.

"I'm not prepared to make a decision on it right now because I'm still so upset with you. I'll sleep on it and let you know in the morning if you can stay in the class."

Roxie nodded her head. This was not the answer she had hoped for, but at least her professor was spending some time deciding her fate in the class. Marlee reminded Roxie of the name of the motel they would be staying at in Chamberlain that night and said goodbye.

The students on the sidewalk all turned as they saw Marlee approaching them, acting as if they had not heard every single word in the exchange between their professor and Roxie. "We need to get on the road to Chamberlain. It's about an hour and a half drive. That's where we're staying tonight. Anyone have any questions about how to get there or find the motel?" Everyone shook their head and Marlee continued. "After we check in tonight, we need to meet for a few minutes. We have a big day tomorrow and need to be at the juvenile facility by 8:00 a.m. sharp. We will all meet in the breakfast room no later than seven-thirty so we can go over a few things before we leave. Okay?" Everyone nodded and left for their vehicles.

"Whew!" Marlee said to Marcus as they got into her car and slammed the doors shut. "I've never had a student go off like that before." Marlee was a professional and did not want to discuss her thoughts on students with other students, but Marcus had graduated and was technically no longer one of her students. She felt free to vent to him about her frustrations with the class and the students, knowing he would not repeat her comments.

"I didn't know what to do!" Marcus repeatedly shuffled a sheaf of papers from one hand to the other as he struggled to make sense of Roxie's blow up.

"I didn't either. I'm deciding about kicking Roxie out of the class. She promised she won't say another word on any of the other tours this week, but I don't know if she can keep that promise. She was so fired up and I wonder if she will be able to control herself when she sees something else she disagrees with." Marlee wrestled with the pros and cons of keeping Roxie in the class.

"It made the other students really uncomfortable too," he said. "Some of them said they don't want her in the class because they won't learn as much if Roxie keeps acting this way."

"That's a good point, Marcus. I'll think on that. I have nine other students to worry about and I can't just focus on the one with bad behavior all week. If her behavior is disruptive to them, then it hampers what they can learn in the class." Marlee rubbed her eyes and forehead, hoping for a simple solution to the dilemma.

Before leaving Pierre, Marlee went through a drive thru so Marcus could get a Coke and a burger. Marlee was still full from supper at the prison and didn't want any caffeine to stimulate her further. Plus, she had a bottle of rum in her suitcase and would fix herself a stiff drink once they arrived at the motel.

The students were excited to discover the Lakeside Motel had an indoor pool. After everyone checked in, Marlee had difficulty corralling them into the motel lounge for a brief visit about what they had seen and done that day. All of the students were present except for Roxie. She must have slipped out after getting her room key. Marlee thought she might have decided to leave the class on her own rather than potentially be kicked out. Students had some great questions and good insights, but Roxie's outburst at the women's prison was the pink elephant in the room that nobody was discussing.

As soon as they finished the group meeting, most of the students made a bee-line for the swimming pool. It was a good way for them to relax and also spend some time together as a group, talking about the day. Marcus said he might go for a swim later, but wanted to get settled in his room first and call his girlfriend.

Marlee had other ideas about relaxing. The day wore on her and she was not equipped to deal with so much interaction with so many people. She felt like collapsing onto her bed and sleeping for the next twenty hours. As exhausted as she was, Marlee would not be able to calm down and rest for a while. She still had a big decision to make regarding Roxie.

She pulled the clothes out of her suitcase that she planned to wear the following day. Taking one of the plastic motel cups from the sink area and unwrapping it, Marlee opened her bottle of rum and poured in two generous glugs and drank it straight. The next drink would be on ice and mixed with pop. Then she would call her boyfriend to complain to him about all the injustices she had to endure. She grabbed the brown ice bucket and fumbled around in her purse until she gathered up a handful of quarters. Marlee's room was located on the second floor of the motel on the west side while all of the students' rooms were on the first floor on the east side. She arranged this purposely so as not to hear the inevitable late night partying and gossiping that occur when groups of people get together. All rooms could only be accessed from the outside and with any luck, Marlee would make it back to her room with pop and ice before any of her students could flag her down with questions or problems.

The professor walked outside to the pop and ice machines located on the second floor. Standing by the vending machines looking at the selections, Marlee knew she needed to purchase a beverage without caffeine and preferably without sugar. She had been doing well on her low carb diet for a few weeks now and didn't want to sabotage it with a sugary drink. As she was pushing the button for caffeine-free Diet Coke, she heard loud voices coming from the patio area on the floor below her.

Against her better judgment, Marlee turned around after she picked up her plastic bottle of pop from the dispenser. A female voice was yelling, but Marlee could not make out the words. A car door slammed and an engine roared. She peeked over the balcony and saw Roxie standing in front of an open motel room door with her fist in the air, still shouting. The large car turned and spun out of the motel driveway.

Marlee shook her head. She had no intention of getting involved in Roxie's personal business. Plus, she just did not have the energy to care what was going on with her students and their private lives right now. Marlee rubbed her eyes again. On top of everything else, her eyes were deceiving her. Marlee could have sworn Mean Dean Green was the person in the car who zoomed away from the motel.

You never really know what people think of you until you're gone.

Chapter 7

Marlee returned to her room and without hesitation fixed herself a rum and caffeine-free Diet Coke on ice. She sat on the wooden chair next to the tiny table in the small, dingy room.

Could it have been Dean Green who was arguing with Roxie? Marlee sipped on her drink and pondered what she thought she saw. *But that doesn't make any sense. She accused him of sexual harassment, he was fired over a number of things, and he left town already. Why would he track Roxie down?*

Marlee continued to think through the pros and cons of her possible Mean Dean Green siting. By the time she drank her concoction and prepared for bed, she knew she'd made a mistake. She was mentally and physically exhausted when they arrived at the hotel that night and then she drank straight rum before going to the ice machine. As she turned in for the night, she knew two things: she had not seen Dean Green at their motel, and she would have to kick Roxie out of the class tomorrow morning.

An annoying beeping roused Marlee from her sleep. She had brought her own travel alarm and also asked the front desk for a wakeup call. No sooner had she silenced the alarm, than the phone began to ring. Since it was a small, family run motel, there was not an automated answering service providing the wake up announcement. A lady with a grandmotherly voice advised her of the time and wished her a peaceful day.

Marlee pushed back the pink flowered bedspread that was reminiscent of one her great-aunt had years ago. With a deep breath, she stood up and began to prepare for the big day ahead of the class. Their first stop that day was at a juvenile correctional facility. Although it had undergone a number of name changes over the years, the mission remained the same; to rehabilitate youth so they could return to society as law-abiding, fully functional citizens. Most of the kids placed there were from South Dakota, yet a surprising number came from the big cities. When street gang members were arrested and court ordered to a correctional program, they had to be split up. Putting multiple members of the same gang in the same facility was asking for trouble. They would simply reunite within a correctional facility and resume gang activities while locked up. When members of a big city street gang were arrested, the members were sent to various facilities all over the United States, including the Youth Adjustment Program, or YAP as it was termed, in Chamberlain. Juveniles from Los Angeles, Chicago, and New York all occupied space in the rural South Dakota facility. Unfortunately, they would recruit new members from within the facility and start new branches of their gangs among South Dakota communities.

At six forty-five, Marlee headed down to the front office where the free breakfast was provided. She hoped to get in some caffeine and food before dealing with Roxie. The decision she made last night to evict Roxie from the class was a decision she remained committed to that morning. She just hoped there wouldn't be a huge scene in front of the students and other motel patrons.

Marlee was on her second cup of coffee and had already consumed a container of blueberry yogurt, a banana, and was contemplating a donut when the first group of students arrived for breakfast. They sat at a table next to hers and chatted about the upcoming events for the day. By seven fifteen, almost all of the students were in the breakfast nook eating and commiserating about the early hour and their need for more sleep. At seven thirty, everyone was present and ready to depart for the tour. Except Roxie. She would not be going on any more of the tours, but Marlee needed to talk with her before the class departed for YAP.

"Has anybody seen Roxie this morning?" Marlee asked. Several students shook their heads indicating they had not.

"I'll have the front desk call her room." Marlee approached the front desk and talked to an elderly lady she presumed was the grandmotherly-voiced wake up-call person.

"Can you please call the room of Roxie Harper? She's with our class and I need to speak with her."

"Sure," said the clerk as her gnarled fingers reached for the telephone atop the desk. After a long pause she said, "No answer."

"Hmmm... did she happen to check out already?" Marlee hoped Roxie had checked out of the room early and left town, thus taking herself out of the class.

The gnarled old fingers rapped on the computer keyboard much quicker than Marlee could type. After tapping for a few seconds the clerk replied, "No, she hasn't checked out."

Marlee went back to her table. She had a dilemma on her hands. She really needed to talk to Roxie, yet she could not delay the class's first tour of the day. Pulling Marcus aside, she asked him to take the class to the Youth Adjustment Program and act as the role of leader until she arrived. She briefly noted that she needed to speak with Roxie and would be along shortly.

"No problem," he replied. "I remember how to get there, so there shouldn't be anything to worry about. I'll explain the situation when we get to YAP."

The professor knew she had chosen wisely when selecting an assistant. "Thanks, Marcus. I shouldn't be too long. Tell them I'll be there as soon as I can and I'll catch up to you guys."

Marlee approached the students and announced that Marcus would be acting as their tour leader until she arrived at YAP. No one questioned it and she was thankful she didn't need to provide additional detail about her delay.

After the class cleared out from the motel, Marlee walked over to Roxie's room. The front desk clerk readily gave her Roxie's room number when asked. Marlee pounded on the door repeatedly but there was no answer. She peeked in the window, hoping to catch a glimpse of movement. All she could see were clothes strewn across the floor and the edge of the bed with possibly a foot sticking off of the edge. More pounding on the door yielded the same results. Frustrated, Marlee stomped back to the motel office.

"Can I get you to open the door to Roxie's room? I think she's in there and isn't answering. I pounded on the door but there was no sound. I think I saw her foot on the bed." Marlee was not entirely sure it was a foot she glimpsed through the ill-fitting plastic drapes, but she needed to convince the clerk that Roxie could be sick and in need of help.

"Well…" the clerk hesitated. "That's not something we usually do unless the police ask us. Or if a roommate gets locked out."

Marlee was at her wit's end. She did not know what else to do, so she just stared at the clerk without saying another word. From her past careers in dealing with people, she knew most Americans were quite uncomfortable with silence and would often acquiesce just to break the tension. This situation was no different.

"Okay, but if she raises heck about it, I'll need you to tell my boss you made me," said the elderly woman.

"Who's your boss?" Marlee was curious as to who would be able to control this capable senior citizen.

"My daughter," she said with a grimace.

"If Roxie causes a problem, I promise to take full responsibility," Marlee assured the clerk. She had no intention of getting her into any sort of trouble.

The elderly clerk grabbed an old-fashioned jumbo key and the two proceeded to Roxie's room. Marlee knocked again to see if there would be an answer. There was not, so Marlee motioned for the clerk to open the room door.

Sure enough, Roxie was lying in bed with the flowered bedspread pulled up around her shoulders. One foot extended through the covers and hung just off the edge of the bed. Clothes, shoes, and personal hygiene items were thrown about the room. Empty beer and liquor bottles littered the floor, table, dresser top, and bathroom vanity. Marlee walked toward the bed, careful not to step on the mish-mash of items.

"Roxie, wake up," Marlee said with a gentle tone, not wanting to startle the woman who was in a deep alcohol-induced sleep. There was no response.

"Roxie! Get up!" Marlee yelled, yet there was still not a sound from the sleeping woman. The professor walked up next to the bed and shook Roxie's shoulder, which was covered by the bedspread. "Get up, Roxie! I need to talk to you!"

Still no response.

Marlee looked at Roxie's face up close. It had an odd color. A cold sweat started at the base of Marlee's spine and worked its way downward. She touched Roxie's cheek. It was ice cold.

"Oh my god! I think she's dead!" Marlee shrieked.

The elderly clerk sprang into action. She grabbed the phone on the bedside table and dialed 911. As the old woman was relaying what little information they had about Roxie, Marlee checked to see if she was breathing or had a pulse. She had neither. Roxie's lips were blue and her eyes were wide open and glazed over. Marlee shook her head at the clerk, indicating that the ambulance need not rush over.

Coffee, yogurt, and banana all roiled in Marlee's stomach until she could not hold it down. She had the foresight not to puke in the bathroom, knowing this was possibly a crime scene and should not be contaminated. The professor ran out of the room and yakked up her breakfast a few feet from the front door. The clerk, not knowing what to do, began picking up Roxie's towels to take to the laundry room.

"Don't move anything. The cops will need to investigate this to see if it was an accident or a natural death. Or if she was killed. Let's just wait outside." Marlee and the clerk stood outside the room, near Marlee's puke pile, and waited until the police arrived moments later.

Two middle aged officers arrived in a squad car and Marlee and the clerk took turns apprising them of what they saw in Roxie's room. One ran inside right away to determine that she was, in fact, dead. Once he was satisfied that was the case, he returned to the small group outside the room to ask questions.

"Did you see anyone enter her room?" asked the eldest of the two male officers.

"Last night I went to get a pop and ice and heard Roxie yelling at someone," Marlee said, unsure if she should reveal her suspicion last night that Mean Dean Green was at the motel arguing with Roxie.

"Who was she yelling at? What did she say?"

"I couldn't hear what she said, but she was definitely mad. Then I heard a car door slam and a guy drove away in an older car. A Buick, I think. I don't know, I'm not very good with car makes and models. Roxie had her hand over her head in a fist, still shouting."

"Did you get a good look at the guy who drove off?"

"No..." Marlee hesitated.

"What is it?" questioned the elder cop.

"I'm not sure that I believe it myself, but it really looked like the Dean of the College of Arts and Sciences at Midwestern State University in Elmwood. That's where I teach and I'm leading a criminal justice class around the state touring various jails, prisons, and juvenile facilities. Roxie was in the class. Actually, I was going to kick her out of the class because she caused a huge commotion at the women's prison yesterday..." Marlee knew she was rambling, but could not stop herself. Shock had set in and she was unable to stop chattering on. She'd be discussing her Christmas shopping list if someone did not stop her soon.

"Wait. Wait," said the younger of the two officers. "What did the man who drove away look like? And what kind of car was he driving?"

Marlee took a deep breath in an attempt to clear her head and focus her thoughts. "The car was very large, four door, and silver. Sorry, I don't know car makes and models. It looked like Ira Green because he was around seventy years old. He had gray hair, a gray mustache and beard. He was a big guy. Not really fat, but just big."

"And this description fits Ira Green from your college?" the elder cop asked.

"Yes, it does. I never saw the driver standing up, but I could tell by looking at him in the car that he was a big–boned, older guy. But I just want to say that I'm not at all sure it was Dean Green." No matter what her feelings were for the dethroned dean, she would not try to get him into legal trouble. Especially when that legal trouble was murder. She was torn. If he had something to do with Roxie's death, then he should be held accountable.

"There's something else," Marlee said. "Again, I don't know if it was Dean Green, but I do know there was a problem between the dean and Roxie. The rumor mill has it that she filed a sexual harassment claim against him at MSU, which led to an investigation that revealed he had falsified information on his application. There were also other sexual harassment claims against him at other universities too. He was just fired and left town over the weekend according to the campus gossip. Nothing official came out from administration about Dean Green this weekend and I've been on the road all day and haven't accessed my campus email."

"So Roxie got the dean fired from his job? That sounds like a motive for murder," said the younger officer.

The elder officer shot him a hard look. "No jumping to conclusions. We know the lady is dead but we don't know that it's a murder. It could have been an accident, a suicide, or natural causes. Until the coroner makes a ruling after the autopsy, we keep our mouths shut about murder. Is that clear?"

"Yes, sir." The younger officer appeared appropriately chastised and looked down at his feet, letting the senior officer handle the questions.

"What can you tell us about the victim, Roxie Harper?"

"Not a whole lot. I guess she's in her late thirties or early forties. She was a student at MSU, majoring in criminal justice. She's been in one of my other classes, but never really talked, so I didn't get to know her very well. I was going to kick her out of this class though because she came unhinged at the women's prison yesterday and started shouting at some of the women on the inmate panel. She was being very judgmental and rude and she even made fun of one inmate's mental health condition."

"Is that why you had the clerk open the door to her room?" the elder officer asked.

"Yes, I wanted to talk to her in person to let her know she couldn't continue in the class. Last night, I told her I was considering it and would let her know my decision this morning. When she didn't show up at the departure time, I was worried and eventually talked the clerk into opening the door for me." Marlee was not worried about getting into trouble with the police for asking the elderly clerk to allow her access to Roxie's room. She was more concerned about the clerk getting into trouble with either the police or worse, her daughter.

"Do you know anything else about the victim?"

"Well, no. I can't think of anything other than she was a work-study student at the library on campus. I heard that's where the sexual harassment by the dean took place. Other than that, nothing. Some of the students in this class might know her better than I do. You should probably talk to them. They're at YAP right now on a tour with my assistant but will be finishing up in about half an hour."

"Yes. We want to talk to all of them, and your assistant, to see what they know about the victim," said the elder officer. Marlee provided the police with her requested background information so they would know how to contact her if they needed to question her further. Then she drove her vehicle over to the Youth Adjustment Program with the police car following her. The elder officer drove over to question the students while the younger officer remained behind to secure the crime scene. Detectives had been called and would be there soon to conduct an investigation.

What am I going to tell the students? Marlee thought as she drove to YAP. Even though it was only the second day of the class, a bond between most of the students had already been established. She was not sure that Roxie was included in this bond, but it would be hard on the students when they learned one of their class members died over night.

People are judged by the best and the worst things they did during their lives. Was she a good person or a bad person? Depends on who you ask.

Chapter 8

"Dead?" several of the students said in unison when Marlee told them in the Youth Adjustment Program entryway of Roxie's demise. The tour was over when she arrived and Marcus had kept everyone inside the building awaiting Marlee's further instructions.

"Yes, I'm afraid so. At this point, we don't know anything. The police are here and want to speak with each of you about Roxie," Marlee said, gesturing to the officer who was now walking in the front door.

"He thinks one of us killed Roxie?" shrieked Violet Stone. At just eighteen years of age, she was the youngest student on the tour. A single tear ran down her cheek and her lip trembled.

"No, he just wants to know what you know about Roxie and if you saw or heard anything last night or this morning. Just tell the truth. None of you are in trouble. We'll wait until everyone is questioned before we leave for our next tour, okay?" Marlee asked. "When you're finished being questioned, you can wait in here or in your cars but don't leave until everyone's ready."

Students nodded as the officer had them come outside one by one to talk with him. Within minutes, two additional officers arrived on the scene to help with interviews. Marcus was the first to be finished with his police interview and joined Marlee inside the YAP facility where she sat waiting.

"Wow, this is incredible. I can't believe what happened." Marcus' eyes lit up in both fascination and shock.

"What did the officer ask you?" Marlee inquired. Marcus gave a rundown of the questions he was asked and they all seemed to be in line with what Marlee was asked earlier about Roxie's background.

"Did you see Roxie at all last night or this morning?" Marlee asked.

"Yeah, she came to the pool last night right before it closed. She wasn't even wearing a swim suit. She just jumped in wearing a t-shirt and shorts. Then she started swimming over to all of us and talking crazy again like she did at the women's prison," Marcus reported.

"Really? What did she say?"

"She was talking about the women at the prison and making mean remarks about them, just like she did when we were there. Then she kept trying to get us to agree that she was right," Marcus said. "Roxie was even worse last night than at the prison."

"Who was at the pool?" Marlee asked.

"By then it was me, Dom, Jasper, and Donnie, and the three USD students. We were all standing around in the pool talking and splashing each other when Roxie jumped in. Lucky for us, the clerk came in and told us the pool was closing and to get out."

"Was it the clerk at the front desk this morning?"

"Nah, she was younger than that lady. She was really grouchy, but I was okay with it because it got us away from Roxie. I went back to my room and I don't know what everybody else did. I didn't hear or see anything after I went to my room. I kept the TV on all night. It helps me sleep," Marcus said.

Within the hour, the three officers finished interviewing the nine students. While she waited for the last of them to be questioned, Marlee placed a call to the department secretary at MSU. She was not sure what to do since she needed to notify someone on campus of Roxie's death. Her immediate supervisor was the dean, but since he'd been fired, she wasn't sure who she needed to report to. Marlee decided talking to the secretary would be a good first step. She didn't think it was a good idea to just call up the president of the university and relay the information of a student death while on a class tour. Perhaps Louise, the department secretary, would have some insight.

Taking her small TracFone outside the building, both for better reception and for privacy, Marlee called Louise and related what few details she knew of Roxie's death. Then she asked who she should report the incident to, since Dean Green was gone.

"Hank Barnaby from Biology is going to be the Interim Dean until someone is hired to fill the spot. I'll let you talk to him," Louise said.

Marlee was happy to hear this. Hank was a good guy and was not one to play games. Marlee had talked to him about confidential work matters in the past and he seemed to be a solid person. He was a straight shooter and wouldn't go out of his way to make trouble for the faculty.

"Hello! Barnaby here!" Hank's booming voice packed a punch and Marlee extended her cell phone out away from her ear.

"Hey, Hank. I hear you're the boss now. Hope you don't think I'm going to be treating you with respect," Marlee joked.

"Heh, heh. Absolutely not. What's going on? Aren't you on your prison tour class now?"

"Yeah, I've got some bad news and I'm not sure what to do. One of the students was found dead this morning in her motel room. Roxie Harper. I don't know if you know who she is... was, I mean. She was majoring in criminal justice," Marlee stated.

"What? That's terrible. What happened?"

"We don't know. The police are investigating. The desk clerk and I were the ones who found her when she didn't show up this morning. When she wouldn't answer the door, the clerk let me in and we found her dead in bed. She was covered up and I didn't see any wounds or weapons, but her room was a mess and I was kind of in shock, so I don't know for sure if there was a weapon there."

"So where are the other students?"

"I sent them with my assistant to the Youth Adjustment Program to start a tour before we found Roxie. I met up with them here and now the police are questioning each of them. We're almost done and then I guess we're off for another tour. We have some extra time, so I thought I'd gather everyone together so we can talk. I don't have any new information, but I think the students will need to discuss it," Marlee said.

"That sounds like a good plan. I'll notify President Ross. I'm sure reporters will be around asking questions soon. I'd like you to check in with me every day so I can keep the president apprised of how the students are doing," Hank said.

"Okay. I'll do that. The police just finished with the last of the interviews. I imagine detectives and crime scene people are at the motel now. Then the body will be delivered to the coroner for autopsy. I'll keep in touch with the police on this and report any findings right to you," Marlee said. She wanted to make sure to cover all her bases and keep her new acting dean in the loop. One thing she learned as a probation officer was the fine art of CYA: Cover Your Ass. With any big decision or event, always run it by your supervisor. That way, if there was a fallout after the fact, you could say it was reported to the supervisor and you were given the go-ahead.

After finishing her conversation with Hank, she motioned all the students to the parking lot. It was mid-morning in late May and the weather was flawless. Not a cloud in the sky and only a light breeze. The temperature was in the low 70s and it promised to be a beautiful day. Had it not been for Roxie's death, Marlee would have been in good spirits.

"I just wanted to talk to you guys for a few minutes before we leave for Mitchell. That's our next tour, but we have a little time before we need to be there," Marlee began. "I know this is really upsetting; having a classmate die and then be questioned by the police. I really don't know why she died and I don't think the police know anything either. Roxie's body will be autopsied to determine the cause of her death."

"Do you think she had a heart attack?" Dom asked.

"It could have been some sort of medical problem like a heart attack, or aneurism, or even an ongoing health issue Roxie had. It could have been a suicide or someone could have killed her. I can tell you that the clerk and I found her and I didn't see any signs of foul play or suicide, but that doesn't mean it didn't happen. At this point, none of us knows what happened to her."

"Why did the cops question all of us? What do they think we know?" asked Becca Troutman, one of the students from USD.

"It's standard protocol that the police interview the people who were around the victim and who knew her. They interviewed me at the scene. Since they don't know why she died, they have to ask questions about what everyone saw, heard, and knew. My guess is that they asked you all pretty much the same questions and asked for your contact information so detectives can contact you if there is a need to follow up or ask further questions." A few students nodded, as they had already compared what had been asked of each other.

"What if somebody did kill Roxie? We might be in danger too!" Becca twisted a fast food napkin in a knot and then untied it and then retied it, small shreds of paper falling to the ground.

"I doubt somebody killed her, but I don't know. For everyone's protection, I suggest you stay in your rooms with the doors locked at night. All of you have one or more roommates, so that should help everyone feel a bit safer. Don't leave the motel after we get there. If you really have to go somewhere, take one or two others with you. No one should be left alone, okay?" Marlee was not a parent, but at a time like this, she felt protective of her students.

"What about you? You're in your own room alone. Do you want to room with us?" asked Paula Stone. Her sister, Violet, nodded in agreement.

Marlee was touched that a student would make such an offer. Still, she knew she wouldn't be comfortable rooming with her students. "Thanks, Paula. I really appreciate the offer, but I'll be fine. Once I get to my room I'll just stay there."

Switching gears, Marlee asked, "Do any of you want to leave the class? If you do, I'll make sure you get your money refunded to you. I don't want anyone to stay if they are fearful for their lives. Personally, I think we're safe, but I have no idea why Roxie died. I plan to continue the class but if anyone wants out, just let me know sometime today."

After discussing Roxie's death and the impact on the students a bit further, the class got into their respective cars and drove east on the interstate toward Mitchell. "What do you make of all this, Dr. M.?" asked Marcus, turning in his seat so that he could get a better view of the professor as she spoke.

"I really don't know. I'm still kind of in shock. How well did you know Roxie?" Marlee asked.

"Not very well. I had classes with her, but she never talked. Not even when we had group activities. She only spoke if she absolutely had to. I think yesterday was only the second time I'd ever heard her talk," Marcus said.

"Did you have any sort of impression of her before yesterday?"

"Not really. She was a non-trad and I'm not trying to be mean, but students tend to make fun of the non-trads in their classes," Marcus said.

"What caused them to make fun of Roxie?" asked Marlee.

"Nothing that really meant anything. I remember sitting behind some people in a class and they were talking and laughing about her clothes and her book bag because they were out of style. But I never heard anything other than that," he said.

"So just superficial stuff?"

"Yeah, nothing of any importance."

"Can you think of any reason somebody would want Roxie dead?" Marlee inquired.

"No, not at all. Like I said, she was quiet as a mouse in classes and other than a few people laughing at her clothes, I've never even heard anybody mention her before. It's almost as if she didn't exist," said Marcus.

The two conversed about Roxie's death the remainder of the way to Mitchell. Once there, they pulled into the parking lot for Step By Step, a group home for girls. Many of the females placed there had alcohol and drug addictions, mental health problems, and had been victims of physical and sexual abuse. Some of the girls would return to their homes after completion of the program, while others would never be able to go back home. Step By Step helped some of the residents move into independent living; a supervised situation in which the underage girl would live on her own but be monitored to ensure she was working, paying her bills, abiding by the law, and following her treatment program.

The Criminal Justice To Go class entered the large, two story structure and waited for the facility director. Lola Greenfield greeted them and insisted on giving everyone a hug. She was a petite blonde in her sixties. Her caring and goodwill spilled from her eyes as she smiled and welcomed the class to Step By Step. Lola introduced two of the girls who were residents of the program and advised they would be leading the tour through the facility and answering any questions the group might have. Following the tour, the class would join the residents in the dining room for lunch and conversation.

Charlotte, a tall, slim Native American girl, spoke as she led the class up the stairs. She showed the commissary where they could buy snacks, hygiene items, magazines, and other luxuries. Then Charlotte led them to the classrooms, and talked about the units they just finished in her classes.

Tina, a shy white girl followed more toward the back of the group. She appeared uncomfortable in her position as co-tour leader. Marlee, who was walking beside her, tried to bring her out of her shell by engaging her in conversation. "So, Tina, how long have you been here at Step By Step?"

Tina shrugged, but then answered, "About a year.

I might get to go on a home visit this summer." "Where's your home?" Marlee inquired.

"Rapid City. My mom lives there with my brothers," Tina said, now making limited eye contact with Marlee.

"How do you feel about going home for a visit?"

"Happy, mostly. But a little scared. I don't want my old friends to come around 'cuz they'll try to get me to use. I've been clean since I got here and I don't wanna relapse," Tina mumbled, using the common verbiage of treatment programs.

"What can you do to make sure you don't relapse while you're home?" Marlee had not been a probation officer for years, yet she still focused on behaviors and consequences when talking to young people.

Tina looked at Marlee and grinned. "You sound like the counselors here."

"I used to be a probation officer, so I'm used to helping people figure out how to stay out of trouble," Marlee disclosed.

"I'll stay away from my old friends. I won't tell them I'm coming back home so they won't be able to bother me. And I'll attend AA and NA meetings too," said Tina. "And I'll stay in touch with my counselor here at Step By Step. He helps me stay on track."

The group continued to one of the sleeping rooms the girls shared. The rooms provided a twin bed for each girl along with a desk, chair, and small closet. A shared bathroom connected two of the rooms together. Most of the beds had homemade quilts atop them, a small touch that personalized each girl's bed. When asked about the quilts, Charlotte went on to explain that a church group in Mitchell donated them so each girl would have something of her own to keep after she left Step By Step.

Following the tour, Marlee and the students gathered in the dining room. They lined up as directed and went through the serving line to receive chili dogs, corn chips, fresh fruit, and a chocolate brownie on their plastic trays. The class sat at one long table with the director at the head so she could answer questions about the program.

"How long do the girls stay here?" asked Paula.

"Anywhere from a few months to a few years, depending on their issues and how well they're working the program. Some girls come in with a multitude of problems; legal, addiction, abuse, mental health, you name it. For those girls, it takes longer to deal with everything. Other girls who have just one or two issues can move through the program more quickly if they choose to do so. It all depends on how hard they work their program," said Lola.

"Are most of the girls successful when they're released from Step By Step?" asked Bart.

"We have some girls who go through the program and have to come back because they couldn't maintain sobriety or hadn't fully dealt with their problems when they were here the first time. Some age out of our program and have to be released because they are too old to be housed in a juvenile group home. Those girls often go on to get into more trouble. The overall success rate for programs like ours is low, but I'm proud to say we have one of the highest success rates in the state. Keep in mind, it depends on how you define success. Staying sober and

94

out of legal trouble is the pinnacle of success for most of our girls, but we have a few who go on to college and technical schools."

Following the give and take of information, Marlee stood and thanked Lola Greenfield and the girls for the lunch and for providing them with a tour of the facility. On the way out, Marlee pulled Lola aside and explained about Roxie's death. "Since you have a background in counseling, I was wondering what advice you could give me in dealing with my students when it comes to this issue."

"Keep talking to them about it, both in groups and individually. Reassure them they're safe and ask them to come to you with their fears and concerns. Right now they probably just need to feel safe and to have someone listen to them, even though you won't be able to provide any solutions. Don't let anyone isolate themselves or spend too much time alone," Lola advised.

Marlee kept Lola's words in mind as the group drove to their next stop, the medium security prison for men in Springfield. Her inclination was to isolate when tense, tired, or confused. She would have to overcome that, at least for the next few days, to make sure the students felt comfortable in the class. So far, no one had approached her about dropping the course.

"Marcus, has anyone talked to you about dropping the class? I gave the students until the end of today to decide if they wanted out."

"No way! Everyone wants to see how this plays out. I think they're all on edge, but not really frightened for their own safety. Even though Roxie wasn't one of their favorite people, two of the students mentioned to me how important it is that we find out what happened to her," Marcus related.

Realizing that she forgot to call Vince the night before, Marlee reached for her phone and called her boyfriend at work. She left a message when he didn't answer. It was Tuesday and those were always busy days because Mondays were big court days for him. The day after court was spent putting out fires and implementing the judge's new orders.

I'll try calling Vince at home tonight, she decided.

The tour of the men's prison at Springfield mirrored the tour they had the day before at the women's prison. A tour was followed by a meal in the chow hall and then a panel of inmates was brought into a secure room to speak to the students about their lives, the convictions, and being in prison. The tour consisted of the housing units, the work quarters, and the recreational areas. Then the students joined the inmates in a noisy, chaotic dining hall for a bland meal of a meat gravy substance covering a piece of corn bread.

The men's prison had the distinct odor of sweat, soup, and farts. The noise level there was mind-numbing at times. Being confined would be hard to deal with, but Marlee thought the excessive noise would be the worst part.

"Some of these guys look like my dad's friends. You know, just regular ordinary guys," said Bart.

"There's no specific type of person who fits the description of 'criminal'. Every one of us is capable of doing anything any of these men did. There's very little difference, deep down, between the people who are incarcerated and the people who are on the outside," Marlee said as she glanced around the dining hall. There were men of all ages, shapes, and sizes. About half were Native American, with the other half Caucasian. There were a few African Americans and Asians, as well as some Latinos. Since the majority of the population in South

Dakota was Caucasian, and Native Americans were the largest minority, the racial breakdown was not surprising. What was shocking was that Native Americans only constituted 8% of the population in the state yet they comprised nearly half the inmate population. This begged the question of unequal treatment for Native Americans in the criminal justice system.

"When I think of somebody doing hard time, I think of a guy like that," Jasper said nodding his head in the direction of a grizzled, tattooed man who looked as if he has seen a lot of living and dying in his life. "I don't think of guys like that," Jasper continued, now looking at a slight, middle aged man with wire framed glasses and short brown hair. "He looks like an accountant or a real estate agent."

"And he may be a murderer, or a rapist, or a thief. We can't tell much about people just by looking at their appearance."

Jasper nodded, agreeing to a point, but still glancing around the chow hall to find better examples that fit his notion of a criminal. The tour leader asked them to wait in the dining hall until all of the inmates left. Then he escorted them to a recreational area which had been cleared out for the students to listen to the inmate panel. Marlee and the students seated themselves on the folding chairs lined up before the long table with four inmates seated behind it.

After a series of opening remarks and announcements, Major Aspen, the tour leader, introduced the inmate panel to the class. Tom was a fifty-year-old man who was doing a five-year sentence for drugs. Terrence was a sixty-year-old man finishing up a seven-year term for sexual contact with a child. Alex had killed his parents and was doing a life sentence. Bradley was the baby of the group; at twenty years of age, he was serving two years for robbery.

"I'm Tom and I'm in for drugs," began the wiry, bald man. "I'm a veteran and got hooked on heroin in Vietnam. I went to treatment several times when I got back, but never completely kicked it. It's hard to hold down a job for very long when you're on heroin. You either can't concentrate because you need a fix, or you miss a few days because you're using what you bought, or else there's a drug test and they fire you. Anyway, I started dealing, which was one thing I told myself I'd never do. I never sold to kids, just adults who knew what they were getting into. I sold to an undercover cop and that's how I got busted. After I came back from 'Nam, I really didn't have much left waiting for me. My wife and kid had left and my parents had both died. So I used drugs because I needed to get away from how awful life really was." He turned to the next person at the table, signaling that he had finished talking.

"I'm Terrence and I got locked up for sexual assault of a child," said the pudgy man with a crew cut and small, brown eyes. "I pled guilty to the charge but I didn't really do it. I just plead guilty to get a lesser sentence because I knew they would convict me at trial. The kid and her mother convinced the police I molested her but I never did. They got the wrong guy." As Terrence was talking, Major Aspen spoke into his walkie-talkie and two male correctional officers came into the room and motioned for Terrence to stand up. They handcuffed him and escorted him out of the room.

"What did I do? What did I do?" Terrence shouted as he was led away.

The major stood and faced the group. "One of the qualifications of talking in an inmate group like this is that the inmate must accept responsibility for his crime.

Terrence told us he had done so and we believed him. Then he gets in here today and starts denying he had any sexual contact with the victim. We can't have someone on the panel who doesn't acknowledge what they did and accept that it was wrong."

"Can I ask a question before the rest of the group speaks?" Marlee asked. When Major Aspen nodded, she continued. "Is being part of this inmate panel something you all wanted to do?"

The three remaining inmates nodded their heads as the major began to speak. "It's a privilege to talk to a group of students. They like to do it because it's a break from the boredom of everyday life in prison and it gives them a change to interact with regular people from the outside instead of just criminals and corrections officials. We had numerous men who wanted to be on the panel, but we could only choose four. Before and after they come into this room to speak, they're strip-searched to make sure they're not bringing in, or taking out, any contraband." With that declaration, the major nodded to the next man on the panel.

"Hi, I'm Alex and I'm doing life for killing my parents in 1988," said the average-built Caucasian man with non-descript features and a mild manner. "There's really nothing I can say that justifies what I did. They were good people. I was into meth and needed money. They wouldn't give it to me so I stabbed them and took the cash they had in the house along with some things I could sell, like the TV, VCR, and some of Mom's jewelry. They had cut me off a couple years earlier, but would let me come over for a meal and to take a shower once in a while. Mostly I lived on the streets in Sioux Falls and couch-surfed at people's houses until they kicked me out. Mom and Dad lived out in the country on an acreage. I went there knowing I would get money but I didn't plan to kill them."

Taking a deep breath, Alex continued. "I took a hunting knife with me just to threaten Dad into giving me some money. He wouldn't give me anything and called me a loser. He told me to get out and not come back anymore. Mom was crying and I just sort of snapped and stabbed Dad. Then I knew I had to kill Mom because she would turn me in. They were both retired and nobody found them until about a week later when the mail carrier noticed they weren't picking up their mail. She peeked in the window and saw them. By that time, I took off for Denver and was using meth as often as I could. Probably would have died from it if the cops hadn't caught me and brought me back to South Dakota. I admitted everything right away. No point in denying it. Who else would kill two nice, elderly people?" Although Alex was not crying, he became choked up and unable to speak further. Marlee suspected he had plenty more to say but had reached his limit in the telling of that part of his story.

"Hey, I'm Bradley and I'm in here for home robberies." The athletic young man was handsome and had his dark, wavy hair styled with gel. His skin was flawless and he looked as if he would have been more at home on a runway than prison. "I got caught when the idiot I was working with left his cell phone behind at one of the houses." Bradley laughed a bit before he continued, "The cops found the phone and then found him. He rolled over then the cops got me. I don't have a whole lot of time left in here. I'm going back home to Pierre and work for an uncle who has a used car dealership." There was something about Bradley that bothered Marlee more than the others on the panel. He was young and cocky. He didn't seem to have much remorse for his crimes, although he was smart enough not to deny them as Terrence had done earlier. Bradley had even laughed while telling his story, which suggested to Marlee that he was a long way from rehabilitated.

Major Aspen opened the forum up for questions and Paula was the first to speak. "I always hear about rape being a common problem in prisons. Is it a problem here?" The three inmates looked at the table top and no one spoke at first.

After a few moments of silence, Tom started to talk. "Sex among inmates isn't rare. I'd say about half the guys in here have some sort of sexual contact with another guy. Most of it is agreed upon by both of them. Most of them would say they weren't gay. They just want the sex. As for rape, yeah, it happens. Especially to child molesters. They're the lowest of the low on the prison totem pole."

"But we do everything we can to prevent rape. If we find out about an inmate being sexually assaulted, we take every measure possible to separate him from his attacker," interjected the major. "We have almost no reports of rape or sexual violence in any given year here at this prison."

The inmates gave each other knowing glances. It was the administrator's job to downplay any physical or sexual violence to outsiders. One of the reasons most people in South Dakota were so pro-punishment is that they didn't fully comprehend what occurred in prison. Being locked up and separated from family and friends was only a small part of the misery.

"Do you have families? Do any of you see your families?" Katie asked.

Tom, the vet, shook his head. "I haven't seen my kid since he was a baby. I don't even know how old he is now. I think about him a lot, but the truth is that he's probably a hell of a lot better off without me."

"I never had any kids. Shootin' blanks they called it, when I was tested one time. My second wife really wanted kids and we weren't having any luck, so she made us both get tested. After she found out I couldn't produce, she left me," said Alex.

"I have four, maybe five kids," said Bradley. "The fifth one isn't a sure thing yet. I'm waiting on a paternity test."

"Bradley, why don't you tell them about your girlfriends?" suggested Major Aspen, crossing his arms as he looked at the young inmate.

Just when Marlee thought she could not like Bradley any less, he dropped another unflattering nugget of information. "Well, that's a long story. Hit it and quit it, y'know what I'm sayin'?" he said with a chuckle. "I don't like to get tied down, y'know? I never make any promises to a girl, but they all think that just because we do it that we're married. Unless I put a ring on her finger, we're not together and I can see whoever I want. So I've been getting hassled a lot by the Department of Social Services about paying child support for those kids. Since they have different mothers, DSS tries to make it look like I'm a deadbeat dad. Guess I have to go to court on that when I'm outta here."

After the question and answer session was finished, Marlee and the students walked to the parking lot. "We're staying in Yankton tonight and will be touring the Federal Prison Camp tomorrow morning. When you get to the motel in Yankton, wait in the lobby until we're all there so we can get checked in together. Then we'll have a quick meeting and call in a night."

Marlee asked Marcus to drive her car from Springfield to Yankton. It was a short drive, but Marlee thought she could best utilize the time making some phone calls and catching up on the status of Roxie's death.

Her first call was to the police department in Chamberlain. She was advised that Detective Ramos was in charge of the case. The dispatcher took Marlee's cell number and advised the detective would be notified of her call. Marlee no sooner hung up than her phone rang.

"Hello. Yes, Detective Ramos, thank you so much for calling me back. Can you tell me anything about the investigation of Roxie Harper's death? I'm meeting with my students shortly and I'd like to be able to give them an update if I can."

After a minute-long pause, Marlee thanked the detective and ended the call. She turned to her assistant and said, "The initial autopsy findings won't be made available until tomorrow, but Detective Ramos thinks she was poisoned. Roxie had some blue crystalized substance around her mouth, which didn't appear to be normal food or drink. He doesn't know if she ingested the poison intentionally or accidentally. Or if someone killed her with poison." Marlee's stomach fell as she relayed the information to Marcus. Deep down, she suspected foul play but was hoping maybe Roxie had a medical condition that claimed her life. There was no good solution to Roxie's death. She was still dead regardless of the reason. A murder, however, was almost too much to process.

Marcus was equally upset as he turned to talk to Marlee as he drove. "Who would poison Roxie? She's been acting weird on this trip, but not so bad that someone would try to do her in."

"I have no idea. I guess it's possible that she poisoned herself, but it also could've been someone else. I'm sure there are some facts the detective didn't share with me. I wonder what else he's uncovered," Marlee mused.

Once she finished talking to Marcus about her conversation with the detective, she called Hank

Barnaby's work number and left him a message detailing the information on Roxie's suspected cause of death. She would've liked to talk to the new acting dean in person, as he was a calming presence and had a way of putting things into perspective.

Once the group arrived at the motel in Springfield and checked into their rooms, Marlee held a meeting in the corner of the motel lobby. She encouraged her students to pull their chairs up close and keep their voices low so as not to alert the other motel patrons and the front desk clerk that they were discussing an ongoing death investigation.

Marlee related her conversation with Detective Ramos and his assertions that Roxie's cause of death may have been poisoning. "Since this is a bit of a difficult place to chat about such a sensitive subject, I'd like to come to each of your rooms and chat with you in small groups, if you don't mind. There's no swimming pool here, so there won't be much to do tonight."

"Do we have time to go get some food? Supper at the prison was beyond disgusting!" Katie Daniels said and several other students nodded.

"Sure, how about if I wait an hour or so. That'll give you time to eat and get back here. Remember, don't go anywhere alone. I'm sure there's no reason to believe someone will try to hurt any of us, but it'll make me feel better if you stick together. Okay?" Marlee was back in mom-mode.

After agreeing all of the students and Marcus would go together to get something to eat, Marlee went to her room and pulled the next day's clothes out of her suitcase and spread them over a chair back in hopes of releasing some of the wrinkles. She found her bottle of rum in the bottom of her suitcase and set it on next to the sink by the plastic cups. *Better wait until I finish talking to the students before I have a cocktail,* she thought, not at all excited that she would have to wait to have a relaxing drink.

Remembering that she hadn't talked to Vince since she left home on Sunday, Marlee dialed his home number. After two rings, the phone was answered but it was not Vince's voice she heard. It was Spud. "Well, hey there! Nice to hear from you. Glad you called to chat," Spud said in his creepy voice.

"Actually, I'm trying to reach Vince. Is he there?" Marlee asked, hoping to ditch Spud as soon as possible.

"Nope, he has intramural volleyball tonight and then he's going out for drinks with some of the others on the team," Spud reported. "So how's your class going? Do you miss me yet?"

Marlee ignored Spud's sickening attempt at flirtation. "What time do you think Vince will be home?"

"Late. He said Suzanne was in town and he wanted to see her," Spud said with a degree of smugness. He was enjoying tormenting Marlee with the fact that Vince would be seeing his old girlfriend, Suzanne.

Suzanne Austin and Vince dated for over two years until she broke it off and moved out of town for another job. Her parents and most of her other relatives still lived in Elmwood, so she visited on occasion. Marlee met Suzanne back when she lived in Elmwood and was envious of her beauty. Suzanne was everything Marlee was not; she was tall, slim, had long blonde hair, and model good looks.

"Marlee, are you still there?" Spud asked with a chuckle.

"Yep. I'll call him tomorrow. Bye." With that abrupt ending to the conversation, she turned off her cell phone and slammed it on the bed, watching it bounce three times before coming to a halt near a pillow.

What would Vince be doing with Suzanne? Where was he meeting her? At the bar? At a motel? Was she moving back to Elmwood? Were they getting back together? Marlee's imagination ran wild as she thought of all types of scenarios, most of which involved her being dumped and Vince and Suzanne reuniting to live happily ever after. She continued to torment herself with thoughts of Vince and his ex-girlfriend until it was time to meet the students.

Marlee started first with the room shared by Dom, Jasper, and Donnie. They were members in the Criminal Justice Club which was founded two years before when a professor was found dead on campus. In order to discuss the case and process their feelings, the students urged Marlee to develop the club, which she did. Mean Dean Green had the final approval on any campus clubs and he denied her petition. Marlee got around that by holding informal Criminal Justice Club meetings at her house, local diners, coffee shops, and other places off-campus and out of the dean's reach. She knew Dom, Jasper, and Donnie very well, and trusted their judgment. She was anxious to hear their collective take on Roxie and what happened to cause her death.

She heard laughing coming from the room before she knocked, then the room went silent. Marlee knocked again and said, "It's Dr. McCabe."

Dom opened the door and peered out to verify it was indeed his professor before unlatching the chain lock. "Come on in. We just finished eating but have some fries left. Do you want them?"

"No," Marlee said laughing, realizing it was the first time in the past couple days she found anything amusing. She sat down in one of the chairs beside the dresser. Donnie was sprawled across one queen sized bed while Jasper was sitting on the edge of the other. Dom pulled up another chair and pulled it closer to Marlee so that he was facing her.

"Basically, I'm here to find out what you guys know about Roxie," Marlee said. She was also there to make sure they were handling their classmate's death, but first she wanted to get their impressions of Roxie.

Donnie spoke first, rising from a prone position to sitting upright on the bed as she talked. "Roxie was in several of my classes. We're both non-trads, so I think we kind of gravitated toward each other at first. She's quite a bit older than me, but we were both older than the regular students and worked together a few times on group projects. She seemed shy and unsure of herself. That's why I was blown away by her behavior at the women's prison. Roxie hardly ever talked except when she absolutely had to, so I found it hard to believe what I was seeing and hearing as she just went off on the inmate panel."

"Did she ever confide in you, Donnie? Anything about problems or concerns she had?" Marlee asked.

"No, not really. She was stressed about tests and projects and grades like we all were, but nothing out of the ordinary."

"What about you two?" Marlee looked at Jasper then Dom. "Did you guys know Roxie at all?"

"Nope, but I've seen her on campus. Never knew her name or anything about her," said Jasper.

"She was in one of my classes but I never talked to her. I don't remember seeing her other than that one class last year," Dom reported.

"I'm going to tell you three something and I don't want it to leave this room. It will probably become common knowledge later, but I don't want the story being spread around because I said anything. Agreed?" Marlee asked.

The three students nodded with enthusiasm, sitting up just a bit straighter in anticipation of top-secret information being shared with them. Marlee then relayed the story of Roxie being sexually harassed by Dean Green and the dean's ultimate dismissal from MSU based on other information that came to light.

"What?" exclaimed Jasper, not sure he had correctly comprehended the story.

"Have any of you heard anything about this?"

"No," the three students said in unison.

"Have you heard anything at all about Dean Green being handsy with women on campus?" Marlee asked.

Dom and Jasper shook their heads but Donnie hesitated. "One of the girls I worked with at the information desk in the Student Union said something about him one time. I don't think he did anything to her, but she seemed to know something about him harassing one of her friends."

"Who was this girl you worked with, Donnie?"

"Her name is Bethanny Hayes. She's on campus this summer, taking a couple classes and working, but I don't know where. They don't keep the information desk staffed in the summer because so few students are around.

I can ask one of my friends how to contact Bethanny," Donnie said.

"That would be great. If possible, can you call your friend tomorrow and get Bethanny's contact information? I'd like to talk to her as soon as possible and see what she knows." Donnie nodded her agreement and Marlee continued, "The reason I'm asking about Dean Green's behavior is that I think I saw him driving away from the motel in Chamberlain that night we stayed there. Roxie was arguing with someone and a man looking a lot like Ira Green drove out of the parking lot. At first I thought my eyes were playing tricks on me, but now I think my first hunch was right. Maybe Bethanny knows something about Dean Green's behavior with other women on campus. That might link in to Roxie's death."

"Wait, you think Dean Green killed Roxie?" Dom asked.

"No, not necessarily, but he has some explaining to do if it was him arguing with Roxie at the motel on Monday night. I'm just trying to find out more information about Roxie and in doing so, I have to find out more about Dean Green's behavior," Marlee said, not quite understanding her own line of thought. "Did any of you see Roxie on Monday night after we finished talking in the motel lobby?"

"Yeah, she came to the pool and acted just as crazy then as she did at the women's prison," said Jasper. The other two nodded in agreement.

"Did you see her at any other time that night? Or hear anything from her room or outside?" Marlee asked.

Donnie, Dom, and Jasper all denied hearing or seeing anything out of the ordinary after they left the pool.

Before she left the students' room, Marlee felt she should ask them about their feelings and how they were dealing with Roxie's death. They all assured her they were handling it in an acceptable fashion and that they were talking to each other continuously about Roxie's demise.

She left their room feeling like she had done her job as a caring professor, but also that she gained a bit more information about Dean Green. How that would apply to the death investigation of Roxie Harper, she wasn't sure.

The next stop was the room shared by the Stone sisters, Violet and Paula, and their long-time friend, Johnny Marble. Marlee knocked on the door and it was opened by Paula, who had changed into a long green nightshirt, and held her toothbrush in her hand. She motioned the professor in and Marlee entered and looked around the room. It was exactly like the previous room she had been in, as well as her own. Violet sat on one of the two beds with her head propped up with four pillows, two of which she must have brought with her because they were extra fluffy and depicted Betty Boop. Johnny was nowhere to be seen. The toilet flushed and he walked out of the bathroom wearing knee length sport shorts and a ratty off-white MSU t-shirt.

The spiel about why she was visiting all of the students' rooms was repeated. Since Violet was in her first year at MSU, she was taking mostly general classes and not too many in her major. Thus, she didn't have any information about Roxie. "I've never even had a class with her," Violet reported.

Paula Stone knew Roxie, as they had shared several of the same classes, although Paula could not report any relevant details about their now deceased classmate. "I've known who she was for a couple years now, but I don't really know her. I noticed she always sat alone, so I sat by her a couple times and tried to strike up a conversation before class. She just didn't want to talk about herself."

Johnny Marble, also a criminal justice major at MSU, had little knowledge of Roxie other than what he had heard about her since starting Criminal Justice To Go. "Not really anything I can tell you. She seemed nice enough until she exploded at the women's prison."

"Did you guys go swimming last night?" Marlee asked.

Paula shook her head. "We wanted to watch Dancing with the Stars finale last night, so we didn't go swimming. We thought that was more important. I heard Roxie was acting bizarre at the pool."

Marlee launched into her speech about coming to her if they had any problem dealing with Roxie's death. "If you want to talk or just want company, let me know." Johnny gave a noncommittal nod and Marlee doubted he would be running to her with his thoughts and feelings anytime soon. Paula and Violet, on the other hand, were enthusiastic over the offer and Marlee suspected she might have opened the floodgates with those two.

The room with the USD students was Marlee's last stop. She intentionally left them until the end because they would not have any information on Roxie other than what they observed along with the rest of the class. This stop would be a quick check in, and then she could go back to her own room and relax.

After knocking three times, Bart flung the door wide open. "C'mon in," he slurred. Marlee could see that Bart had been drinking and she could also smell it. Marlee entered the room and saw a red cooler placed in the middle of the room. The lid was up, exposing cans of beer and two bottles of hard alcohol. Marlee really didn't care if the students drank after they were through with the tours for the day. As long as they were not drunk or hung over during the tours, she had no problem. She was not naïve enough to think the students would remain alcohol-free the whole week. Most of the students probably brought something with them or bought it in the towns they stayed. She had her own bottle of rum in her suitcase, so to forbid the students from drinking seemed hypocritical. Plus, they would do it anyway. It was best to give up the farce of a no-drink rule on the trip.

Katie walked past the cooler and gave it a hard kick on the side, as if stubbing her toe. It had the effect of knocking the lid shut and hiding the drinks. "Come in, Dr. McCabe." She motioned to the chair beside the dresser and Marlee sat down. She ran through the purpose of her visit for the third time that night.

"Did any of you know Roxie before this class?" Marlee asked, assuming that none of the three knew Roxie since they all attended USD and were only taking this class because it was the only course like it offered in the state.

"No. I never said one word to her," said Becca who was standing in the corner near the television, searching for the remote to reduce the volume.

"I said hi to her, but that was it. She didn't seem very friendly," said Katie, sitting on the edge of the bed near the cooler.

"Me neither," slurred Bart, now leaning against the dresser in what Marlee guessed was more for stability than anything else.

"Did you guys see her at the pool on Monday night?"

All three nodded and repeated the same story she heard from Marcus, Dom, Jasper, and Donnie. With that, Marlee finished by reminding the students to talk to her if they needed any support or just wanted to vent about Roxie's death. With that, she stopped by the pop machine on the way back to her room. With a caffeine-free diet Pepsi in hand, Marlee entered her own room and fixed herself a cocktail in one of the plastic cups provided by the motel. It was after ten o'clock, and she was itching to call Vince's house again. She desperately wanted to know why he had met with his old girlfriend that night, but she was also afraid of the answer. This was a conversation that could be delayed until the following day.

There are two types of prisons. One is the place where criminals are sent. The other type of prison takes the form of restrictions we place on ourselves.

Chapter 9

It was Wednesday and, if past instances of Criminal Justice To Go were any predictor, this would be the day the shit would hit the fan. The past two summers she taught the class, Wednesday was the day from hell. The novelty of the class had worn off at that point and the students were starting to get on each other's nerves. Cliques had formed and alliances made. Roommates were spatting and a few people ganged up on one or more students they found irritating. Marlee tried not to intervene unless the situation became intolerable. Unfortunately, the students tried to pull her into their dramas, wanting her to side with them and sanction their opponents.

Everyone met in the breakfast room of the motel before seven-thirty, and nearly everyone had a sad face. The early mornings, late nights, different foods, and lack of their own personal comforts took a toll. Marlee typically hated each and every one of the students by Wednesday, but this morning, she was in a strangely positive mood. She was halfway through a class that she would despise by the end of it, a student had died while in the class, and her boyfriend was spending time with his super-model ex-girlfriend. Marlee's life was in the crapper and there was not much reason to be happy, yet she was.

After a brief chat with the tables of students breakfasting on sugary rolls, make-your-own waffles, and cereal, Marlee returned to her room to grab the last of her items and place them in the car. Before leaving the room, she decided to give Vince a quick call on his home phone. She usually didn't call him on his work cell because that line needed to be free in case there was an emergency with one of the felons he supervised in the community.

Marlee rang the number and after the third ring, a husky female voice answered, "Hello?"

Marlee ended her call with one swift press of the END button on her cell. She was mad, sad, disappointed, and brewing for a fight all at the same time. Clearly, Suzanne had spent the night with Vince. *How convenient, I'm gone for a week and Vince uses the time to court his ex-girlfriend.* Of course now Marlee was most likely the ex-girlfriend. Marlee was out and Suzanne was in.

"Vince Chipperton, you asshole!" Marlee yelled, turning off her phone and shoving it in her purse. She was so mad, she feared she would cry just to release some of the emotion. Taking a deep breath, she left her room and proceeded to lead the class to their next tour.

Marcus didn't say a word when he saw Marlee's scowling face. He knew something was up, but didn't feel he should ask. They parked on a side street near the Federal Prison Camp and walked into the main building lobby to be screened and given further directions. Only males sentenced in federal court could be imprisoned in the Federal Prison Camp.

The Bureau of Prisons oversaw the custody, control, and care of individuals sentenced to a term of prison in one of the country's federal correctional institutions. After being sentenced in federal court, the BOP decided where the offender would be located. Being a South Dakota resident did not ensure they would be housed within the state, or even the Midwest. Although the BOP tried to place offenders close to home, that was not their main goal when designating someone to a prison. Placement issues in the federal prison system were based on the type of offense committed, length of the sentence, prior offenses, and the level of violence in the offender's past.

The BOP also sought to keep offenders separate from their co-defendants and other known criminal associates to reduce the chances of them forming alliances or planning future criminal activities. Non-violent offenders were placed at prisons that had lower security levels and allowed more privileges. Those convicted of violent offenses were typically placed at prisons with much higher levels of security since they were deemed more of a threat to society.

The only federal prison in South Dakota was considered a country-club prison because it housed only non-violent offenders, most of whom were convicted of white collar crimes. The lack of fences and gates, the visibility of a volleyball court and other recreational areas, and the fact that two streets bisected the prison grounds perpetuated the idea that the prison in Yankton, South Dakota, was indeed for those who committed crimes like securities fraud and embezzlement, and could only be punished in posh surroundings.

The BOP designated the facility in Yankton as a prison camp because camps had the lowest security of all federal institutions. The lack of bars, wires, and armed guards made the general public wonder what kept inmates from just walking away. Occasionally, this did occur, but most inmates realized there was a high probability they would be caught and then incarcerated at a much more secure facility. Plus, more time would be added to the sentence as punishment for the escape. Since it was a low security prison, any inmate who walked away from the prison camp would be much more likely to embezzle from a victim's bank account than to perpetuate a murder, rape, or robbery. An escapee wouldn't be an immediate danger to the community.

The prison had, at one time, been a college campus and was later repurposed into a prison. The recreation areas were holdovers from the college days, as were the large, stately buildings. Inmates were kept busy tending to the grounds with non-powered push mowers and small hand tools. Other inmates were occupied with maintaining the polished and pristine interior of the old buildings. Brooms and dust mops were in the hands of most inmates inside the administrative prison buildings at Yankton. The work of the inmates was evident in the shining wood floors, stairs, and banisters in the buildings and the well-tended green space outside.

The general public tended to lament the prison population for refusing to work while incarcerated. This was far from accurate. Most inmates wanted to work to help pass time. Twenty four hours spent in a cell or barracks passed very slowly when there was nothing to do. Although it was possible for inmates to refuse to work, most wanted to work to fight boredom. Plus, they earned a small amount of money which could be used to purchase snacks and hygiene items at the prison commissary.

Marlee and the students awaited their tour guide after being greeted by Deputy Warden Michael Fluharty and given an overview of the prison and its programs. The group had already been screened and approved for a tour, so now all they needed to do was wait for their guide to appear. They sat on overstuffed couches as inmates in tan pants and shirts walked to and fro, seemingly without any restriction on their whereabouts.

Rosalita Diaz joined them, introducing herself as a case manager in the prison and their tour guide for that morning. Rosalita was in her late twenties, heavy set, quick witted, but tempered with a kind personality. She was immediately liked by Marlee and the students.

She explained that her work as a case manager involved making sure the inmates followed the directives of the court while in prison, such as paying restitution, fines, court fees, and child support. Most inmates were restricted from contacting their victims by telephone, mail, in person, or through a third party, and Rosalita worked to ensure that none of those contacts occurred. In addition, she encouraged inmates to complete their education, participate in support groups, and work in various parts of the prison such as groundskeeping and automotive repair. She also made contact with the U.S. Probation Office that would be providing supervision to the inmate once he returned home. For those who could not return home, due to estrangement from spouse or family, or because the house had been seized in their federal investigation, Rosalita helped the inmates find other living arrangements. Some she would assist in placing in a halfway house, which would provide them a group facility to live in in the community, allowing them to work and participate in everyday activities. Once inmates saved enough money for an apartment, they were able to leave the halfway house and live independently, although still on supervision by the federal court system through their probation officer.

Rosalita showed them the talking books program. Inmates read books out loud in one of the studio rooms. The audio tapes were provided to people in the state with vision impairments.

One of the new regulations implemented in the federal prison system was a ban on smoking. Prisoners were irate when they found out they would no longer be allowed to smoke anywhere on the prison grounds, thus turning them into non-smokers. "We had a really angry bunch of inmates for a while, but then, they calmed down after the nicotine left their systems. Once in a while somebody smuggles some in, usually through the visitor's lounge, but otherwise we don't have much of a tobacco problem anymore. Just the new guys. The ones who are just brought in have a really hard time giving up their smokes."

"Before the smoking ban, where could the inmates smoke?" Marlee asked. She knew the answer to the question, but since none of the students commented on it she decided to ask.

"There were designated smoking areas outside. Smoking hasn't been allowed inside the buildings for years. Now they can't even smoke outside," Rosalita replied.

"What about staff here? Can they smoke on prison grounds?" Marlee inquired.

"Nope. I know of one correctional officer who sneaked in a smoke here and there outside, but he was written up twice and all of a sudden he was gone. I can't swear the smoking is what got him fired, but it had to be a major factor." If Marlee were a betting woman, she would place cash on the supposition that Rosalita was a smoker. She seemed sympathetic to the inmates and the fired correctional officer as well as a bit put out by the infringements on smokers' rights.

After touring the prison camp at Yankton and observing the well-kept buildings and nicely tended greens, several students noted that it was nicer than their home campus at Midwestern State University. Marlee was proud of MSU and its appearance, but nothing could compare with the level of care put into the prison camp. A captive population with an incentive to work had that effect.

Gathering near the parked cars on a side street, Marlee had a quick meeting with the class. "Our next stop is Sioux Falls. We're touring The Right Trail tonight. It's an all-boys residential facility in a rural area. We're also eating supper there and then it's tradition that the class plays softball with the boys. I can tell you that in my two previous years of teaching this class, The Right Trail boys have won both times. It's my understanding that they won most, if not all of the time when my predecessor led this class."

"I knew we were playing a softball game with them, so I brought my baseball shoes and my glove," Becca Trautman said with a smile.

"We're gonna kick their asses," Bart said, oblivious to the fact that the focus was on the sportsmanship and camaraderie rather than winning against a group of kids placed in a group home for juvenile delinquents.

"Keep in mind that you guys are role models. They're really impressed that college kids want to come see where they live and then play softball with them. I'm not telling you to go easy on them during the game. What I am saying is make sure you demonstrate good sportsmanship," Marlee said. A few of the students nodded, while others plotted the demise of The Right Trail's softball team.

Marcus drove Marlee's car again while she made phone calls. More than anything she wanted to call Vince and rip him a new one. How dare he cheat on her with Suzanne! She knew better than to place that call while Marcus or any of the students were present. What she was about to say to Vince wouldn't be good for her professional image.

Instead of confronting her boyfriend via telephone, she called Detective Ramos, the lead investigator handling Roxie Harper's case. After identifying herself, Marlee launched in to her reason for the call. No use wasting time on pleasantries.

"So what did Roxie Harper's autopsy reveal?" Marlee asked. She had previously informed the detective of her past work history in quasi-law-enforcement positions and also shamelessly dropped the names of her friends in the Elmwood Police Department and the FBI office. She hoped this would entitle her to unlimited information from the detective handling Roxie's death investigation.

"Just as I thought. It's poisoning, but the coroner thinks it's murder and I agree. He ruled it suspicious because he can't confirm it as a murder. He also can't rule it a suicide or an accident." Detective Ramos reported.

"So why does he think a murder was committed, even if the evidence isn't there to prove it?" Marlee asked.

"After talking it over, we agreed that she was probably poisoned by someone else. There was some bruising around her mouth and neck, which is consistent with being forced to ingest something. Also, it looked like there had been a struggle in Roxie's room. From what the staff at the library told me, Roxie was a neat freak, so it doesn't make sense that her room was such a mess. I'm still considering that she could've taken her own life, but at this point, it doesn't seem probable. We didn't find a note in her motel room or in her car. Roxie was a shy, introverted person, but there's nothing to suggest she was depressed, despondent, or wanting to kill herself."

"What about Dean Green? Have you talked to him?" Marlee asked.

"No. He's a slippery bastard. We keep calling his cell and leaving messages but he won't return our calls. We know he's on the road, but aren't sure where. Yesterday we put out an APB on him, hoping law enforcement somewhere will hold him for us if they stop him for speeding or some other violation," Ramos said.

"Do you think he poisoned Roxie?" Marlee was torn. Dean Green was evil and had caused her a great deal of trouble since starting at MSU. On the other hand, she never had the sense that he was a murderer. Of course, there were a lot of people walking around, un-convicted of murder, just because no one suspected or caught them.

"It's something we definitely want to check out. As far as we can tell, Ira Green was the last person to see Roxie alive and they had some kind of verbal fight. There's also her claim that he sexually harassed her on campus and then he was fired. Green has a motive for killing her, that's for sure." Detective Ramos stated. Then there was an uncomfortable pause.

"What is it?" Marlee asked. "I feel like you wanted to say something else."

"What do you know about Roxie's past? She's 39 and in her third year at MSU. What did she do before that? Is she from South Dakota? Was she married? What prompted her to go to MSU and major in criminal justice?"

"Hmmm... I can't answer any of those questions. I'll talk to the students in this class some more and see if I can find out anything. If there's anything to report, I'll let you know."

After signing off, Marlee paused for a moment to reflect on her conversation with the detective. Then she turned to Marcus and said, "If Roxie was so shy and introverted, then why did she go off on the inmates at the women's prison on Monday? That seems very uncharacteristic of her."

Marcus shrugged his shoulders. "I don't know. It's really weird."

Roles can change in an instant. Sometimes it's hard to tell who's the helper and who's the helpee.

Chapter 10

The afternoon was warm and some of the students changed into athletic gear for the big softball match against the boys at The Right Trail. This was the one tour the whole week in which students could wear shorts. The prisons and many of the group homes had strict dress codes which prohibited shorts, tank tops, and other revealing clothes being worn by both the females and the males. Young, nubile students in correctional facilities were distracting enough without adding skimpy clothing into the mix.

Since the previous clothing incidents with Bart wearing the t-shirt depicting a man having sex with a horse and Becca having a metal chain somehow incorporated into her underwear, Marlee had taken to giving each student the once-over each morning before they departed for their tours. She could not prevent them from wearing metal underwear, but she could intervene if she observed another nasty t-shirt design.

That afternoon she would have missed Becca's outfit because she got in their car before Marlee came to the parking lot. The class was preparing to depart for The Right Trail. Marcus was the one to tip her off to the problem. "Um... have you seen Becca this afternoon?"

"Not since we checked in. About an hour ago. Why?"

"You might want to take a look at what she's wearing before we leave," he advised.

Marlee walked over the car which held the three USD students. Becca was in the backseat. Before Marlee was even up close to the car window, she could already see the problem. Becca was wearing a V-neck tank top and no bra.

"Becca, you can't wear that to a juvenile facility. It's too revealing and totally inappropriate."

"Everybody's wearing shorts!" Becca was taken aback that she was being singled out for her clothing choices.

"Your top is too revealing. You need to go change quickly before we leave," Marlee said with a firm but patient voice.

Becca sighed heavily and dragged herself out of the back seat of the car as if it were the hardest task she ever had to complete. When she was standing, Marlee saw she was wearing perhaps the shortest red shorts Marlee had ever seen. Becca's lower butt cheeks were exposed as she was standing, so who knew how far they would ride up during the softball game.

"You need to change out of those shorts too. They're way too short."

"But these are the only shorts I have with me!" Becca exclaimed.

"Then put the jeans on that you were wearing earlier today," Marlee said.

"But I'll be so hot during the game."

"Not my problem. Do you think wearing shorty-shorts to a group home for delinquent boys is a good idea?"

Becca ignored the question but as she stomped toward her motel room she said, "This is so embarrassing."

"Well, we agree on one thing," Marlee said with an eye roll as she walked back to her vehicle to wait for Becca. She took her time and it was nearly ten minutes past the group's scheduled departure time before Becca returned to the parking lot wearing jean shorts and a short-sleeved shirt with a rounded neckline. *Guess she had some other shorts after all*, Marlee thought to herself as she got into her car.

"Thanks for letting me know about Becca's clothing situation, Marcus. Taking her out to The Right Trail dressed like she was could get the class banned from touring next year. Geez, what was she thinking?"

Marcus just shrugged and smiled as he drove out of the parking lot. Marlee needed to make more phone calls and thought the half hour drive to the juvenile group home would be an ideal time to do so. She wasn't going to call Vince until she was alone in her room that night. In fact, she might not call him at all. She might just wait until she returned to Elmwood and then let him have it. *Maybe this time I'll hit him with my car on purpose*, she thought with a little smile.

Marlee had a quick chat with Hank in which she relayed that all of the students seemed to be handling Roxie's death appropriately and that she did not have any worries about them suffering from post-traumatic shock.

"Well, that's great to hear. President Ross has been calling me a few times a day for updates, so he'll be happy to hear about this. Do you know anything about the police investigation?" Hank Barnaby asked, chomping on something crunchy as he spoke.

"Detective Ramos had a lot of questions about Roxie's past and I had no information for him. I imagine he will be talking to some people on campus soon if he hasn't already. He wanted to know what she did before she started classes at MSU, where she lived, and stuff like that."

"Has he talked with Ira Green yet?" Hank asked. He had already dropped the title of dean from Ira Green's name, as would other faculty as time marched on.

"They're trying to get in touch with him but he won't return their calls. He's on the road, Ramos thinks, and they don't know where," Marlee said. "Any ideas on where he might be going? I don't even know where he considers his home."

"He was in Lancaster, Pennsylvania, for quite a few years when he taught and then later was the president of Keystone University, but I don't think he's from that part of the country originally. I'll look through some records I have here in the office and see if we can figure out where he might be headed. If I find anything, I'll let you know." With that, Hank hung up the phone, leaving Marlee wondering where exactly ex-Dean Green might be going.

The students were in a collectively foul mood by the time everyone arrived at The Right Trail. They were tired, hungry, and ready for the class to end. Plus, a couple of them resented that they would have to play softball with the boys at the facility.

Gene Graft greeted the class as they approached the main building. He was a dark haired white man in his mid-forties, dressed in western jeans, cowboy boots, and a polo shirt. Gene had a wide smile and put the class at ease almost immediately. After talking briefly about the program and the goals it hoped to accomplish with the boys living there, he introduced them to Tyrone, a young white man who would lead the class around the facility and answer their questions.

Tyrone was a gregarious teen and began chatting up everyone as soon as he started the tour. "I'm almost finished with the program. Just one more level and then I get to go home," he replied in response to Violet's question about how much longer he would be at The Right Trail. "I came here two years ago and I was a mess. I didn't care about anybody or anything. My brothers always went to school and didn't give our parents any problems. I was the wild child; getting kicked out of school, stealing, vandalizing buildings, taking off with cars. Just didn't care what happened. Since I've been here, I've learned about consequences and having empathy for others. If I finish up this last level over the summer then I can probably get back into school this fall in Custer. That's where I'm from."

Tyrone's story had captured the students' attention and they crowded around him as they walked toward the far edge of the facility where four log cabins stood in a horse shoe shape. "This is where we live," he said. "I'll show you just one of the cabins. The one where I live. They're all about the same so we don't need to go through all of them."

The class followed Tyrone through the cabin he and several other boys called home. Upstairs, the sleeping quarters consisted of large, open rooms with several single beds lined up in a row. This was the bedroom for older boys who were nearing release from the program. There was also a large bathroom, which housed four individual shower stalls as well as the other accoutrements of most restrooms.

Downstairs held a large living room, complete with a wide screen television, DVD player, a stack of movies, and multiple video games and controllers. Teen boys were slouched on chairs, couches, and on the floor, engrossed in a movie. "If you violate the rules, the first things taken away are your TV and gaming privileges. That's the worst, especially in the winter when there's nothing to do." Tyrone's smile was gone now, suggesting he had undergone the multimedia restriction himself on at least one occasion.

A small table and four chairs were clustered into a kitchenette area. "We don't eat here. We go over to the main building for all our meals. This is just where we make popcorn and snacks and stuff," Tyrone advised, motioning to the area with a flourish of his arm. "Now I'll take you to the best part of the whole program," he said with a grin. They walked across uneven ground to a fenced-in barn yard, complete with horses. Tyrone opened the gate and ushered the class through before walking up to a horse tied to the fence and petting her. "This is Mable. She's my favorite," he said. "We feed and clean up after the horses and we get to ride them too. And we even have a horse drawn wagon in parades around Sioux Falls every year." Half of the students nodded, familiar with the horses and wagon from the program.

"We also do equine therapy. Do any of you know what that is?"

The students looked at each other and shook their heads.

"It's using horses in therapy with humans. We're taught to be kind and gentle with the horses, just like we need to be with other people. It gave me a feeling of control. It's hard to explain, but it works. I can swear to it," Tyrone said with an emphatic nod of his head.

The students asked a few questions about the horses and their care before Tyrone took the students back to the main building. He showed them the classrooms, which looked like classrooms in any other high school. Then he concluded with the kitchen and dining room.

"We do all the clean up after the meals. Each cabin takes a turn washing the dishes and putting them away, stacking the tables and chairs in the corner, and mopping the floor after supper. It's a lot of work, but it goes fast since there are so many of us in each cabin."

Gene rejoined the group and invited them to sit in the dining room. Ten tables, which could each comfortably accommodate eight people, were set up with accompanying chairs. He told them they could sit anywhere and the whole class started gravitating toward one table. "Hey, why don't you guys break out to some of the other tables and chat with the boys. We don't all need to sit together," Marlee suggested. A few of the students looked uncomfortable, but did as advised. After they were all seated, platters of food were brought to the table and they were served family style, helping themselves to the barbeque chicken, scalloped potatoes, vegetables, and fresh baked rolls.

"We have an excellent cook. His name is Robert and he makes all his own bread and desserts," said a boy of about twelve with closely cropped red hair. "We get to tell him what we like the best and then he cooks it for us. But he makes us eat vegetables, too." Marlee smiled as the young boy made a face regarding vegetables.

Following the meal, Gene stood and announced that the Criminal Justice To Go class would be playing a game of softball with them. This resulted in a round of cheers and excited chatter. "But first, Dr. McCabe wants to say something," he said motioning toward Marlee.

"Thank you all for letting our class come here and learn more about your program. We appreciate your hospitality and to show just how much, students from my class will do the kitchen clean up tonight!" Marlee exclaimed.

Even louder cheers and chatter rose from the cabin who was assigned to clean up that night. Her own students looked at her with feigned upset and groans. They were no longer in grumpy moods and were merely playing along with the chores their professor had assigned to them.

Marlee helped with the clean up too, although she made herself scarce from the kitchen. She assisted in folding the tables and moving the chairs and then helped with mopping. After nearly an hour of clean up, the students proceeded to a large open area where the softball game would be held. Gene gained everyone's attention and announced how the game would be played.

"Everyone gets to bat, but no one can bat again until everyone else has had a turn." A flip of the coin put The Right Trail boys first at bat and they lined up. There were over fifty boys who were going to play ball that night, as opposed to the college class, which consisted of only eleven people; nine students, Marcus, and Marlee. They moved to the outfield and divided up the positions each would play. Dom and Jasper gave each other knowing looks, suggesting that winning the game would be like shooting fish in a barrel.

The game went a bit differently than any of the students anticipated. The boys in the program were used to playing softball and had perfected their game, while the college students were not all athletic or in shape. The students, most of whom were not used to regular physical exercise anymore, huffed and puffed as they ran around the bases. The game ended in a trouncing for the college students with a score of 17-4. Marlee was proud of her students, not for their playing ability, but for their good sportsmanship. After they lost the game, they lined up and said "good game" to the boys as they walked by and slapped their hands. Gene took the ball used in the game and placed it on a small brass pedestal, proclaiming The Right Trail boys to be the winner, yet again, of the softball challenge between them and the class from Midwestern State University.

As they walked toward their cars, ready to go back to the hotel, Marlee overheard Dom and Jasper talking. "We did a good thing by letting them win," Jasper said.

"Yeah, that's our good deed for the week," agreed Dom.

Marlee smiled as she listened to the face-saving conversation her students were having. The boys from The Right Trail had clearly beaten the college students fair and square without any pity or charity. Marlee decided to hold their class meeting in the parking lot at the group home since it was a nice evening and they would have their privacy since the boys were all moving toward their cabins.

"So did you guys enjoy yourselves tonight?" Marlee asked.

"Yeah!" chorused most everyone in the group. The students had been tired and grumpy earlier on, but now were all smiles after engaging with the boys in the residential program.

"What was your favorite part and why?" Marlee asked.

"The horses. I never heard of equine therapy until today. It's really cool and I want to find out more about it," said Paula.

"I liked the supper," said Jasper and everyone started laughing. "No, not just because of the food. I liked talking to the kids at our table. They seemed really excited to talk to people from outside the program. Just to have someone listen to them and ask questions. It was an amazing experience."

The rest of the students answered the question and Marlee was impressed by the depth of their answers. She was excited that they had a real chance to connect with the boys in a somewhat relaxed setting. The contact the students had with prison inmate panels, while informative, did not allow for the casual effect this program had. Students had questions and the group talked until it became too dark to see each other. At that point, they called it a night and drove their cars back to the motel.

Marlee no sooner reached her room than the phone on the bedside dresser rang. "Hello?"

"It's Detective Ramos. I need to meet with you tomorrow."

Once a door is opened, it can be difficult to close.

Chapter 11

Marlee tossed and turned much of the night. The bed was comfortable and she was relaxed from her nightly caffeine-free pop and rum cocktail. What was bothering her was her latest phone conversation with Detective Ramos. He wouldn't say why he wanted to talk with her, just that it needed to be done the next day. The detective would be traveling two hours to Sioux Falls from Chamberlain. Marlee agreed to meet him at a nearby Perkins restaurant for breakfast at 9:00 a.m. The first tour the next day was of a juvenile facility and could be handled by Marcus. The second tour was at one o'clock at the State Penitentiary and she wanted to be present for that.

She finally fell asleep, only to be awakened a few minutes later by her travel alarm and then by the desk phone in the room. Once again, she felt beat to hell and was not sure how to get through the day. Fighting the temptation to reset her alarm for a half an hour later, she got up and walked zombie-like to the shower. She was ready in record time, deciding to let her wavy hair air dry and not putting on any make up. They would be staying in Sioux Falls again that night so she didn't need to pack everything and haul it out to her car. Marlee grabbed her purse and went to the breakfast room in the motel and poured herself two large cups of coffee. *This will at least wake me up a little*, she thought.

The students made their way to the breakfast room, in better moods than they were at breakfast the day before. Once everyone was there, she told them about her meeting with Detective Ramos and that Marcus would be in charge for their tour of Dream Catcher, the juvenile residential facility which emphasized culture and education. She instructed everyone to meet in the parking lot at the State Penitentiary at twelve-thirty for their tour of the high security facility.

After slurping down two cups of coffee, Marlee went to the Perkins restaurant where she was to meet the detective. It was an hour before their meeting, but this would give her a quiet place to think and drink coffee until he arrived. She asked for and received a pot of steaming black coffee and a glass of water. She pulled a plastic baggie out of her purse and used the plastic spoon inside to scoop beige powder into her coffee. She preferred her own non-dairy, artificially-sweetened powdered creamer over the real cream and sugar that restaurants provided.

Marlee drank her coffee and placed a notebook in front of her. She had been writing notes of her conversations regarding Roxie's death. She wanted to review her notes to help her think up additional questions to ask Detective Ramos. It was twenty minutes before their scheduled meeting, so Marlee was a bit startled when a handsome man in his late forties walked up and introduced himself. He had short, dark hair that was graying at the temples and caramel-brown eyes behind small framed glasses. He didn't look anything like the grizzled old detective she'd been expecting. He looked like a professor. A very foxy professor.

The detective sat and the two made small talk waiting for the waitress to bring Ramos his coffee and then take their breakfast orders. "So you made really good time getting here," Marlee commented.

"Yeah, I turned the lights on and drove like hell," the detective said with a chuckle.

After they both ordered various versions of eggs, bacon, and toast, Marlee spoke. "I can't take it any longer. Tell me why you needed to meet with me right away!"

"I was in Elmwood yesterday doing some interviews again and going through Roxie's apartment. I got into her computer and found her diary that she keeps in a Word file. Did you know she had a child that she gave up for adoption?" Ramos asked.

"No, I don't know anything about her personal life," Marlee said, a bit disgusted that the detective was asking her questions she already answered for the officers on the scene.

"According to her diary, she had a child when she was a teenager. She didn't mention how old she was when she gave birth. Somehow she figured out who the child was. Or at least she seemed convinced that she knew who the child was," Detective Ramos reported and then paused for effect.

Geez, was this guy in community theater or what? Marlee thought. She raised her eyebrows and nodded to show him she was still listening.

"Roxie never referred to the child by name or even the child's gender. She called the child 'it' and 'X'. And you'll never believe this…"

Again with the pauses. Marlee rolled her eyes and let out a deep sigh. "Just tell me!"

"Roxie thought the child she gave birth to was a student at MSU," the detective said.

"What? How did she know that?" Marlee asked.

The detective shrugged. "We don't know. Yet. Her diary doesn't start until just a little over two years ago, when she was about to enter Midwestern State University. So what I'm wondering is: did Roxie seem focused on any particular student on campus? Did she try to get near anyone?"

"Whew... I really don't know. This is only the second class she took with me, but she had general courses like biology and English too. Plus, she took some classes from other profs in my department. Honestly, I can't remember her staring at or focusing on any one student in this class or Intro to Criminal Justice. I never really saw her other than in the classroom, so I don't know what she did beyond that," Marlee said, flustered at the information the detective just dropped on her.

"I'd like to talk to students who knew her, but really couldn't find any on campus yesterday. I want to talk to the students in your class about her and see if any of them noticed anything suspicious." Detective Ramos finished his cup of coffee and poured another. Marlee noticed he was not wearing a wedding ring and he noticed that she noticed.

"Uh, fine by me. We should be done with our tour of the State Pen by three o'clock if you want to talk to them then." Marlee said. "We're staying at the Red Roof Inn off of 41st Street and can be there after three until whenever you're finished." Marlee stumbled over her words, a blush creeping to her cheeks. Not only did Ramos catch her looking at his ring finger, but now she just told him where she was staying.

"That'll be fine," the handsome detective said with a grin.

Marlee poured herself another cup of coffee and took the baggie of creamer from her purse. As she opened it up, Ramos said, "Coffee creamer, huh?"

"Nope. It's cocaine. I thought we'd do a line."

Ramos' loud laugh at her lame joke made her smile. Some people just did not get her, or her attempts at humor. This guy did.

The two finished their breakfast and chatted until the coffee was gone and the waitress started giving them the stink eye for holding the booth too long. During the conversation, Ramos disclosed that his first name was Hector, that he was divorced, and had two adult children. Marlee talked about work, past and present, and life in the fast-paced city of Elmwood, population twenty-five thousand. Hector spoke about life in Chamberlain and how work prevented him from having a social life because every time he stepped out of his apartment, he was faced with people he had already arrested in the small town.

"Well, I suppose I should be going. I'll have to meet the students in a bit at the Pen. I'll see you later," Marlee said, not wanting to leave.

When Marlee left the Perkins restaurant, she decided to run back to her motel room to grab a light jacket. She was already planning to hurry back to the motel after the tour of the State Pen so she could freshen up a bit before seeing Hector Ramos again.

Wait, why am I thinking about Detective Ramos? I have a boyfriend. Marlee thought. Then she remembered Suzanne's sleepy voice answering the phone at Vince's house. *Or do I?*

It was nearing noon and Marlee called Vince at work, thinking he might be in his office. Her call was transferred to his voice mail and she hung up. She really could not think of what she wanted to say to him, but she knew she didn't want to unleash her feelings in a message on voice mail. She called Vince's house and after only two rings, the phone was picked up.

"Hello?" said the same sultry female voice that answered the last time Marlee called Vince's house.

"Who is this?" Marlee demanded.

"Who's this?" the sultry voice shot back.

"This is Vince's girlfriend," Marlee snapped.

"This is the first I'm hearing of a girlfriend," the voice hissed. Then there was a click and the line went dead.

Everyone talks about lack of communication like it's a bad thing. Sometimes it can be a blessing in disguise.

Chapter 12

Marlee slumped onto the multi colored bedspread. Her blood pressure had risen to the level where she could feel her heart beat in her eyeballs. A tear rolled down her cheek and she wiped it away with a sleeve of her light-green spring jacket. She did this in a quick motion, as if to make sure no one would see, even though she was alone in the room. Marlee was not a crier and she hated that she was reduced to tears. *That asshole. He doesn't even have the courtesy to break up with me. He lets his new girlfriend do it.*

She felt like mixing up a large cocktail just to settle her nerves, but she knew better. Her reputation meant a great deal to her and she didn't want to be known as the lush professor. Plus, alcohol could be smelled on her breath and she would not be allowed inside the prison if she reeked of rum. This breakdown would have to wait until after the tour of the prison.

It was starting to sprinkle and get chilly. In South Dakota, there were as many cloudy and rainy days in May as there were warm and sunny ones. There was a local saying that rang true: if you don't like the weather in South Dakota, just wait five minutes, it'll probably change.

The clouds and the rain fit Marlee's mood as she drove to the State Penitentiary. She parked near the car of one of the students. She needed to speak with them about Detective Ramos questioning them this afternoon, but didn't want to have the conversation out in the rain. They made haste to the main building and, after passing through the screening process, were ushered into a waiting room. While waiting, Marlee addressed the students and advised them of the detective's upcoming talk with each of them.

"But you said we had free time this afternoon and didn't have to be back until our group supper and meeting tonight at seven o'clock," whined Becca, stomping her foot.

"I know, Becca," Marlee said with more patience than she felt. "But this can't be helped. If a law enforcement officer wants to talk to you about an ongoing investigation, that takes precedence over going shopping at the mall."

Several students nodded in agreement, realizing the gravity of the situation. "Do we have to talk to him?" asked Bart.

Marlee glared at Bart Lamont. "Why wouldn't you talk to the detective?"

"Oh, I'll talk to him. I was just wondering the legalities. You know, can he force anyone to talk in this type of situation?" Bart said.

"No, of course he can't force you to talk." Marlee was tiring of the questions, attitude, and immature behavior. Her tone and expression must have conveyed that, because no other questions were asked until their tour guide approached them.

Major Marie Hawkins stood before the group in her tan uniform. She was over six feet tall and looked as if she could wrestle a bear and win. Her blonde hair was pulled back in a tight ponytail and her eyes revealed that she had already heard every story in the book and would not put up with any nonsense from anyone. The students sensed this and all stood a bit straighter and paid more attention than normal when she spoke. This lady commanded respect and the students in her presence knew she was not one to joke around with.

"Unfortunately, we'll be cutting the tour a bit short today," Major Hawkins announced. "Every staff member here is busy because we had an incident last night, and we're dealing with numerous disciplinary hearings."

"Can I ask what happened?" Paula squeaked, raising her hand.

"Some of the inmates made hooch and got drunk. One of the guys worked in the kitchen and stole some bread. Another guy took out orange juice every morning. They mixed it up and let it brew for a while. Last night, they had a little party in one of their cells and sixteen guys got sick from it. Too high of an alcohol concentration. We're still doing cell searches for contraband in many of the units and the guys who drank the hooch are all getting disciplined." The major was very matter of fact in her reporting of the incident. This type of thing was not new, just a nuisance to the prison officials who had to deal with the aftermath.

"What kind of punishment will they get?" Violet asked, encouraged by her sister's bravery in asking the first question.

"It depends on their level of involvement. Those who made the hooch are facing more violations because they had possession of contraband items in their cells to make it. Then, they brewed it and distributed it to others. Some of them might be looking at a stint in the hole. Some might get moved back to the higher security unit of the prison."

"What's the hole?" Donnie asked.

"That's solitary confinement. It's one of the worst punishments an inmate can get because they spend all of their time alone in a cell. The only time they get out is for an hour twice a week to shower. Otherwise, they're brought their meals and they don't have contact with any of the other inmates. It's a rough way to go and a lot of guys can't handle it because there's no television and they only get one book; the bible or whatever their preferred book of religion might be," said Major Hawkins as she motioned them toward the stairs.

The MSU class toured the main building, the high security unit, and Admissions and Orientation where the new arrivals to the prison were housed until they could be fully assessed. The assessment process took about three weeks, then the new inmates were assigned to a prison based on their level of violence, risk to others, past criminal history, and need for treatment. The major took them through the living areas of the prison and even the death chamber. The tour ended at the workshop where the inmates they saw were repairing bicycles to donate to the poor. Major Hawkins again reminded the class of the need to cut the tour short and sent the class on their way without allowing for additional questions.

The class took their time walking back to their cars. It was no longer raining and the sun was peeking through the clouds, so there was no hurry. As they walked, the students asked questions about the upcoming disciplinary hearings, the bicycles in the workshop, and death row. Marlee answered as many questions as she could from memory. For those specifics she could not recall, she promised to find out and email everyone in the class the following week, hoping that by next week the students would forget the questions and wouldn't be expecting an answer.

Before everyone got into the respective vehicles, Marlee reminded them of their meeting with Detective Ramos. "You need to be there no later than three. That gives you about an hour. Don't be late. When you've each finished your interviews, you're free to go do whatever. Just be at the restaurant by seven." Marcus waved to Marlee and got in the car with Donnie, Jasper, and Dom. They planned to make a quick stop at a convenience store for snacks before returning to the motel.

Marlee drove straight back to the motel. For the last hour she had been able to keep her mind off of the phone conversation she had with Suzanne. Now it was all coming back to her. She was mad, sad, and felt like a fool too. Maybe this had been going on for a while and she was just figuring it out. Her face flushed as she imagined Vince and Suzanne laughing at her behind her back, thinking she was Vince's girlfriend. The more she thought about it, the madder she got. She was afraid if she reached Vince on the phone that she'd start yelling at him and then become so upset she would begin to cry. She wouldn't give him that kind of power over her. Marlee decided to contact Vince after the class dinner and meeting that night. Then she would knock back a few drinks, call Vince, and tell him off!

Roaring into the motel parking lot, Marlee did not see as Detective Ramos waved at her as he was getting out of his white four door car. She parked the car, slammed the door, and began to stomp toward her room.

"Hey, what's your problem?" Ramos called out.

Marlee whirled around, ready to give whoever was talking a glare and a smart comment. Then she saw it was

Hector Ramos. She stopped in her tracks and her jaw went slack. "Uh, hi," she said, at a loss for words.

"You looked really pissed about something. Are your students giving you problems?"

"Something like that," Marlee said, her mood improving already. "I told the students to be here by three to meet with you. Some of them should be here shortly."

"Great. I'll see what I can find out about Roxie and if she seemed particularly obsessed with any one student on campus."

Marlee nodded, not sure what else to say to the suave detective.

"I'd like to talk to you further after I'm done meeting with each of your students," Ramos said.

"Sure. If you find out anything from the students you can let me know," Marlee said.

"Do you have tours later this afternoon or evening?"

"At seven, we're meeting at The Tree Top for a class dinner and a meeting. We're doing it a little differently this year. Last year we asked some corrections officials to come to our supper and talk to us on an informal basis over a meal. It was our treat. Well, they sort of took advantage of us. Two of them ordered all the drinks they could hold and got drunk. One guy was belligerent and I felt like punching him in the face. I decided this year we wouldn't have the corrections folks come in."

Hector chuckled as she told the story, Marlee again appreciating that he liked her sense of humor. "So no speaker this year, huh?"

"Nope. Not unless you want to do it," Marlee said off handedly.

"Okay. Sure. I'll do it," Hector said.

"Uh... really?" Marlee was not prepared for this. She just threw out the offer more as a joke than anything else. She really never expected him to accept the offer.

"Yeah. What do you want me to talk about?" he asked.

"Maybe you could talk about some of the cases you've worked on, why you got into law enforcement, the best and worst things about being a detective, and so on. You can talk about whatever you want," Marlee said, thinking on her feet.

Donnie Stacks drove her car in the lot and parked near Marlee and Ramos. Jasper, Donnie, Dom, and Marcus exited the car and approached the professor and the detective. Marlee made the introductions and it was agreed that he would talk to each person individually in his car. Donnie volunteered to be the first interviewed and got into the passenger side of the detective's car. Marlee asked Marcus to wait in the parking lot and make sure all the students waited there for their interview.

Walking toward her room, she glanced over at Ramos' car. He made eye contact with Marlee as he was talking to Donnie and smiled. Marlee smiled back and made her way to her room. She had butterflies in her stomach and realized she was nervous and excited to see the detective later that night.

Poor judgment and risky behavior will follow you into adulthood if you aren't careful. And even sometimes when you are careful.

Chapter 13

After a two hour nap, a shower, and change of clothes, Marlee felt completely restored. The rest did her a world of good, even better than a few cocktails. She was still mourning the loss of her relationship with Vince Chipperton, but the sting was blunted by the spark she felt for Detective Hector Ramos. She took a little extra time getting ready before going to the restaurant to meet the class. Marlee put on an extra coat of mascara in hopes of lengthening her already long lashes, and lipstick a shade darker than she usually wore. Her usual beauty routine consisted of a dash of mascara and some Chapstick, so this was a major glamour session. The sunburn from a few days ago had faded and miraculously, Marlee's skin had not peeled.

She selected blue dangling earrings and a coordinating silver and blue ring. Her wavy auburn hair was curlier than usual, due to the humidity in the air from the afternoon rain. She pulled part of it back and fastened it with a barrette, letting the curly tendrils fall about her face. Marlee pulled on a V-neck summer sweater in cornflower blue and a pair of navy capris. She finished off the look with navy sandals with a bit of a heel. *Not too bad, if I do say so myself*, she thought as she twirled in front of the full length mirror attached to the bathroom wall. *As soon as I lose another thirty pounds, I'll be looking good!*

Marlee arrived at The Tree Top a bit early to ensure the class had a table reserved. Reservations were made weeks ago and she had called to confirm just last week. Being ever careful, the professor was worried the class might not have one big table in a private room. Her worries were unfounded when a woman Marlee's age led her to a back room with twelve chairs placed around a circular table so they could all see each other. She was just about to ask for another chair to be brought in for Detective Ramos when she remembered there was already an extra chair at the table. The chair that was meant for Roxie. She gulped as she remembered that one of her students had died while under her supervision. The details of Roxie's death replayed in Marlee's mind as she waited for the others to arrive.

The meeting room was decorated with stuffed deer heads and walleyes mounted on wooden plaques and hung on the walls. The host explained that this room was most often used by hunting enthusiasts in various clubs and had been decorated with their tastes in mind. Marlee sat with her back to the wall, facing the entrance to the room, for two reasons. First, when she was a probation officer she never wanted anyone to be able to sneak up behind her so she always sat so she could see people approaching her. Some habits die hard. The second reason was there were no stuffed carcasses hanging by the door and she wouldn't have to look at a dead animal's glassy stare. It was hard to enjoy a thick steak or grilled fish if you were looking its brethren in the eye.

Dom, Jasper, and Donnie arrived next and seated themselves to Marlee's right. Donnie leaned over and handed her a piece of paper. "It's Bethanny Hayes' number. You said you wanted to contact her about some information she might have about Dean Green being inappropriate with others on campus."

"Yeah, thanks. Good work, Donnie. Did you talk to Bethanny?"

"Nope, just got her number from a mutual friend. Bethanny's not around much this summer. She went home to Fargo to work," Donnie reported.

By this time, the remaining students were filtering into the room and Hector Ramos was with them. He grabbed the chair to Marlee's left and gave her a wide smile. "How's it going?"

"Great. How about you?" Marlee asked.

"Can't complain. I'm ready for my talk," the detective said as he took a sip from his water glass.

A server came through and took everyone's drink orders. A limited menu with a set price was set at each place setting, offering one dish each of fish, beef, chicken, or vegetarian. "So we pick one of these, right?" asked Bart.

Marlee smiled and nodded. Leave it to a student to inquire if they could order more than one meal. She stood and cleared her throat to get the room's attention. "Hi, everybody. Hope you had a nice afternoon. Thank you all for being here on time. Tonight after our meal, Detective Ramos will speak about life in law enforcement and answer some questions for you. We should be finished here by eight-thirty and then you have the remainder of the evening to yourselves. Remember, we are meeting at 10:00 a.m. tomorrow to visit a halfway house. Then we meet for a group lunch and meeting and then the class is finished until next week when we meet on Monday for a few hours to go over what was learned and observed during our week touring various correctional facilities."

The server came back with the drinks and Marlee sat down. The orders were taken and while they waited for their food, Marlee and Hector talked about everything but the Roxie Harper murder case. He liked fishing, canoeing, and playing sports. Marlee talked of her love of travel, books, and bicycling. The love of cycling was exaggerated, as she had not been on a bike in over two years. She wanted him to think she was more athletic than she really was, although he could most likely tell by looking at her doughy frame that she was not a regular at the gym.

The detective and the professor talked to each other while the rest of the class members entertained themselves with discussions of what they would be doing for fun later that night. Those who were twenty one or older intended to hit the more popular bars in town, while the underage students talked about shopping and swimming at the motel pool. Marlee had to congratulate herself on booking hotels that had pools. It helped the students work off some energy, get exercise, and provided an alternative to drinking in the bars and in their motel rooms. She thought about bringing her swimsuit on the trip, but didn't want anyone in her class to see her in the shallow end of the pool doing flutter kicks and jogging in place. Not only was she embarrassed to be seen in her one piece bathing suit, but Marlee had never learned to swim. It was a task she intended to master one of these days.

After a completely forgettable meal, Marlee pushed back her empty plate and introduced Detective Ramos, even though everyone in the room had been interviewed by him earlier that day. Marlee was surprised by his eloquent and well-planned presentation. The students listened with intent as Ramos talked about his early years as a patrol officer in Taos, New Mexico, and how policing is handled similarly between South Dakota and the desert Southwest. Then Ramos discussed some of the typical cases he investigated as a detective and finished with the general qualifications one needs for being accepted into a career in law enforcement. His presentation was met with a hearty round of applause and several questions from the students.

An hour after first standing to speak, the detective returned to his chair next to Marlee. "Wow, that was great!"

"You sound surprised. What did you think I would say?" Ramos asked feigning disappointment.

"No, I didn't mean that," she corrected. "I meant that you did a nice job of explaining the work in a realistic manner, yet not scaring the students. Sometimes I have speakers who tell every gritty detail of their work and the students get so creeped out that there's no way in hell they'd want to go into that line of work. Then other speakers are all pie in the sky about their jobs and don't address any of the realities of law enforcement. You did very well in not going to either extreme."

"Ah..." Hector said with a smile as he looked straight into her eyes.

Realizing that the students were all still sitting at the table, ready to be released from the mandatory supper, Marlee stood and reminded them of their schedule the following morning. "Our tour tomorrow isn't until 10:00 a.m., so you get to sleep in a bit. Have a good night, and see you tomorrow." Chairs squeaked as they were pushed back from the table with force in the students' haste to get on with their plans for the remainder of the evening.

"What are you doing for the rest of the evening?" Ramos asked as pushed back his chair and slowly rose to a standing position.

"I've got a bottle of rum in my room with my name on it. It's been one of those kinds of days," Marlee said. "Are you heading back to Chamberlain?"

"No, I'm staying in Sioux Falls tonight. I had a couple other things I wanted to follow up on before I left. Do you want to go somewhere for a drink? I have a couple other things to tell you about the investigation," Ramos said.

"Uh, sure. Any place in particular you want to go?" Marlee was getting more and more excited to find out the new information on Roxie's death. *Had he found out something from one of the students?*

"I noticed there was a bar across the street from the motel," Ramos said.

"The motel where I'm staying?" Marlee asked.

"I got a room there too. Since I spent half the afternoon interviewing your students, I thought it was a good place to stay, in case I needed to follow up with any of them in the morning."

"Okay, I'll meet you at the bar in twenty minutes." Marlee picked up her things and walked to the restroom before going to her car. She was unsure if Hector was hitting on her. They were both single and seemed to get along well. It felt like there were sparks between them, but she didn't know if she could trust her own instincts when it came to matters of the heart. Most likely he was just lonely and found her interesting to talk with because of her background in criminal justice.

Marlee ran to her room in the motel before going to the bar. She checked her face to make sure no new zits had cropped up and brushed her teeth to lessen the spices of her supper from her breath. The professor felt stupid for the excess attention to grooming, but she wanted to make sure she looked her best for the attractive single detective. Before leaving her room, she placed a quick call to Bethanny Hayes. When there was no answer, Marlee left a quick voicemail message asking for a return call.

Chaser's was a small dimly lit bar with two video lottery machines near the entrance and numerous booths with cracked and peeling red vinyl lining the walls. A small area in the middle was open, presumably for dancing, although there was really nowhere for a band. The jukebox behind the last set of booths was the most likely explanation for the dance area. Chaser's one waitress was barely over five feet tall and in her late sixties. She had a gravelly voice as if she had spent the past fifty-five years chain smoking. She walked over to Marlee after she sat in the booth furthest away from the jukebox. Country tunes were playing and Marlee was not a fan. She preferred hard rock from the 80s and 90s, what was now being called hair metal.

Marlee ordered a Bud Light from the waitress and waited for Ramos to join her. She looked around and noticed four people sitting individually at the bar, talking to no one and looking either down at their drinks or up at the small television broadcasting a baseball game. The people in the booths had multiple empty bottles and glasses in front of them. The waitress either didn't have the time or the inclination to clear them. All in all, it was a sad bunch. The depressed on the bar stools and the alcoholics in the booths. Marlee started to feel a bit sad for the group at Chaser's just as the front door opened and in walked Hector Ramos. Her jaw dropped a bit even though she was expecting him any minute. She waved her hand so he could see where she was sitting and he walked over. On his way, he saw the waitress and ordered a beer. She looked him up and down as he placed his order, not missing out on one bit of his handsomeness.

BRENDA DONELAN

Sliding across from her at the booth Ramos said, "Fancy meeting you here. What's a nice girl like you doing in a place like this?"

Marlee laughed as she took a nervous gulp of beer. The waitress caught her eye and she motioned for another beer.

"How many of those have you had so far?" Hector asked with a laugh as the waitress brought over both of their bottles of beer.

"This is just my second." Marlee killed the first beer and lifted the second one to her lips. She was nervous and she had a tendency to drink too much when feeling socially awkward. If she didn't slow down, she would make an ass of herself within the hour.

"Sure, whatever you say," Ramos teased.

"So, what's the big news about the investigation that you couldn't tell me at supper tonight?"

"We have a lead on Ira Green. He was spotted yesterday and he's still in South Dakota. I didn't want to announce that at supper because I didn't want to scare the students. It's doubtful that he's the one who killed Roxie and I didn't want to get them all upset about their safety." Ramos took a long swig on his Leinenkugel and waited for Marlee to respond.

"Where was he seen? Who reported it?"

"It was an anonymous tip. He was seen in Yankton."

"We were in Yankton yesterday. Are you sure he's not keeping our class in his sights? I mean, it just seems weird that he showed up in Chamberlain and then in Yankton, both on the days we were there." Marlee was worried again. Although the students were all adults and legally on their own, she felt responsible for them and their welfare. Especially when they were majoring in criminal justice or in one of her classes. She wasn't

162

worried about her own safety. She'd been on her own for a long time and could take care of herself.

"I don't think he's a threat. Besides, you already talked to the students about sticking together and not going off by themselves, right?" Ramos asked.

"Yeah, I think I made it very clear. But you know how it is when you're in your late teens and early twenties. You think you know everything. You're invincible!" Marlee raised her beer in the air in a salute. *Good God, I'm getting tipsy and I'm only halfway through my second Bud Light.*

Hector laughed, enjoying the conversation, even though they were talking shop. "Any idea why Green is touring South Dakota when he no longer has a job here?"

"That is odd. I don't know. As far as I know, he and his wife came to South Dakota without knowing anyone. He's really outgoing and was dean for a couple years, so maybe he has some friends or acquaintances he's stopping in to see. Dean Green's the type of guy that would just show up at somebody's place unannounced even if he'd only met them once. He lacks boundaries, that's for sure." "What do you know about his wife?" Ramos asked.

"Very nice and polite. She's quiet and seems very deferential to him. He's definitely the dominant one in the relationship. I think she just lives to please him," Marlee said, recalling the two occasions she met Mrs. Dean Green. She was not even sure of her first name. One time she met Mrs. Green at a campus function; another time they were at a picnic and brought their enormous canine with them. That dog had the biggest balls Marlee had ever seen. At first glance, she thought he might have been a small bull, but after speaking to the Greens face-to-face, observed that it was indeed a dog.

"Why do you think she puts up with him? I can't imagine sticking with anyone who was sexually harassing women or even just being an incurable flirt," Hector said looking her directly in the eye.

"I don't know. I can't imagine it either. She's very submissive. I'd guess she doesn't feel very good about herself and is wowed by Dean Green's power and bravado. I think it's at least a second marriage for him. If they're recently married, maybe she doesn't know about his indiscretions." Marlee said. Mrs. Green was an enigma. She did not have a presence on campus nor the Elmwood community. Gossip on campus had it that Mrs. Dean Green, as she was always referred to, stayed in their apartment near campus and only left when Dean Green accompanied her.

The waitress, who they now knew was named Marge, came by their table and they both ordered another beer. "You two out on a date?" asked Marge. Marlee blushed and the detective just smiled and raised his eyebrows. Then they both laughed to relieve the tension.

"We've got some other detectives looking into Green and his whereabouts, so we'll find him sooner or later. Enough talk about the investigation. Why were you stomping around the motel parking lot this afternoon? You looked like you were ready to punch somebody." Hector said with a concerned look.

"I was ready to punch someone. Boyfriend problems. Or ex-boyfriend problems, I should say. You don't want to hear the whole story." Marlee shook her head, both in disgust at Vince Chipperton and Suzanne and also at herself.

"Ex-boyfriend, huh? Can't say that I'm sorry to hear that," Hector said looking at Marlee as he took a long draw from his beer bottle.

"Um, what?" Marlee was very good at reading people and she could swear Ramos was flirting with her, but she wasn't sure.

"Look, I'd like to take you out some time. On a real date. Not just drinking in a dumpy little bar." Ramos paused, looking at Marlee as if trying to read her mind. If he could read her mind it would have been a bunch of muddled words not culminating in any complete thoughts.

"I... uh... okay," Marlee stammered and then laughed at her own bumbling approach to romance.

"Alright then, it's settled. We will go on an official date," Ramos said reaching across the table and placing his hand atop Marlee's.

They drank and talked for a few hours when Marlee felt her face getting hotter and hotter. She wondered if someone turned on the furnace or if she was having a hot flash. *Wait, I'm too young for hot flashes! Aren't I?*

She fanned herself with a bar napkin and lifted her wavy hair off the back of her neck. "Is it getting hot in here?"

"That's what I was thinking," Hector said. "Let's go outside for a bit."

They walked toward the front door, stopping at the bar to pay their tab. Hector insisted on taking care of the bill, so Marlee returned to the table and left a generous tip for the waitress. As she turned to leave the table, Marge approached her.

"You're one lucky gal, you know that?"

"Yeppers," Marlee said, smiling and walking toward the detective.

Hector grabbed her hand and the two walked out of Chaser's, enjoying the cool night air. They took their time walking back toward the motel. "So do you want to go to my room or yours?" he asked.

"Uh..."

"No, I didn't mean it like that. I thought we could just sit and talk some more," Hector said.

"Let's go to your room. The students all know where my room is," Marlee said, knowing the rumors that would be flying among her charges if they saw their professor leaving the room of the handsome detective assigned to Roxie Harper's death investigation. "But first, let me go to my room and grab my bottle of rum."

"This night is getting better and better," Hector said with a flirtatious smile. He gave her his room number and Marlee hurried to her own room to retrieve her bottle of alcohol.

The cell phone on the bed was ringing as Marlee entered her room. She jiggled the lock with impatience, hoping to answer the phone before the caller hung up.

"Hello?" Marlee breathed as she grabbed the phone in the darkness of the room.

"Marlee, it's Vince."

She walked back to the front door and turned on the lights. "Uh huh?"

"Look, I really need to talk to you," Vince said in his usual, cool, matter-of-fact tone.

"Guess what, Vince? I don't need to talk to you. Suzanne filled me in on what was going on with you two while I've been gone. Go to hell!" Marlee hit the off button and threw the phone on the bed. She grabbed the bottle of rum nestled in the bottom of her suitcase and left the room.

"Hey, Marlee," Hector Ramos said when he opened his door. He took her hand and led her into his room.

When the devil bares his soul, do you believe him?

Chapter 14

It was after 4:00 a.m. when Marlee awoke. The lights were off and she felt snug under the covers. Still, something was not quite right—and it was not just the beginning of the headache from excess alcohol consumption. A slight movement of the bedspread caused her to smile, as Pippa was rustling around on top of the bed as she always did in the wee hours of the morning. But then Marlee realized she wasn't home and the movement on the bed was not Pippa.

Then it all came rushing back. The drinks, the flirting, and Detective Hector Ramos.

Oh my god, this isn't my room!

Marlee gently pulled the bedspread and sheet back from her body and rose from the bed. Hector stirred next to her as he felt movement.

"Where you going?" he asked in a sleepy voice.

"Uh, I think I need to get back to my own room. I don't want the students to see me walking out of here,"

Marlee said. This was uncomfortable. She looked around the dark room, searching for her sandals.

"We're still going out on a proper date soon, right?" Hector asked.

"This wasn't what you mean by a proper date?" Marlee joked to cover her embarrassment.

"It was most certainly a date, but there was nothing proper about it." Hector laughed as he rolled over to face her. "I was thinking I could drive back up to Elmwood this weekend. You know, look for some more leads on Roxie's case and maybe take a certain professor out for a meal."

"That sounds like a great idea," Marlee was a bit uncomfortable right now, but was looking forward to seeing Hector again.

The detective rose from the bed, and switched on the small table top lamp beside the bed. He was bare chested and wearing plaid boxers. Marlee was still looking for her sandals.

"After you crawled in bed, you took off your sandals and threw them toward the bathroom. Then you were asleep in about thirty seconds," Hector said.

"Oh. Well, I'm a little hazy on that part of the evening. The rum really kicked my ass."

"Yes it did," said as he walked toward Marlee and embraced her in a giant bear hug. "Sure you don't want to stick around for a bit?"

"Well, yes I would, but I think I better be on my way." She was tempted to stay in Hector's room, but she had a headache and her mouth felt as if it were stuffed full of cotton balls due to the drinking and then sleeping. She extricated herself from the hug and smiled at him with his rumpled hair and sleepy eyes.

"I'm calling you later," Hector called out as Marlee exited the room.

"You better," she said over her shoulder, still smiling from the evening encounter and anticipating spending more time with the dashing detective.

The motel parking lot was quiet in the early morning hours. The one light cast a faint glow across the lot, but kept much of the entrance in the shadows. A second light pole with a burned out bulb stood near the front of the motel. Marlee fumbled in her purse for her motel key card. She chastised herself for not locating the key card before she left the light of the detective's room. It was impossible to find just by touch next to all the business cards, coupons, and assorted detritus that collected in her purse over the course of a week.

"McCabe! I need to talk to you!" barked a familiar voice.

Marlee whirled around to see Ira Green standing behind her. She jumped with fear, dropped her purse, and put her hands up near her face in a defensive pose. "What the hell?" she shrieked.

"Put your hands down, McCabe! What the fuck do you think? That I'm here to hurt you?" Green growled.

"Why are you here? I know you've been going to the same towns our class has been visiting," Marlee said, wanting the former dean to answer the question yet not sure if she was ready to hear his reasoning.

"It's because of Roxie." Green looked down and Marlee was unable to get a read on his body language.

"Did you kill her? I heard you arguing with her on Monday night at the motel in Chamberlain and I saw you drive out of the parking lot," Marlee said, knowing she was placing herself in danger right now by revealing what she had seen and heard.

"No! I didn't kill her. I would never hurt Roxie! I just wanted to talk to her," Green said, now looking up.

"What did you want to talk to her about?"

171

"It was about the sexual harassment charge she filed against me at MSU. I thought if I could just talk to her and get her to understand that she was wrecking my career that maybe she'd retract her statement. Then I could get my job back at MSU," he said.

"From what I heard, it wasn't Roxie's accusation that got you fired but the fact that you lied about your past work history. Why didn't you tell us that you'd been the president of Keystone University for a few years? Why have you been going by a different name since you came to South Dakota?" Questions were spilling out of Marlee's mouth faster than she was able to process. Finally she paused to let him provide some answers.

Ira Green took a deep breath and began. "South Dakota was supposed to be a fresh start for me. I'd gotten into some hot water in Pennsylvania and didn't want that hanging over my head when I applied for the dean position at MSU. So I used my middle name. That way it would be harder for anyone on the search committee to track me. Look, I was set up by those women at Keystone University. I had a relationship with a couple of them, but it wasn't sexual harassment by any means. Those bitches just wanted my money and to destroy my career."

"You have some pending lawsuits from your time at Keystone, don't you?" Marlee asked.

Green nodded. "My lawyers are still working on them. One I finally had to pay out and another one was dismissed. Two are pending."

"So why are you here tonight? Why are you lurking around our motel?"

"I wanted to talk to you, but someone else is always around. The police want to talk to me about Roxie and I'm afraid they'll try to pin her murder on me," Green said.

"Why do you want to talk to me?" Marlee was confused. When Green was the dean at MSU, he used threats to keep her from becoming involved in police investigations on the campus. On more than one occasion, he tried to have her fired.

"Because you seem to have a way of finding out things. As much as I hate to admit it, I need you to do some sleuthing for me," Green said.

"And why would I do anything for you? You tried to get me fired! You've been a jackass to me since you came to MSU," Marlee said.

"I know. I know," Green said. Marlee knew he was not one to apologize and he would not be starting now. "You're a snoop. And you're good at it. And I also know that you don't want innocent people to be punished for something they didn't do. Plus, you want to find out what really happened to Roxie." That was as close to an apology as she was going to get from the former dean.

All of Ira Green's comments about her were spot on. Still, she felt like making him grovel a bit. Marlee McCabe was a lot of things, but she was no saint. "Maybe I really don't care if you did it or not, but I'm willing to let you take the fall for it."

"I really doubt that," Green barked, staring her straight in the eyes through the dim light.

"And why's that? You don't have any control over me anymore."

"Do you really want your students to know where you spent the night?" Once again, Ira Green had the upper hand. "I was sitting in the parking lot waiting for you to come back to your room. Then I saw you and some guy go into his room and now I see you walking to your own room at 4:00 in the morning and you're carrying your sandals. I may not be a detective, but I can put two and two together."

"For your information, that guy is the detective investigating Roxie's death and he wants to talk to you.

How about if I knock on his door right now and introduce the two of you?" Marlee had no intention of doing that. Not until Green answered some more of her questions.

"Touché, McCabe," Ira Green grumbled. "Look, I wasn't going to say anything to the students. I don't even want to see or talk to anybody who knows me from MSU except you."

"Right. We both know you'd use any dirty trick in the book to get what you want."

"Just listen! I didn't hurt Roxie. I would never do anything to hurt her. When I saw her at MSU I almost didn't recognize her at first. But then when I did, I started going over to the library and talking to her. Then I tried to take things to a different level," Green recounted.

"What? You already knew Roxie? How?"

"Look, it's a long story. Do you think we could sit somewhere and talk?"

"You're not coming in my room and I'm sure as hell not getting in your car. There's a Denny's a block down," Marlee said pointing toward the west. "Meet me there in twenty minutes."

Marlee entered her room, debating what she should do. On one hand, she wanted to meet with the elusive Ira Green on her own and find out what he had to say. Even if it was all bullshit, it was bound to be creative and entertaining. On the other hand, she knew she should walk back down to Hector's door and alert the detective that she knew the whereabouts of the former dean. After brief consideration of all positions on the matter, Marlee decided to meet Green on her own. Of course she would report everything she knew to Hector, but she wanted a bit of time on her own to get information. Besides, Green might clam up if the police became involved right now. He seemed more than ready to talk to her since he sought her out.

Grabbing her cell phone from atop her bed and giving her teeth a quick swish with the toothbrush, Marlee left the room and walked the block to the all-night diner. Denny's was a bit busier than she expected it to be. There was a mixture of early risers, people getting off the late shift, and drunks who found a place to drink after the bars closed at two o'clock and were now famished. The hostess approached Marlee and she asked for a booth in a quiet spot. The sleepy looking hostess seated Marlee in a nearly empty part of the restaurant. A booth on the other side of the wall was filled with four tired looking men in dirty work clothes. They were forking up pancakes, eggs, and bacon in record speed, no doubt hungry from a night of manual labor. One table in the middle was occupied by an older couple who were mainly occupied with the morning newspaper and the never ending cups of coffee. It was the perfect location; quiet but with a few people around in case Ira Green tried to hurt her.

Speak of the devil, Marlee thought as Green stomped in and sat across from her. In the harsh overhead lighting he looked awful. His face was sallow and there were huge bags beneath his eyes. It looks as if he'd been wearing the same clothes for a few days, as he was a rumpled mess.

"Where's your wife?" Marlee asked, hoping she was not outside waiting in his car, although she would not be entirely surprised if that had been the case.

"She left. Went to Florida to stay with her sister. Said we're done, but she'll come back. She always does," the former dean said with conviction.

The waitress swung by their table and offered them coffee. Marlee and Green both passed on breakfast. She was so anxious to find out what Ira Green had to say that she had no appetite. "So how do you know Roxie? You said you recognized her at MSU which means you knew her before you came to South Dakota."

Ira Green nodded, taking a noisy slurp from his coffee. "I knew her back when she was a student at Keystone University. She took one of my classes when I was teaching. We became involved for a short while then I broke it off when she was being too clingy."

"How long ago was this?" Marlee asked.

"About twenty years ago, maybe a little less."

"So why did you approach her on campus at MSU if you were the one to end it twenty years ago? Were you trying to get back together with Roxie?" Marlee asked.

"Hell, no! I was just surprised to see her and thought it would be nice to talk to an old friend."

"Did she consider you a friend?" asked Marlee.

"Well, not really at first, but then she could see I was different from when we were together before. We started meeting and talking and I sort fell for her all over again. That's when Roxie misinterpreted everything and reported me for sexual harassment." The former dean was oblivious to his pattern in dealing with women.

"Doesn't sound to me like you changed much," Marlee shot at him.

"It's not like that. I'll admit that I was a hound dog when I was younger. But now things are different. I really wanted to get something going again with Roxie. Something serious."

"And how does your wife fit in to all of this," Marlee asked.

"It's complicated, McCabe. Don't start judging my personal life. Besides, you have a boyfriend back home. I met him, right? How does your cop friend fit into that?"

"If you're still trying to get me to help you, then you're going about it all wrong," Marlee hissed at Ira Green as she leaned across the table and glared at him. She held his stare for what felt like hours before he broke his gaze and looked down at the table top.

Green nodded. Marlee guessed the nod was not so much about his agreement, but more out of realizing he needed to fine tune his tactics with her.

"If you didn't hurt Roxie, then who did?" Marlee asked.

"It wasn't me. I swear on my dear mother's grave. It wasn't me," Green said with as much sincerity as she'd ever seen from him.

"Well, then who would hurt her? Who had something to gain by killing Roxie?"

"I have no idea. She never said anything to me these past few weeks about being threatened or feeling scared."

"Do you know how Roxie was killed?" Marlee asked.

"No, I assumed she was strangled or suffocated."

"Nope. She was poisoned." Marlee watched Green's reaction and there was none. He remained stone-faced.

"What kind of poison?"

"We don't know the particulars yet like the type of poison or the method of delivery. The autopsy showed poisoning, but further testing was needed to determine the rest," Marlee said, not ready to fill Green in on everything she knew or suspected about the poison. There was still no reaction from the former dean. "So my big question for you is; what exactly did you want me to help you with?"

"The cops are trying to find me so they can ask questions. When they hear how I knew Roxie, they'll suspect me for sure. I didn't do anything to her. I just tried to talk to her about recanting her sexual harassment claim against me. But the police will assume since I was one of the last people to have contact with her and since I had a beef with her that I killed her. I'm not going to prison for something I didn't do!"

"Maybe you should get a lawyer and see if he or she can help you with this. I can't help you hide and I'll have to tell Detective Ramos that we spoke," Marlee said.

"I don't have the fucking money for another lawyer! All these lawsuits have cleaned me out. Plus, there's a lien on what little property I do have. I'm nearly bankrupt." Either Ira Green was a fantastic actor or he was being sincere. He was a manipulator and made a life out of using and abusing people. Still, his story of financial ruin had a ring of truth to it given what she knew of his past and his current situation.

"Again, I'm not going to do anything illegal like hide you or lie to the police about seeing you. I'm sure I'll be in hot water already for meeting you here."

"I just want you to ask around. Ask some of the students in your class about Roxie," Green said.

"I've talked to all of them and no one knows much of anything about Roxie. Why would this help in any way?" Marlee was puzzled.

Ira Green let out a loud sigh. "Because Roxie is the mother of one of the students in your class. And I'm the father."

Here's a toast to those who are lost. May you be found and returned home.

Chapter 15

"What the hell?" Marlee was gob-smacked. Never in a million years had she seen this coming. "How long have you known?"

"Not long," Ira Green stated. Marlee could feel the deception rolling off him while he talked. "This whole matter just came to my attention recently."

"How recently? And is that what brought you to South Dakota in the first place?"

"I gotta go. My car's been in the lot too long and I'm sure your cop friend had an APB put out on me. Cops tend to eat early breakfasts at places like these, so I need to roll. Here's my cell number," he said thrusting a folded piece of paper her way as he exited the booth. "We'll be in touch."

The former dean was out of the restaurant in seconds, leaving Marlee at the table, slack-jawed and wondering what to do next. She thought about following Green, but he had driven to the restaurant while she walked from the motel a block away. By the time she was in her car, he would be long gone and Marlee had no idea which way he was going. After assessing the situation, she pulled her phone out of her purse and placed a call to Detective Ramos.

"Ramos," answered a groggy voice after the fourth ring.

"Hector, it's Marlee. Look, I just found out more information on the case. Do you want to meet me at Denny's just down the block from the motel?" He agreed and joined her within ten minutes.

"What's up?" he asked, eyeing her in a quizzical fashion as he slid into the opposite side of the booth. He was wearing his same clothes from the night before and his hair was disheveled. A small blob of blue toothpaste clung to the corner of his mouth after a hasty brushing.

"I just met with Ira Green," she said, pausing for the detective's reaction, but there was none, so she continued. "He's afraid of being arrested for Roxie's murder since he argued with her on Monday night and was probably the last person to see her alive. Plus, he said he knew Roxie back when she was a student at Keystone University and he was her professor. Ira Green said he was the father of the baby Roxie gave up for adoption! And the kicker is that he thinks the child they had together is in the Criminal Justice To Go class right now!"

"Do you believe him?" Ramos asked, still showing no emotion.

"Yes and no. He's definitely spinning his stories to make himself seem like a good guy and doesn't take much responsibility for any of the sexual harassment claims. He said his wife left him and that he's nearly bankrupt because of all the past and pending lawsuits and lawyer fees. That part rings true. As far as he and Roxie having a

182

child, I don't know. I'm not sure why he would lie about that, but he might have some angle," Marlee said.

"How did this meeting between you two happen?" asked the detective. Marlee recounted the whole story for him, including Green asking her to help find out who really killed Roxie Harper so that he would no longer be a suspect.

"Why didn't you contact me right away?" Hector still did not display anger or any type of emotion.

"Because he said he wanted to talk to me. I thought if I called you to join us that it would scare him away. I made it very clear to him that I wouldn't help conceal his whereabouts and that I'd be telling you all about our conversation," Marlee said.

"Do you know where he went or what else he planned to do?"

"No, he just got up abruptly and said he had to leave. He gave me his cell number and that was it. I called you right away. I thought about following him, but I walked over from the motel so there's no way I could catch up to him if I ran back to get my car. I didn't see him drive up or leave, so I don't know if he's still in the same car or not," Marlee said.

He maintained his stare at Marlee and did not speak. She was feeling a bit anxious about how he would eventually react to the information.

"Are you mad? You seem a little tense."

"Should I be mad?"

"I don't think so, but I can see why you might be peeved that Ira Green was nearby and you weren't able to talk to him," Marlee said.

Just as Hector was about to speak, his cell rang. As he was speaking, the waitress came by holding up her coffee pot. He waved her away and hopped out of the booth as he finished his conversation.

"I'll catch ya later. Gotta go," Ramos said as he fled from the restaurant.

Marlee paid the bill for the coffee and walked back to her hotel. He was inscrutable. She had no idea what he was thinking or feeling regarding her conversation with the former dean. Maybe he was as low key and forthright as he seemed, but Marlee knew most cops tended to have big egos and didn't like anyone else interfering in their investigations. For all she knew, that might be the last time she saw or heard from the handsome Detective Ramos.

The sunrise was beautiful, but Marlee was too tired and too consumed by her conversation with Ira Green to notice. It wasn't even 6:00 a.m. and her class wasn't due to meet for their tour until ten. She flung off her sandals and crawled into bed, setting her travel alarm for nine-thirty.

Marlee's dreams were all of a scary nature and she tossed about as she slept. She jolted upright when the alarm rang, feeling as tired as she did before she went to sleep. With only a half hour to get ready, check out of the room, and eat breakfast, Marlee didn't have time to focus on her burning eyes and foggy brain. She leapt out of bed, took a three minute shower, and used a headband to pull back her wet hair. There was no time for makeup and she quickly swished toothpaste around her mouth. She grabbed clean clothes without paying much attention to how they looked and put them on. Within twenty minutes of her alarm ringing, Marlee was clean and heading out the door with her suitcase.

Throwing her belongings into her car, she walked the few steps to the main office area and turned in her key. Then she grabbed a banana, a cup of coffee, and three donuts from the breakfast area. Her students were all present and ready to embark on their final tour. She motioned them to the parking lot as she ate a donut.

"Last tour today, guys! Woo-hoo!" Marlee was not feigning happiness, she really was thankful to be finishing up with the class. She was exhausted and by looking at the students, she could tell they were all out of steam too. They were reminded of the mandatory lunch meeting which would follow their only tour that day. The tour was of a halfway house in town. It housed both men and women who were newly released from prison or who were on some type of correctional supervision and struggling in one or more areas of their lives. When she was a probation officer, Marlee had personally taken numerous people on probation and supervised release to Helping Hands to deal with their ongoing substance abuse, to obtain a job, or to be separated from other people in their home towns.

Before they left the parking lot, the professor updated the students on the goals and procedures of Helping Hands. "The program uses a level system. Each level carries with it a number of privileges. In order to be out in the community unsupervised for an extended period of time, the offender must have earned that right. The levels are based on the amount of time they've spent here, their adherence to the rules, and how they're progressing in meeting the program goals. If someone breaks the rules or gets kicked out of Helping Hands, they can be brought back before the sentencing court for further punishment."

The class members got into their respective vehicles and drove to Helping Hands. On the way, Marlee was tempted to share all of her new investigative information with Marcus, yet she decided not to disclose too much.

"Marcus, tell me a bit about your family and your younger years. I'm always curious what my students' early lives were like," she said, hoping to immediately cross him off the list of possible offspring of Roxie Harper and Mean Dean Green.

"I grew up around Alpena. Do you know where that's at?" Marcus asked. After Marlee nodded, he continued. "I was adopted as a baby and was raised on a small farm. Our family lost the farm a few years ago and we moved to Yankton. After that, my parents split and Dad still lives in Yankton. Mom moved to Elmwood. I was the youngest of two kids and already in college, so neither of us had to worry about being shuffled from home to home."

When Marcus paused to take a breath, Marlee jumped in before he could recount his years in elementary school. "When did you find out you were adopted?" She was excited to hear what Marcus knew of his adoption. *Could this be the child of Roxie Harper and Ira Green?*

"When I was around five or six Mom and Dad started using the word 'adopted.' I didn't know what it meant, but I knew I was adopted. My sister was too. Our parents just wanted us to be comfortable with the term early on even if we didn't fully comprehend what it meant. That way there wouldn't be any huge shock later on. We were always encouraged to ask questions about adoption and we met our birth mother a few times."

"You and your sister had the same birth mother?" Marlee asked.

"Yeah. She was a distant relative and couldn't care for my sister Cindy, so Mom and Dad adopted her. Then she had me a year later and I was adopted too. She took off for Nevada or Utah, I forget which, with a boyfriend and only came back to South Dakota a few times that I can remember. She was weird and I never really felt any connection to her at all. But I'm glad Mom and Dad made arrangements for Cindy and me to meet her. At least I've never spent much time wondering "what if" like a lot of adopted kids do. I know the way my life turned out was the best possible alternative." Marcus said.

"Is she still with her boyfriend in Nevada or Utah?" Marlee asked.

"No, she had many boyfriends after that and moved all over the country and into Canada for a while too. We found out about three years ago that she died of a drug overdose," Marcus said without any feeling.

"Oh, I'm so sorry. That would be really tough, but it sounds like you had a good relationship with your adoptive family," Marlee said.

"Yeah, I still do. They're great. Even though Mom and Dad aren't together anymore, I still see them quite a bit."

"I've been interested in adoption stories since I was an undergrad. I did some research on kids who were adopted as babies and have always had an interest in the kids and how they adjusted. Do you know any other kids who were adopted?" Marlee was lying through her teeth. She just wanted to find out if Marcus knew of any other adoptees in the Criminal Justice To Go class that summer.

"A few. When my sister and I were in junior high we were in an informal group made up of other adopted kids. We drove to Sioux Falls once a month. It was led by a counselor and I guess the point was to make sure we knew we were loved and cared for even though we'd all been given up by our birth parents." Marcus said.

"How about since you've been in college?" Marlee pried on with her questions. "Any other adoptees that you've talked to?"

Marcus was getting suspicious. "Um, I'm sure there are tons of people who are adopted, but we don't all have a club or anything."

"Oh, I'm sorry. I know. I'm being a bit nosy. It's just all so fascinating to me. I get carried away with my questions."

This statement placated Marcus and he continued on. "No, that's fine. I've talked to a few other people at MSU since I started. Our stories are all so different. So many similarities, but so many differences. Not everybody's had it as good as me." He didn't seem inclined to elaborate and Marlee did not push. She felt certain she could cross him off the list of people in the class who might be Roxie Harper's child.

Moments later, Marlee parked her Honda CR-V across the street from Helping Hands. The remainder of the class parked near her and started walking toward the front entrance.

As she exited from her vehicle, she was more attentive than she had been earlier at the breakfast room at the motel. One student, Johnny Marble, was walking in a zombie-like fashion; eyes glazed, motions stiff, and robotic. When she approached him she didn't smell alcohol but if she were a betting woman, she would have guessed he imbibed last night and early this morning. Not that Marlee was one to cast stones over last night's behaviors.

"How's it going, Johnny?" she asked. "You're looking a little tired."

"I am. Didn't get enough sleep the past few nights," he muttered.

"Why is that?"

"The people in the room next to us were really loud," Johnny said.

"Uh huh," Marlee replied thinking this was the type of excuse she would have used on one of her profs if she had been out drinking all night.

"The people next door had a big party two nights in a row. I called the front desk but they didn't do anything about it. I should've brought my ear plugs on the trip."

"Well, I guess it's good to know that for next time you stay in a motel," Marlee said, not sure if her student was being sincere or just spinning a yarn to cover his hangover.

The group went inside Helping Hands and met with Irving Bladmore, the director of the program. Irving had worked at the halfway house for over twenty years, starting as a counselor and working his way up to program director. He conducted a tour of the facility, which was divided into separate quarters for men and women. Irving explained that the residents had to be out of bed at 8:00 a.m. and were not allowed to lounge around in their rooms. They had to make progress toward their programs and obtaining legal employment. Once they were working, the residents were required to pay a percentage of their earnings toward rent.

As they walked through the facility, residents eyed the students, curious about their presence. Irving explained that they didn't get many tours. Those who toured the facility were primarily parole and probation officers, so it was no wonder the residents looked at the students with a degree of suspicion. Two men in their late twenties eyeballed the class members as they walked by.

Irving Bladmore led them to an empty meeting room in the lower level of the facility where they sat on couches and chairs in the room which simulated a living room. There he explained the components of the critical thinking program, which emphasized personal responsibility and understanding of consequences for actions. Marlee glanced around the room and noticed Johnny Marble was leaning over with his head in his hands. On the side of his neck were two large hickeys.

Marlee guessed they were fresh from the night before, as she hadn't noticed them on him prior to that day.

Following the explanation of the critical thinking program, the tour ended and Irving saw them out to where their cars were parked. Marlee took a moment to speak with him before driving to the buffet restaurant where the class would meet for their final meeting today.

"Irving, I don't know if you heard, but we had one of our students in this class die while we were in Chamberlain."

"Yes, it was on the news. I heard it was deemed suspicious by the police a couple days ago, but haven't heard any updates since then," Irving replied, raising his eyebrows.

"Poison, but we don't know the method of delivery. It could be that Roxie poisoned herself, either accidentally or on purpose. The detective working the case thinks it's murder."

"That's a lot of drama for these students to handle. Is everyone doing okay?" Irving inquired, his counselor background showing through.

"As far as I can tell. What I wanted to ask you was how do I go about questioning people about adoption? I have some information that may or may not pertain to the Roxie Harper's case and it involves an adoption shortly after birth. Are there any no-nos when asking people about their background?" Marlee asked. She knew she'd bungled the talk with Marcus about his adoption and didn't want to make the same mistakes again when questioning other students in her class. Since Irving had two decades of experience as a counselor, she hoped he could impart some wisdom.

"Each individual is different. Some may want to talk about it and some may not. For many people, it's a really complicated process involving abandonment issues dealing with the birth mother. There also might be some unrealistic fantasizing about what might have been if they hadn't been given up for adoption. Then there are the issues surrounding finding out the identity of the birth mother and making contact. Some birth parents want to have contact with the child they gave up, while others will do whatever it takes to make sure their current families don't find out about other children," Irving said.

"So, I need to just be sensitive to what each person is saying. There's no real rule of thumb when discussing adoption?"

"That's right. A question that might offend or upset one person might be completely acceptable to another. You just have to play it by ear. Good luck finding what you're looking for." Irving waived as Marlee got into her car and pulled away from Helping Hands.

Irving Bladmore had a Master's Degree in counseling and Marlee had hoped he could impart some secret counseling trick to elicit information from her students. She was disappointed that she only received common sense approaches to delving into her students' backgrounds.

As Marlee drove, she looked over at Marcus. "You know we were talking about adoption before and I asked you several prying questions. I'm sorry about that."

Marcus turned his head toward her and smiled. "It's fine. It just got me thinking about some things I really don't think about much anymore."

"When I asked about adoption I really had more than a mild curiosity. I can't tell you why, but I need to find out if any of the students in this class are adopted. Can you help me with that?" Marlee asked. Even though Marcus was adopted at birth, his story of a distant relative with a multitude of personal problems giving birth to him and his sister rang true. Unless, of course, he was lying.

"Sure. I can ask some of them today. It's kind of hard subject to get in to, but I think I can probably chat up a few of them at lunch."

"That would be great. Thanks, Marcus," Marlee said as she parked the vehicle.

They walked into the enormous buffet restaurant lobby where all of the students were standing. After they paid for their meals in advance, Marlee talked to the hostess and she steered them to a long table in a back room. It was semi-private, as the majority of the other tables were empty. It was early yet, barely after 11:00 am, plus the room was the furthest from the food.

After helping themselves to massive amounts of meats, potatoes, pasta, soups, and dessert, the group settled in at the table. Marlee saw Marcus at the far end chatting with Johnny Marble and the Stone sisters. With any luck he could elicit information from each of them about their families of origin and then move on to talk to other students.

The hungry group wolfed down their first plates of food and returned for more. When everyone was back in the room following their second run to the buffet, Marlee began to speak.

"Well, gang, this has been a big week. Thanks to everyone for doing their part to make it run as smoothly as possible. I know we're all upset about what happened to Roxie and that she isn't with us today. I don't have any new information on the investigation to tell you yet." She lied because what she did know was not necessarily something she intended to share just yet. After a few more remarks about the class, Marlee reminded the students that they would meet the following Monday on the MSU campus to discuss what they observed during the week long tours and how that changed their previous impressions of the correctional system.

After a few more remarks and giving an assignment, Marlee let the students go. There was a huge uproar as everyone shoved back their chairs, anxious to be on their own time now. Some were on their way back to Elmwood, some were going to their home towns, a couple wanted to hit the mall and do some power-shopping, and the USD students were on their way back to Vermillion.

"Dr. M., I'm riding back to Elmwood with Donnie, Dom, and Jasper. I'll talk to you on Monday morning to see if I find out anything. I didn't get much from the Stone sisters and Johnny Marble. I don't think any of them are adopted," Marcus said as they approached her vehicle. He grabbed his duffle bag from the back of her car and waved over his shoulder as he went to join the students for the ride back to Elmwood.

Driving home, she had plenty of time to think. Marlee had no idea how Roxie and Dean Green being the parents of one of the students in the Criminal Justice To Go class fit into Roxie's death investigation. Maybe there was no connection at all. Maybe none of the students were even related to Ira Green or Roxie. She had glanced around the table at lunch, looking for characteristics in the students similar to the former dean and the deceased non-traditional student. None of them bore a resemblance to either party, yet if she stared long enough, Marlee felt like she could find at least one similar feature or trait in each of them. Violet and Paula had Roxie's curly, light brown hair. Katie Daniels was animated in her conversation, waiving her hands around and increasing her volume until Bart Lamont had to shush her. This was very similar to how Ira Green's wife handled him when he became overly boisterous. Bart had a nose that was a bit too large for his face, just like Ira Green. *Wait, Ramos said the student who was Roxie's child was attending MSU. So, Katie,*

Bart, and Becca could not be her offspring since they're students at USD.

If what Ramos and Ira Green said was accurate, there could only be seven students who could be the love child of Green and Roxie Harper; Johnny Marble, Donnie Stacks, Jasper Evans, Dominick Schmidt, Marcus Johansen, and the Stone sisters. Marlee ruled out Paula and Violet Stone because they were obviously sisters and looked very similar. Reportedly, Roxie had one child she put up for adoption, not two. Marlee knew Donnie, Jasper, and Dom very well and would be quite surprised to find out any of them were Roxie's child. She had already talked to Marcus at length about his adoption and was satisfied that he was not the child of Roxie and Ira Green. Marlee's best bet was on Johnny Marble.

The drive home went by in a flash. It was a three hour drive, but Marlee's thoughts flitted from the death investigation, to her burgeoning relationship with Detective Ramos, and the infidelity of Vince Chipperton with his ex-girlfriend, Suzanne, who was now his new girlfriend. By the time she arrived home, it was late afternoon. She was tired to the point of not being able to relax. Pippa, her sixteen pound Persian sat on the dining room table glaring at her when she walked in the back door toting her suitcase and other belongings.

"Pippa! I'm so happy to see you!" Marlee called and approached the fluffy kitty in an attempt to hug and kiss her. Pippa was having none of it. She was pissed at having been left home alone for the better part of a week. Even though Marlee's friend and colleague, Diane Frasier, checked in on her every day to give her food, clean water, kitty treats, and scoop her poop, Pippa was not to be consoled. The cat rose to all four feet and arched her back, her luxurious fur sticking out in all directions as she hissed at Marlee.

"Whoa! That's not a very nice greeting," Marlee said as she walked by Pippa, not attempting to touch her given the feline's crabby mood. Marlee walked into her bedroom and found a little surprise Pippa left for her. On the new spring quilt, Pippa had yakked up a giant fur ball. Marlee knew her cat planted it on her bed on purpose. Usually when she barfed, it was on the floor. Fur balls in the bed were saved for special occasions, like when Marlee was gone for days at a time or people stayed at the house with their dogs and little children in tow.

Scraping up the dried fur ball remnants with a handful of Kleenex, Marlee sighed. It was good to be home. She threw her suitcase on the floor and went back into the living room. Grabbing her fleece blanket with cartoon kitty cats all over it, she flopped onto the overstuffed blue couch and attempted to take a nap. Caffeine overload, the death investigation, and Marlee's crises of the heart prevented her from settling in and resting. Finally, she flung back the blanket and walked around her small house, unsure of what to do next. She went through her mail that Diane had stacked on the kitchen counter. Nothing but bills, sale advertisements, and charity solicitations accompanied by one hundred stick-on address labels.

Marlee looked at her home phone and saw there were four messages on her answering machine. The first was a hang up. The second and third were from her mother. The fourth was from Ira Green. He asked her to call him when no one else was around.

Grabbing the cordless home phone, Marlee dialed the number Ira Green had given her early that morning. On the second ring he answered, "Yeah?"

"This is Marlee. I got your message. What do you need?"

"I'm coming back to Elmwood to finish up a few things. I'd be willing to talk to your cop boyfriend about Roxie if he promises not to arrest me," Ira Green growled.

"You know I can't promise that," Marlee said, disgusted that her former dean was trying to get her to smooth things over for him with the detective handling the case. "If you'd be willing to meet with Detective Ramos, I could sit in on the interview, if that would make you feel better."

"It wouldn't make me feel any better, but I guess it would be okay. Maybe you could help me make him understand why I was talking to Roxie in the first place and that I wouldn't ever want to hurt her," Green said, his voice softening somewhat.

"I'll do what I can," Marlee said even though she really didn't mean it. If Ramos thought there was enough to arrest Ira Green for that, she had no objections, but she would not be voicing that thought to her former dean.

"Call your cop boyfriend and set up a meeting for tomorrow night. Call me when you have a time. I'll let you know the location." With that, the phone went dead.

Taking a deep breath, Marlee called Ramos on his cell phone. She was unsure if he was upset with her because he hadn't revealed his feelings about her meeting with Ira Green that morning. He might be pissed, feel betrayed, or not care at all. Marlee had no type of reading on this guy when it came to the case.

"Ramos," said the familiar deep voice.

Marlee stated her call to Ira Green and his message about wanting a meeting with the detective the following night.

"How do you keep getting yourself involved in this?" Ramos asked, still without a hint of emotion.

"Hey, he called me. It's not like I'm forcing him to talk to me," Marlee said with an air of indignation.

Technically, she was correct, but deep down she knew her nosiness, her need to help others, and her quest for the truth were just as much to blame for her involvement in the investigation as was Ira Green's call to her. Plus, finding out the secrets of others was just plain entertaining.

"Right." Still no emotion, not even a hint of sarcasm.

Marlee didn't answer. She realized Ramos was using an old investigative trick on her. It involved saying very little in hopes of making the other person uncomfortable so they would say more than they intended. Many cultures are comfortable with silence, but in America it causes discomfort and one party usually steps in to talk.

After an agonizing twenty seconds, Hector broke the silence. "I'll get back to you on this. I have to go." Then there was the click of silence.

Detective Ramos was charming and engaging one moment, then silent and unreadable the next. This back and forth behavior would drive her nuts. Marlee thought it might be best if she swore off dating altogether; for sanity's sake.

Do you know what friendship is? Neither do I.

Chapter 16

After a few quick calls, Marlee was able to round up her four best friends who were also colleagues at Midwestern State University. The women were Diane Frasier, a professor in the Speech department who had started at the same time as Marlee, Gwen Gerken and Kathleen Zens, both professors in the music department, and Shelly McFarland, the director of the campus counseling center. Over the past few years, the five women gathered together on a semi-regular basis to eat, drink, and discuss the goings on at MSU.

The group members each agreed to come over to Marlee's house that night for delivery pizza, margaritas, and gossip. Even though she had just returned home from what felt like a week of boot camp, Marlee was ready for some time with people who didn't want anything from her. As much as she liked her students, the constant questions and having to be "on" was emotionally and physically draining. Her friends would replenish her spirits and help put her back on her feet.

Shelly McFarland and Gwen Gerken were the first to arrive. They were in high spirits and the three chatted happily while waiting for the others to arrive. Kathleen Zens and Diane Frasier arrived separately, although only moments apart. Some of them were not fans of beer and Marlee didn't have any wine on hand, so she blended up a pitcher of margaritas while they decided on what type of pizza to order and from what establishment. The group sat around the dining room table with the patio door opened to allow in fresh air. The screen was shut to keep out mosquitoes and to keep Pippa inside.

Kathleen and Diane were both finished teaching until the fall semester and were happily detailing what they would be doing in the four months they did not have to deal with students. "I'm doing some traveling," Diane reported. She had been seeing a professor from Marymount, a private college in Elmwood. Diane and her new beau were attempting a trip together for the first time. "What's your destination?" asked Gwen.

"We're driving to Maine. Spending time along the coast and then driving to New York. Keith has relatives living in Albany, so we'll visit them while we're there. We leave Monday and will be gone ten days."

"Are you nervous about traveling with Keith for that long?" Marlee asked.

"A little, but we've already talked about how I need my own space and time to myself. If it all goes horribly wrong, then I'll book a plane ticket and fly home," Diane laughed as she revealed her plan for dealing with her new boyfriend.

Kathleen talked about spending time with her family in Wisconsin over the summer as well as attending a music conference in Portland in June.

Shelly was not faculty and thus worked year round. "One good thing about summer is that most of the students leave the area and I have time to catch up on my projects at work. Plus, I'll take off a little time and go visit my sisters in Nebraska."

Gwen had agreed to teach music classes over the summer, both on campus and for one of the local high schools in Elmwood. "It seemed like a good idea when I agreed to it, but now I'm thinking maybe I got in over my head. At least I'll be done by mid-July and then I'll have a whole month to recuperate and prep for fall classes."

"I'm jealous of you guys. You all have exciting trips or new challenges going on. Other than finishing up this Criminal Justice To Go class, I don't have any other summer plans," Marlee said, wishing she had thought ahead and planned a trip to Europe to do some exploring and site seeing. "My life is so boring," she lamented as she slugged down the last of her margarita and walked toward the kitchen to prepare another.

"Uh, hello? I seem to recall that a student died during your class. That seems pretty exciting to me," said Kathleen.

"Yeah, it was exciting, but not in a good way." Marlee walked back into the dining room with a full pitcher of margaritas and placed it on the table. She updated her friends on Roxie's death and the ongoing investigation, including the former dean's pleas for help in clearing him of any wrong doing.

"What are you going to do? Are you going to help him after he was so cruel to you?" Diane asked. She knew all the blow by blow details of how Ira Green attempted on more than one occasion to get Marlee fired.

"I don't know. If he's guilty, then he should be punished. If he's not, then he shouldn't have to go to prison for something he didn't do. But I'd still like to see him suffer a little bit for all the trouble he caused me. Of course, he lost his job and his wife left him, so maybe that's punishment enough," Marlee said.

"Hey, what's new with you and Vince? Aren't you guys planning anything fun for the summer?" asked Kathleen.

"Well, that's a whole other story," Marlee said grabbing the pitcher and topping off her glass again. "Vince Chipperton is a first class asshole and he cheated on me with his old girlfriend!"

"What?" Gwen said. "How do you know?"

Marlee relayed her conversations with Vince's brother and with Suzanne herself who stated she and Vince were back together. "And he didn't even have the decency to tell me himself!" Marlee wailed, taking another gulp of her blended margarita which had the effect of giving her brain freeze.

Her friends provided the requisite sympathy to Marlee and outrage toward Vince and Suzanne as Marlee rubbed her forehead in an attempt to relieve the searing pain from the icy margarita. "I'm just so mad at him. If he'd broken up with me beforehand, I'd be upset and sad, but I wouldn't be furious with him," Marlee said, her anger growing as she told the story and drank alcohol.

"Well, don't you worry. You'll find another guy," Shelly said comfortingly.

"Um, I may have already found him." Marlee detailed her introduction to Detective Hector Ramos and their encounters over the past couple days. "But I think Hector's peeved at me since I talked with Ira Green instead of alerting him right away so he could question the dean."

"Do you think you have enough drama going on in your life right now?" asked Gwen. "Death, deception, and romance, all in one week's time while you're teaching a class. I've never had that kind of melodrama in all my years of teaching put together.

The group of women was still laughing when the doorbell rang. Marlee scooped up the pile of money on the table and ran to the door to retrieve the pizza. She flung open the door and there stood Vince Chipperton.

"What the hell are you doing here?" Marlee growled at her ex-boyfriend.

"I think there's been a huge misunderstanding and I need to talk to you," Vince said, peeking inside and seeing all of Marlee's friends.

"I have nothing to say to you. Go back home to Suzanne." The heavy door slammed in Vince's face. Marlee was proud of herself for not resorting to yelling or name calling while he stood on her step. She hated when the neighbors made a scene in their yards and she was determined to avoid looking trashy if she could.

"He's leaving!" shouted Diane, who had run into the living room and was peering out the living room window. "I can't believe he didn't try to defend himself. Or at least apologize. That guy's a bastard! I never liked him!"

Marlee laughed out loud at Diane's reaction. "He saw you guys were all here and thought he'd get the beat down if he stayed any longer," Marlee giggled. She was glad to have her friends around when matters of the heart were involved.

"Who cares about him anyway?" Kathleen said. "You have a new guy and he sounds a lot more together than Vince." The group moved back toward the dining room table and sat down again, raking Vince over the coals while they waited for their food delivery.

The doorbell rang and Marlee again gathered up the cash and answered the door. The Domino's delivery person stood holding an insulated red bag holding two large pizzas. Her friends all knew their way around each other's houses, and by the time Marlee brought the pizzas to the table, Shelly had retrieved plates and utensils from the kitchen. The doorbell rang again, just as Marlee was reaching for her second slice of pizza.

"I have no idea who that could be. If it's Vince I'm gonna rip his face off and hand it to him!" Marlee said, fortified with an additional margarita in her stomach and the support of her four best pals. She stomped toward the door and flung it wide open, ready to do battle.

Standing on her step was Detective Ramos, looking more handsome than ever. "Hector, what are you doing here?" asked a slightly tipsy, greatly stunned Marlee.

"I said I'd be in touch with you soon. Do you have something going on?" he asked, looking inside.

"My friends and I are having pizza," Marlee said, unsure if she should invite him inside or excuse herself from her friends and join Hector on the step.

"Hey, Hector. Come on in!" shouted Kathleen. "Marlee was just telling us all about you!"

The redness in Marlee's face could have been from the three margaritas she had consumed, but most likely it was due to embarrassment since her sunburn had faded by now. She was at a loss for words, and that didn't happen often.

"Sure, I can come in for a bit," Hector said confidently as he strode past Marlee and walked into the dining room. He introduced himself to the table of women, who were already charmed by his confident manner.

"How about some pizza, Hector?" Gwen asked. "Do you want a margarita?"

"Yes and yes. That would be great. Sorry to intrude on your get-together, ladies," he said locating an extra chair in the corner and pulling it closer to the table.

"How did you know where I lived?" Marlee was still in shock. She had not expected Hector to come to her house. As far as she knew, he was pissed at her for talking to Ira Green earlier that morning.

"Um, I'm a detective. I have my ways," he said as he waggled his eyebrows to the delight of the other women at the table who laughed uproariously at his comments and antics.

Diane rounded the corner with an extra glass and poured Hector a margarita and then set a plate on the table next to Marlee's chair. He pulled his chair to that location and sat down. He was comfortable in this situation and even seemed to be enjoying himself. Her friends were all having fun and liking the surprise visit by the handsome detective. The only one who was uncomfortable and mystified by what was going on was Marlee.

Shelly reached for another slice of pizza and said, "This is the most entertainment I've had in quite a while."

Kathleen nodded. "It's like dinner theater. I can't wait to see who shows up next!"

The women and Detective Ramos made small talk for a few minutes until Diane decided it was time to grill him about his past. "How long have you been divorced? Where do your kids live?"

Hector looked up from his plate and stopped chewing. "I guess you really were discussing me before I got here," he said with a smile, looking at Marlee as she continued to get redder and redder.

"Your name may have come up in conversation," Marlee mumbled, avoiding eye contact.

Hector grinned at her and turned back to the questions at hand. "I was married when I was 18. Shotgun wedding, if you know what I mean. We were married for 19 years and when the kids left home, we found out we

BRENDA DONELAN

really didn't have anything in common anymore so we divorced. I've been divorced for twelve years now."

Marlee closed her eyes and attempted to figure out Hector's age. Math wasn't her strong suit on a good day and especially not when she'd had a few drinks. The detective, surmising what she was doing, leaned over and whispered, "Forty-nine."

"Uh, what?"

"I'm forty-nine years old. Isn't that what you were trying to figure out?" he gave her a rakish grin. "And to answer the question Diane asked about my kids, Shelby is thirty and lives in New Mexico and Marco is twenty-six and lives in Milwaukee."

"Are you a grandpa yet?" Diane asked.

"Nope. Shelby's married, but doesn't seem interested in having kids. Who knows what Marco will do?" Hector said. "Now, any other questions?"

Diane scooted her chair up to the table as if to continue on with the interrogation. Marlee, sensing that this could go on indefinitely, said, "I think that's enough questions for now." The group chatted for another hour before Diane, Kathleen, Shelly, and Gwen decided to leave.

"Whew, I didn't think they'd ever leave!" Hector said after the group filed out of the house. He grabbed Marlee and gave her a big bear hug. "I missed you."

After a smooch fest, Marlee and Hector talked about the investigation. "I had a message from Ira Green on my answering machine when I got home this afternoon. He said he'd meet with both of us tomorrow. I guess he'll call back with a time and location."

"That's good. Did he say where he was at?"

"Nope, just that he was coming back to Elmwood and would be able to meet with both of us on Saturday night. No idea what's bringing him back to Elmwood."

Marlee scrunched up her face as she pondered what it was that might be bringing him back.

"He didn't say why he was coming back? Was it just to talk to us or did he mention another reason?" Hector inquired.

"Ira didn't mention anything, but now I'm wondering if he plans to make contact with the child he had with Roxie. According to Roxie's diary, her child was a student at MSU. That rules out the three students attending USD. I talked with Marcus and even though he's adopted, his back story didn't match up with Roxie's diary. He has a sister adopted by the same family. It doesn't make sense that Roxie would try to locate one child she gave up for adoption but not the other." Marlee stopped to take a breath.

"So that leaves the other six students from the Criminal Justice To Go class," Hector stated. "Any thoughts on which of them it could be?"

"Johnny Marble is my guess," Marlee said. She relayed her thoughts about the Stone sisters as well as Donnie, Dom, and Jasper.

"Well, I think we need to rule them out for sure," Hector said. She liked that he said *we*, meaning that she was a crucial part of the investigation.

"They should all be around town since they have to meet for the final day of class on Monday. I can do some checking and we can talk to them," Marlee said.

Hector nodded in agreement. "I tracked down the addresses before I got here and thought it would be a good idea to go check on them tomorrow."

"You're way ahead of me, Hector," Marlee said with a smile even though she was a bit peeved that he'd already thought of this. "Did you find out any more about the poison used to kill Roxie?"

"Yeah, the results came back and it was ethylene glycol. It has a sweet taste and she wouldn't have had any idea it was slipped into her drink. Somebody had access to whatever Roxie was drinking and put it in when she wasn't looking."

"That would've been hard to do because Roxie drove alone to the locations and had her own room. The only person I know for sure that would've had any alone time with Roxie is Ira Green," Marlee said.

"Yeah, that's what I was thinking too. I know you believe Green's story, but I like him for the murder. He had the motive, which was revenge for losing his job. He had the opportunity because you saw Green leaving Roxie's room the night before she died and he admitted it to you too. He has a PhD in biochemistry, so he knew all about poison and what types could be slipped into a drink and not be tasted," Hector said, laying out his case.

Marlee thought for a moment. Although Hector made a strong case for Ira Green's guilt, she couldn't shake the feeling that he was really innocent. The facts pointed to his guilt, but her gut instinct told her otherwise. "I just don't know," she said shaking her head. "It's not like the killer had to be a genius in chemistry to pull this off. Basic information on poison is easily available on the Internet." They both pondered that thought for a minute, neither voicing their opinions.

"We've been going with the theory that Roxie was killed either by her child or by Green. What if someone else did it? Someone who has no connection to either Green or the child she gave up for adoption?" Marlee asked, breaking the silence. The more they discussed the case the more confusing it became.

"Could be anyone. Who else would have a motive besides Green or Roxie's child?" Ramos inquired.

"None of the students I talked to seemed to know much of anything about Roxie. Those who had her in previous classes said she never talked and didn't mingle before or after class. Have you checked the library to see what they know about her?"

"Of course, but they had much the same experience. Roxie was a good worker, but kept to herself and didn't speak to anyone unless they started the conversation. She didn't hang out with any of the other work-study students, which isn't too surprising since they're all quite a bit younger than her. Roxie didn't have any friendships with the librarians or support staff who are all closer to her age." Ramos reported.

"What leads are you following on this trip to Elmwood?"

"Tomorrow I'm going to her apartment building to talk to her neighbors. Maybe somebody there knows something about her. I can't believe she's a complete mystery to everyone. Roxie mentioned a guy named Pete in her diary. I don't know if he lives in Elmwood, but thought I'd try locating him too. Plus, there's another very important lead I want to follow," Ramos said, as he moved closer to Marlee on the couch, a devilish smile on his lips.

Who do you listen to...the angel or the devil?

Chapter 17

It was nearly 1:00 a.m. when Marlee shoved Hector out of her house. He told her earlier that he'd booked a room at the Super 8 motel, but wasn't showing any indication of leaving as the clock struck midnight. "Time for you to leave, Buster. I have to get my beauty rest," Marlee said, grabbing Hector's hand to pull him up from the couch where they'd been sitting.

"Maybe I'll have one more margarita before I leave."

"No, I don't think so. We don't want you getting a DUI. The Elmwood cops love to arrest drunk drivers. I think it's their main form of entertainment since not many other crimes happen here. Well, except for a couple of murders..."

Hector got up from the couch with a reluctant sigh and allowed Marlee to steer him toward the front door. "Ok, see you tomorrow," he said as he gave her a long kiss.

Marlee smiled as she closed the door behind the detective. It would've been very easy to let him stay overnight, but she wasn't quite ready to move things along that quickly. She moved about the house, picking up empty margarita glasses, crumpled napkins, and used plates. A pizza box on the kitchen table was closed and she grabbed it to throw in the trash when she heard and felt some movement. Opening it up, Marlee saw one slice left. *I don't want to throw it away, but it seems pointless to put it in the fridge. One piece of pizza isn't much of a meal. It was more like an appetizer, really.* With her decision made, Marlee grabbed the remaining slice and took a bite. *I don't want my energy to get low while I'm trying to figure out who poisoned Roxie.*

Marlee thought sleep would be evasive that night since she was amped up over the new developments with Hector and their discussion of the murder investigation. Sheer exhaustion won out and she was asleep within minutes of hitting the pillow. A beach scene appeared in her dreams and she saw herself sitting in a striped lounge chair under a large umbrella reading a book. Marlee felt the cool breeze skipping off the water and onto her pale face. Her left foot swung off the side of the chaise, her toes squishing in the sand. She reached for the icy mojito next to her when—

BANG BANG BANG!

Marlee jumped out of bed, still halfway in dreamland. "What the hell was that?" she shouted out loud.

BANG BANG BANG!

Marlee realized someone was pounding on her front door. *Jeez, didn't the idiot see there was a doorbell?* She flung open the door without looking out the window first to see who was there.

Hector Ramos stood before her, grinning, with two cups of coffee and a bag from Bagel House in his hand. "Morning, Sunshine!"

"What the hell, Hector! What time is it? And why didn't you ring the doorbell?" Marlee became self-conscious when she realized she was wearing an old Guns n' Roses concert t-shirt, flannel shorts, and fuzzy socks; her usual sleep attire.

"It's eleven-thirty, and I've been ringing your doorbell. Didn't you hear it?" Hector walked in and set down the coffee and bag on the coffee table.

Marlee remembered her doorbell had been working intermittently, as she had been advised by an irritated Diane a couple weeks ago when she called Marlee from outside the door. "Uh, I think it might need fixing."

Hector tilted his head and looked at her, still grinning. "You're really not a morning person, are you?" He handed her a cup of coffee which she gratefully accepted.

"Thanks, I think I'll hop in the shower. Make yourself at home. I won't take long," Marlee said, not sure if she was going to like Hector's pop-in visits. She might have to have a word with him about calling first so she could be prepared.

"If you need any help in there, just let me know," Hector said, laughing as he reached for the TV remote.

Marlee selected clothes and took them into the bathroom with her. She looked into the mirror while brushing her teeth and was mortified to see her curly hair dented on one side and sticking straight out on the other. *There's nothing I can do about it now.* Within twenty minutes, she was showered, dressed, and even put on a small amount of makeup, hoping to redeem her image from her pre-shower greeting with Hector.

Her hair was wet, but drying it in this humidity would just make it frizz. Elmwood was dry in the winter months, leaving the residents with itching skin, dry hair, and chapped lips for months on end. The summer months were characterized by humidity which caused the curly haired residents to resemble Bozo the clown.

Sashaying into the living room wearing her jean capris and a mint green V-neck t-shirt, Marlee found Hector sprawled out on the couch with one foot up on the coffee table. The television was on and he was watching an old *Law & Order* episode. *He sure seems to make himself at home.* Marlee wasn't sure how she felt about his invasion of her personal space.

"Hey, what's up?" Marlee asked.

"Just waiting for you. I already went to Roxie's apartment this morning and talked to a few of her neighbors. They didn't know anything about her, and had no idea who the Pete was that she mentioned in her diary."

"What did Roxie write about Pete? Do you think that was his real name or was she using some kind of code?" Marlee asked, recalling that Roxie had referred to her baby as X.

"I don't know if it was a real name or not. She mentioned getting together with Pete a few times, mostly at restaurants, but I couldn't tell what the nature of their meeting was. It really didn't sound romantic, but she didn't mention any type of business they might have had either. It sounded more like Pete was a confidant," Hector said, taking the bagels and containers of flavored cream cheese out of the bag and setting them on the coffee table.

Marlee sat next to Hector as they ate in silence, both trying to make sense of the details in their minds. "I think we should track down Johnny Marble and talk to him today," Marlee said.

"I do too. I found his address. He lives off-campus in an old apartment building to the north of the university. Tell me what you know about this kid."

"I know he's good friends with Violet and Paula Stone. They shared motel rooms on our trip last week. I don't think there's anything romantic between Johnny and either of the Stone sisters, but he did have hickies on his neck Friday morning. From what I remember, they're all from the same hometown and are just friends. Johnny is a criminal justice major and is a fairly good student. I think he could work a little harder than he does, but he gets decent grades, shows up for class, and turns in his papers on time." Marlee searched her mind for any other details she knew about Johnny Marble.

"Do you know anything about his background? His family or anything?" Ramos persisted.

"I really don't. I'm not sure what he's doing this summer either. Some students stay here and work, while others take classes as well as work. Most of our students work part-time or even full-time jobs while taking a full course load during the regular school term. During the summer, only a few classes are offered, so the students who take them tend to be those who want to graduate early or need to make up a failed class. Most of them are happy to take a break from classes over the summer," Marlee reported.

"Do you know what the Stone sisters are doing this summer? If they're around we could talk to them about Johnny," Hector said.

"Actually, I do know what they're up to. Last week they mentioned that they had an apartment together and were both working at Pizza Ranch over the summer."

"Let's plan to track them down first to see what they have to say about their friend, Johnny Marble. Then we can talk to him. The Stone sisters might tell us something that Johnny wouldn't reveal. From what you tell me, Johnny is more introverted and the Stone sisters are chatter boxes. It's always good to interview the chatty ones first to get all the information." Marlee rolled her eyes, but the detective didn't catch it. Hector was forgetting that she was a fairly good interviewer herself and already knew these tactics. If he continued with the lecture on dealing with witnesses, she would have to set him straight.

Hector went to his vehicle and retrieved his briefcase which contained his file and case notes on the Roxie Harper murder investigation. He rifled through a pile of documents, which appeared to be in no particular order, and pulled out a bent manila folder labeled INTERVIEWS. In the folder he located his interviews of Paula and Violet Stone which contained their contact information.

"Let's go to the Stone sisters' apartment now and see what they can tell us," Hector said standing up.

Marlee, not quite caffeinated enough to conduct interviews, ran to the kitchen and made a pitcher of instant ice tea. She poured the tea into an oversized insulated mug, added ice cubes, grabbed a straw and was ready to go. *Thank god for instant tea.* It tasted like crap, but was good in a time crunch.

They got into Hector's car and drove to a newer apartment building east of campus. It was a 4-plex, so the neighbors quite likely knew the Stone sisters unless they had just moved in. When she was a probation officer, Marlee often found out vast amounts of information on her supervisees from neighbors. No one knows what you're up to quite like your neighbors; especially if the neighbors are nosy.

Luck was on their side when Violet opened the door to the small apartment. "Uh, Dr. McCabe...what are you doing here? And...Detective?"

"Hi, Violet," said Marlee in a soothing tone. "I know it's unusual for a professor to drop by your apartment, but I'm helping Detective Ramos follow up a few loose ends with his investigation. I came along because I thought you might feel more comfortable with me here." It was a load of horse shit, but Violet bought it.

"Sure! Come on in." Violet motioned them into the apartment and hurried over to the couch which was covered with clothes, a laptop computer, magazines, and other assorted detritus. "Have a seat. Do you need to talk to Paula too? She's at work and doesn't get home until four."

"No, that's fine, Violet. We can talk to her later," Hector said, sitting down on one end of the sagging sofa which looked well-used given the stains and cigarette burns on the arms of the couch. Marlee joined him, sitting discreetly on the other end of the sofa and Violet pulled up one of the two mismatched chairs from a small kitchen table.

"So, we're still trying to find out more information about Roxie and thought maybe some of the students in Criminal Justice To Go might have more information on her than they first realized. We're just here with a few follow up questions about that. But first, we wanted to ask you about Johnny Marble. He's a friend of yours, I understand?" Hector asked.

"Yeah, we're all from Mobridge. It's a small town and everybody knows everybody. Johnny and Paula graduated together in 2004," Violet said.

"Any romance between either of you and Johnny? I mean, he's a good looking guy. I can see why the ladies would like him," Hector said, giving Violet an easy opening to reveal a relationship with Johnny.

"Nope. Just friends. He and one of my friends went out a few times in high school, but that didn't last long. She cheated on him. I don't know of anybody Johnny's dated since then," Violet reported.

"I noticed he had hickies on his neck Friday morning. Who gave him those?" Marlee asked.

Violet just shrugged and looked away.

"What do you know about his home life?" Marlee asked, easing into a discussion of possible adoption.

Violet looked from Marlee to Hector and then back at Marlee again. "Well, his parents live in Mobridge. They both work for the government, but I don't know what they do for sure. Johnny doesn't talk about them much, but he always got along with them."

"Does he have any brothers or sisters?" Hector asked.

"Yeah, he has an older brother. He said his parents wanted more kids but weren't able to have any more. I guess it was a blessing when they had him because they had nearly given up," Violet said. "Why? What does this have to do with Roxie's murder? You don't think Johnny did it do you?"

"No, no. We're just trying to get a more complete picture of the case and in doing so, we need more information on everyone in the class. Just for our records," Hector said, lying through his teeth.

"You said Johnny's parents had given up on the notion of being parents. They must have been older then when he was born," said Marlee.

"Yeah, I guess so. His mom and dad are a lot older than my parents, that's for sure."

"Do you think Johnny was adopted?" Marlee inquired.

"No. I mean, he never said he was adopted. I never heard anything like that," Violet said, confused.

"Did Johnny say anything to you about Roxie before her death?" Hector asked.

"No. Well, I mean he sort of made fun of her when we saw she was in the class. We all did," Violet was a decent kid and looked ashamed for poking fun at someone who was now deceased. "Then after she went crazy at the Women's Prison we all talked about how weird she acted. That's all. Johnny's comments weren't any worse than anyone else's."

"And you said that you, your sister, and Johnny all stayed in your room to watch TV on Monday night. Is that right?" Hector asked.

Violet nodded.

"Did any of you leave the room at all after you started watching TV?" Hector inquired.

"No. Well, actually, Johnny left to go to the snack machine. But he was only gone a minute or two."

"What about you and Paula? Did either of you leave the room at all that night?"

"No, not at all."

"Violet, can you tell me about your family?" asked Marlee. She had already ruled out Violet and Paula as possible perpetrators of the crime, but felt she should be thorough and ask the Stone sisters a few questions too.

"Same as Johnny. Small town, lived with my parents and Paula. Mom is a teacher's aide and Dad works for the city of Mobridge. We had a great childhood and we all got along well. We still do. Paula and I are sisters and we fight a lot, but we're also best friends," Violet said.

"Neither you nor Paula are adopted?" Marlee asked.

"No. Why all the questions about adoption?"

"Just trying to fill in a few blanks," Hector stated as he snapped his notebook shut and stood. "Thank you for your time and if I need anything else I'll be in touch."

Marlee and Hector left the apartment, leaving a quizzical and troubled Violet behind. As soon as her professor and the detective left, Violet grabbed her phone and made a quick call to Johnny Marble. The second call Violet placed was to Pizza Ranch, where she had her sister paged.

All I ever wanted was a family. My own family.

Chapter 18

Johnny Marble wasn't home when Marlee and Ramos stopped to see him. A roommate, dressed in cutoff sweatpants and a stained white t-shirt advised that Johnny was at work at Target but would be off in an hour and he usually came straight home right after work. As they walked away, Hector noted, "You weren't kidding when you said these kids all have jobs."

"Midwestern State University is made up of mainly working-class students. They have to work to pay for school and for food, rent, and everything else. There aren't very many privileged kids with silver spoons here. Sometimes I wonder how they can work full time, go to school full time, and raise a family too. Many of our students are single parents," Marlee reported.

"That's quite a load. I remember the struggles of work, college, and a young kid at home. My ex-wife took care of the baby when I was in college," Hector recalled.

"I always had part-time jobs in college and I thought I was overloaded! I can't imagine two full-time gigs plus raising kids," Marlee said.

The two chatted amiably as they drove to Pizza Ranch. Although they had just eaten bagels not that long ago, both decided they could eat some lunch and make contact with Paula Stone at the same time. It was nearing 2:00 p.m., and the parking lot was packed, which was not unusual for a buffet restaurant on a Saturday. Elmwood residents had large appetites and an eye for value, like most people in the Midwest. Hector circled the parking lot, finally settling on a place near the rear of the building. Approaching the back entrance, they saw a familiar figure. Paula Stone was standing near the employee entrance, one hand holding a cell phone to her ear and the other hand gesturing wildly. When Paula saw Marlee and the detective walking her way, she pulled the phone away from her ear and put it in her pocket.

"Hi, Paula," Marlee called out as they neared her. She appeared frazzled and was wringing her hands. Her curly hair was pulled back in a ponytail, but the wind whipped several pieces loose. She wore the requisite uniform of the restaurant, a navy t-shirt with the Pizza Ranch logo and tan pants. "You remember Detective Ramos, right?"

Paula nodded. "Yeah. Hi." She looked from side to side, as if seeing if they were being watched.

"Hi, Paula," said Ramos, looking her square in the eye. "Were you just talking to your sister?"

"Um, no. I mean, yes, I talked to her a few minutes ago. But that wasn't her I was talking to right now," Paula stammered.

"So she let you know we were going to ask you more questions about Roxie's death?"

"Well, yeah. She mentioned you'd been by earlier. But that wasn't the main reason she called. It just came up in conversation," Paula insisted. "Violet really didn't say much about it at all."

"Okay," Marlee said, not believing Paula's story. "So, Detective Ramos just has a few questions for you to fill in some gaps in his investigation. No big deal. I came along because I thought you might feel more comfortable since you already know me."

Paula nodded, but she looked anything but comfortable. "I need to go inside and tell them I'll be on break for a bit." She turned and went in the back door which led into a loud, chaotic kitchen. The heavenly scent of fried chicken and other grease-laden delicacies wafted out the door.

"Well, that's suspicious. She's acting nervous and guilty. Paula knows something," Marlee said and Hector nodded in agreement.

When Paula returned, no time was wasted on pleasantries or social graces. Hector cleared his throat. "I need to know a bit more about each of the students on the trip, so I'm asking everyone the same types of questions." Hector was a smooth liar. *I'll have to keep an eye on that.*

Hector and Marlee asked Paula the same types of questions about Johnny that they just asked her sister not more than an hour earlier. Her responses were similar to those provided by Violet. Paula's demeanor continued to be nervous and suspicious, her eyes wildly darting about. When the questions turned to her parents, Paula became even more upset.

"Paula, tell us why you're on edge. You look like you're ready to freak out," Marlee said pointedly but with kindness.

That statement was all it took. Paula broke down into tears and relayed her story. "Violet and I aren't sisters.

225

We're cousins. My parents adopted her as a newborn because my aunt couldn't take care of her. Actually, she didn't want Violet, so Mom and Dad took over right away."

"Okay, so Violet is adopted. What has you so upset?" Hector asked with a gentleness to his voice.

"Violet doesn't know she's adopted. I only found out a few years ago by accident when I was snooping through some old papers in the basement," Paula said between sobs.

"You're afraid Violet's adoption will come out during this investigation and you're worried how she'll take it," Marlee said, putting words in Paula's mouth.

Paula nodded. "Mom and Dad know that I know, but they made me promise not to tell Violet. Nobody else around town even knew she was adopted because we look so much alike. Mom said she was out of state for a while getting the adoption arranged, so when she returned with a baby everyone just assumed she had another child. Mom said she didn't show much when she was carrying me, so I suppose everybody in town thought it was the same situation when she brought Violet home."

"What about the relatives? Didn't any of them say anything?" Hector asked.

"Nobody else knew except for the aunt who gave up Violet. I never met our aunt, but I heard she was a complete mess. Mom said she was an alcoholic, couldn't hold a job, and would steal anything that wasn't nailed down."

"Where's your aunt now?" Marlee asked.

"No idea. We've never had any contact with her. I don't even know her name," Paula said. "Mom and Dad just called her "auntie" when they told me about her. I don't know if she's Mom's sister or Dad's."

Hector gathered the names and contact information for Paula's parents. Paula was in tears again as she begged them not to tell Violet she was adopted. They said they'd do their best to keep the family's secret, but because of the criminal investigation, they couldn't make any promises.

As they walked toward the front entrance of Pizza Ranch, Marlee turned around and faced Paula. "Who were you talking to when we first saw you? You said you talked to your sister earlier."

"I was talking to Johnny," Paula said as she pulled open the back door and quickly entered into the noisy kitchen.

"Wow, that was a bombshell!" Marlee exclaimed, looking at Hector, trying to read his take on this new development.

"Yeah, I wasn't expecting that. As soon as we saw Paula today I knew something was up, but I never expected this," Hector said.

The pair decided they wanted to discuss Violet's adoption over lunch, but didn't want Paula to overhear. They nixed Pizza Ranch and drove to Bernie's, a small mom and pop café that Marlee knew would be empty this time of day. It was hidden in an older part of town and did the bulk of its business in the mornings. It was an early morning hot spot for people seeking a cheap, greasy breakfast or those wanting to connect with a group that drank endless refills of coffee and effortlessly solved the problems of society.

Bernie's parking lot was nearly empty when Hector pulled his car into the lot. They entered the establishment and observed only one occupied table near the front of the diner. Marlee led Hector toward a rickety table in the back corner, which was still in full view of the kitchen and the entrance. The smell of grease permeated the air and made Marlee hungry for something fried.

A waitress, whose nametag identified her as Barb, rushed over to their table with two plastic glasses of water. As she set them down on the table, water from Marlee's glass sloshed over the top and onto the table.

"Sorry 'bout that," Barb said as she grabbed a towel tucked inside the band of the apron covering her clothes. She handed them menus and advised that the lunch special, which would be in effect for another hour, was rattlesnake chili accompanied by a slice of cornbread. Still in a hurry, even though there were only three customers in the café, including them, Barb raced off, leaving them to ponder the menu.

"Rattlesnake chili?" Hector asked with a grin.

"Whatever you do, don't order it. They use frozen rattlesnake and everybody knows rattlesnake has to be fresh or else it's tough and chewy," Marlee said with a straight face.

Hector broke out with a loud laugh. Barb raced back to their table and asked for their orders. Since Bernie's served breakfast all day long, they both ordered eggs, bacon, and toast. After Barb scurried away to put in the order, Marlee and Hector began to discuss Violet Stone's adoption and the impact it could have on the Roxie Harper investigation.

"It seems odd that there are so many adopted students involved in this class. Violet and Marcus are adopted for sure and there may be more," Marlee mused. Even though two was not a large number, there were only ten students and one assistant in the class.

"It does. And it seems really strange that the Stone parents kept Violet's adoption secret from both of the girls and that Violet still doesn't know about it. Violet's eighteen now, but Paula was acting like it would be the end of the world if she found out they weren't sisters." Hector sipped his water as he glanced around the small cafe.

"We still need to talk to Johnny Marble this afternoon and also talk to the Stone parents. They don't live that far away from Elmwood, so it shouldn't take much time. Of course, who knows how much they'll tell us," Marlee said.

"And we still need to hear from Ira Green about meeting with him today," Hector added.

After wolfing down their meals, Hector and Marlee drove back to Johnny's home. He answered the door and was still in his Target uniform of a red polo shirt and khaki pants. The hickeys on his neck from the previous day were covered with flesh colored Band Aids.

"Hi," he said with a flat tone as he motioned them inside. The living room was furnished with a large-screen television and three overstuffed recliners.

As they all sat down, Marlee gave the same spiel to Johnny that she used on Violet and Paula earlier. He listened intently and nodded as she spoke, but didn't speak and gave no hint of emotion.

"I already talked to Paula and Violet. They both said you had questions about adoption," Johnny said, circumventing the lead up questions the professor and the detective were going to use to build rapport.

"Yeah," Marlee began. "We're trying to fill in some gaps and wanted to know a bit about the backgrounds of each of the students that took Criminal Justice To Go. One of the questions we've been asking everyone is if they are adopted."

Marlee and Hector waited for Johnny to answer. He looked around the room, contemplating his answer. Finally he spoke in a quiet tone. "I'm not adopted. My parents are my birth parents and I look like both of them. Here's a picture that was taken at their 30th anniversary party last fall." Johnny handed Marlee a photo encased in a silver frame.

Glancing at the photo of a middle aged couple seated with two males behind them, Marlee could see that the boys did indeed resemble both of their parents, albeit in different ways. Johnny had his mother's eyes and fair complexion but his father's build and premature baldness. Most of his brother's facial features resembled the father's but his smile was identical to the mother's.

"What's your brother's name?" Marlee asked as she handed the photo to Hector for his perusal.

"Jason. He's ten years older than me," Johnny stated.

Hector handed the photo back to Johnny. "Yes, you do look like both parents. So does your brother. What can you tell us about Paula and Violet Stone? They're both good friends of yours from what we hear."

Johnny's answer did not reveal any new information on the Stone family. If he knew or had suspicions about Violet's adoption, he didn't share them. "Why all the questions about adoption? How does that have anything to do with the murder investigation?"

"I'm not at liberty to discuss that part of the investigation," Hector said, straightening his posture in an effort to appear more professional.

"I've never seen routine questions about adoption in any of the cop shows I watch," Johnny said pointedly.

"You can't believe everything you see on TV, Johnny," Hector said sternly as he rose from the comfy recliner. This kid was sharp and already smelled a rat. "We need to be going now. If you think of anything about the case, just give me a call." Hector fished a business card from his wallet and handed it to Johnny.

As they were leaving, Johnny said, "I know you can't tell me, but I think you're looking at the students from Criminal Justice To Go to figure out which one of us killed Roxie."

In the car, Hector turned toward Marlee. "Johnny is a smart guy. I wonder which student he thinks did it?"

"Johnny is sharp, even though he slacks off in his classes. It might be worth coming back to talk to him again after he's had some time to think about this. Maybe he will remember something or point us in a direction we hadn't thought of yet. Hector nodded in agreement.

Before driving to Mobridge to meet with the Stones, Hector swung by Marlee's house to see if there were any messages from Ira Green on the answering machine. Marlee jogged inside and her heart skipped a beat when the flashing light indicated she had two new messages. Depressing the play button, she awaited the first message. It was a recorded call from Weight Watchers reminding her that it was swimsuit season and she should join their organization so she would be beach ready.

Marlee deleted the first message in disgust and listened to the second message.

"McCabe, it's Ira Green," barked the familiar voice. "I'll be in town at nine. Meet me then at Easy Street. I'll talk to your cop boyfriend too, but not any other cops." The message ended as abruptly as it began.

Marlee locked the house and jogged back to Hector's car to report Green's message. "Great," he said. "We have plenty of time to drive to Mobridge, interview the Stones, drive back, and maybe even go out for supper before we meet Green."

"Ooooh, we're going out for supper? How romantic. Where are we going? Will it be as nice as Bernie's?" Marlee teased. Hector just smiled as he pulled the car away from the curb.

The drive to Mobridge was uneventful. They used the lack of visual stimulation along the highway to process the details of the murder investigation and all the loose ends associated with it.

As they coasted along Highway 12, Marlee put her thoughts into words. "We're going with the premise that Roxie was either killed by one of the students in the Criminal Justice To Go class because he or she was given up for adoption by Roxie or that Ira Green did it because she indirectly got him fired when she filed a sexual harassment claim against him."

Hector nodded in agreement. "We really don't have any other motives that have surfaced."

"Here's what's bugging me about Ira Green as the killer: people get fired all the time. They usually don't go ballistic and poison someone over it. Roxie wasn't the direct cause of Green's termination, but if they hadn't started looking into his background after Roxie filed the harassment suit, MSU administration might not have figured out he was a big fraud. It all seems a bit weak to me."

"Agreed," said Hector, keeping his eyes on the road. "But you're operating from the standpoint that the job was all Green had to lose. He has pending lawsuits against him for other sexual harassment claims, he may have been worried about this being the final straw with his wife, and with another academic termination on his record he would have a tough time finding a new job. Plus, there's the financial aspect. All of this has to be costing him a ton of money and he's unemployed now. I think when you factor those things in, his motive to kill Roxie becomes a lot stronger."

"True. I keep coming back to my intuition, which is telling me he didn't do it. I know intuition isn't worth much, but it's how I operate. Plus, I really dislike Ira Green, so I really wouldn't mind if he was the killer." Marlee fidgeted with the seatbelt strap as she thought more about it. "It doesn't fit that he's the killer."

"We'll have a better sense of what's going on after we meet with him tonight," Hector said.

"So the other premise we're working from is that one of the students in the class was Roxie's adopted child," Marlee recalled.

"This theory is the weak one. Lots of kids are adopted and it impacts them in different ways, but killing the parent is pretty farfetched."

Marlee was having a multitude of feelings she couldn't sort out. She knew there was an answer in the information they already had but she couldn't bring it to the surface. Her mind wasn't through making sense of it yet.

She cleared her throat before she began to talk. "For someone to kill their birth parent, they'd be dealing with a lot of rage and abandonment issues. Maybe their adoptive home wasn't great and they blame being abused and neglected on Roxie giving them up for adoption."

Hector wasn't convinced. "But why wouldn't they just confront Roxie? That seems a lot more practical than killing her."

"Whoever killed Roxie didn't want her around anymore. It could be because they hated her or were seeking revenge. Or it could be because she knew information about something that the killer didn't want known," Marlee said. "At least that's what it looks like from the two theories we've been dealing with." "Clear as mud," said Hector.

There's only one person you can depend on and that's yourself. Not one hundred percent of the time, but most of the time.

Chapter 19

It was nearly 5:00 p.m. when Marlee and Hector pulled into the Stone's driveway. Their ranch style home was situated on the very edge of the town of Mobridge, population 3,452. Similar ranch homes stood to the east of the Stone residence while a pasture with grazing cows and their newborn calves was located on the west. A green Toyota Camry was parked in the driveway and Marlee could hear a television through the open windows facing the street.

"They're home." Marlee was pleased that the trip hadn't been a waste of time.

Climbing the front steps and approaching the door, Marlee heard sounds of sizzling and caught a whiff of fried onions and peppers. Someone was cooking supper and it made her hungry even though they'd just eaten. Hector rang the doorbell and they both stood off to the side of the door. Law enforcement training had taught both of them not to stand directly in front of an opening

BRENDA DONELAN

door. It was easy for the person opening the door to knock you off the front steps or draw a weapon. Although Marlee hadn't been a probation officer for years, the safety training still made some of her actions automatic.

A tall woman with wavy light brown hair opened the door with a questioning look. She appeared to be in her early forties. Her makeup and hair were impeccable and she wore a fitted pale yellow dress which showed off her slim physique. "Yes?" she asked with caution when she realized she did not know Marlee or Hector.

Marlee and Hector introduced themselves and asked to talk with Mrs. Stone and her husband. The color drained from her face as she motioned them toward the kitchen with a shaking hand. Her husband stood at the stove stirring the contents of a cast iron skilled.

"Burt, turn that off. The police are here to talk to us," she said.

Burt whirled around, the sizzling from the skillet having blocked out the sounds of visitors in the home. He was a hefty man in his forties with thick glasses and a sunburned face. His brown hair was sparse, revealing a sunburn on his scalp as well. Burt was also well-dressed; wearing navy slacks, a white shirt, and a loosened navy tie.

His suit jacket hung over the back of a kitchen chair.

"What's going on, Connie?" he asked his wife.

"They want to talk to us about an investigation," Connie Stone said, motioning for Marlee and Hector to sit at the kitchen table. She joined them, placing her hands before her on the white lace table cloth until she realized they were still shaking. Folding her hands in her lap, Connie made attempts at small talk while Burt turned the fire off on the stove and came over to join them. "We just got back from a graduation party and were making a quick supper before we go to a fundraiser at the VFW tonight."

236

Hector began the questions without further ado. "We're investigating the death of Roxie Harper. She was a fellow student in the class Paula and Violet took. We've talked to both of the girls and the topic of adoption came up. Paula told us Violet was adopted but she doesn't know it."

Burt's jaw dropped at hearing the news and he turned to look at his wife. Connie took a deep breath. "Yes, Paula called me after she talked to you earlier today. Both girls already told me about the murder investigation plus it's been on TV. I really don't know what my girls have to do with any of it. Neither of them saw anything. They told you everything they know!" Connie attempted righteous indignation but failed miserably.

"Some questions came up during our conversations with Paula and Violet about adoption. We want to hear more about it. Specifically, we want information on Violet's birth mother and how the adoption took place," said Marlee.

Burt and Connie looked at each other and neither spoke for a full minute. When Connie broke the silence she did so with confidence. "Yes, Violet is adopted. It was a family adoption. Violet's birth mother never wanted to have the baby but by the time she found out she was pregnant, it was too late for her to get an abortion. We wanted more children but after I had Paula the doctors said it would be very unlikely that I would be able to carry a baby to full term. Paula wasn't two yet when we found out about Violet's mom and decided it would be the best for everyone if we adopted her. It was all very simple."

"What was the name of Violet's mom?" Hector asked pointedly.

"Roxie Harper," murmured Burt, looking down at the table. During the course of the brief conversation, his sunburn had turned to a sickening pale.

"So Roxie was your sister?" Hector asked, looking at Mrs. Stone.

"Yes, Roxie was my younger sister. She was a wild child as long as I can remember. When she came home from college and was pregnant, Mama and Daddy were beside themselves. Burt and I had been married for about four years, had Paula, and wanted another baby. It just seemed to be the best thing."

"And Roxie was okay with it too?" asked Marlee.

"She agreed to the adoption at first, but then after it was official, she changed her mind. About a year after Violet was born, Roxie dropped out of college and moved back in with Mama and Daddy for a few months. She used to come over all the time to see Violet. It got to be too much, and we decided Roxie couldn't have contact with her any more. It would be too confusing for Violet as she got older and Paula was already asking questions. Roxie took off and we rarely heard from her," Connie recalled.

"When did you last hear from her?" Hector asked, jotting down notes in his Moleskine notebook.

"Hmmm... I don't remember. Burt, do you remember?" asked Connie.

"No, it's been several years. She never went back to Peachtree. That's the little town in Georgia where we grew up. We got a letter from Roxie when Violet was about three years old. She wanted to see Violet. The letter was sent from a women's correctional facility in Virginia. We wrote back and told her she couldn't have any contact with Violet. Ever."

"Why is it that you never told Violet she was adopted?" Marlee asked.

"It never seemed like the right time. We were going to tell both of the girls before Violet started kindergarten, but she was so little. We didn't want to upset her. She and

Paula have always been the best of friends and we didn't want that destroyed," said Connie.

"How would that destroy the relationship between Paula and Violet? They could still be the best of friends. They would still be cousins, after all," Hector stated.

"We were afraid Violet would want to meet Roxie and Roxie might try to take her away from us. Roxie was always a bit impetuous and unstable. Then she was in prison for what I don't know. Having Roxie step into Violet's life would've been horrible. There would never be a good time for Roxie to be involved in our family," Burt said, matter of factly.

"But if Roxie knew where you lived, she could come by anytime whether you liked it or not, right?" Marlee inquired.

"She didn't know we lived here. We moved since the last time she wrote to us," Connie said.

Hector and Marlee looked at each other, confused. "Where did the adoption take place?" Marlee asked, attempting to put together a time line of events.

"In Wyoming. We've lived in several places because of our work," said Connie.

"What is it you both do?" Hector asked.

"I'm a teacher's aide and Burt works for the city of Mobridge." The color still had not returned to Connie's face.

"You weren't transferred were you? I mean, the relocations were all your choice?" Hector asked.

Connie nodded, not giving up any information on their moves. Burt fidgeted with his already loosened necktie as he looked at his wife.

"Did you know Roxie was living in Elmwood and attending MSU?" Hector asked.

"No. Not until after she died and we heard about it on the news," Burt said. "We had no idea she lived so close or that she was taking some of the same classes as our girls."

"So will you still keep Violet's adoption a secret now that Roxie's dead?" Marlee asked.

"Oh, yes! There's no reason to stir up everything now. Paula won't tell and no one else knows. Please don't tell Violet any of this," Connie begged as she looked at Hector.

"I can't promise that, Mrs. Stone, but we won't go out of our way to tell her," Hector stated.

Marlee and Hector left the Stones looking upset and disheveled. Half an hour ago they looked like middle-aged models for a clothing catalog. Now they were rumpled, confused, and out of sorts. As soon as the professor and the detective drove away, Connie Stone placed a call.

Hector navigated the car back toward Elmwood, while Marlee thought out loud. "I think Connie and Burt Stone were more worried about the impact Roxie would have on their lives rather than just Violet's."

"I got the same impression," Hector said, glancing over. "Adoptions usually don't turn into this type of a mess."

"It seems Roxie would've had some involvement in the Stone family's life, regardless of whether the Stones wanted it or not. After all, it was a family adoption. The parents could've told Roxie where Violet was living," Marlee said.

Hector pulled his cell phone from a cup holder on the counsel. Pushing one number he made contact. "Yeah, can you check on an adoption for me? State of Wyoming. Yeah, I need the information as soon as possible. I need you to check on something else too. Is there a record of Roxie being in prison?" He clicked the phone off after giving the names and details of Violet's adoption and

Roxie's imprisonment. "Now we need to check on Roxie and Connie's parents. Let's see what they have to say about the adoption and Roxie."

Marlee nodded. Connie said the adoption took place in Wyoming, but that her parents were now in Peachtree, Georgia. "What does Wyoming have to do with this? Neither of the Stones are from there. It doesn't sound like they lived there either. Roxie lived with her parents for a time after Violet's birth and the Stones were nearby because Connie said they had to sever Roxie's contact with Violet. Was that in Georgia?"

"I don't know. The Stones' story really isn't adding up," said Hector as he slowed the car and pulled into the driveway leading to a farm and putting the car in reverse. "Let's say we head back to the Stone home and follow up with a few questions."

Professors keep talking about needing a degree and work experience to land your dream job. If you need education and experience to get a job, why weren't the people in the helping professions able to help me? Those so-called professionals didn't know shit!

Chapter 20

The green Camry wasn't in the driveway at the Stone's home and there was no answer when Marlee and Hector rang the doorbell. The smell of onions and peppers still wafted out the open windows. Marlee stood on her tiptoes to peer in the window at the top of the door. The once-orderly home was now in disarray. Clothes, boxes, papers, and other items were strewn about the living room.

"I think they took off!" Marlee shouted. "They told us a pack of lies and knew we'd discover the truth so they left!"

"They've only been gone a half hour at the most, so they can't be too far away."

"The question is; which direction did they go? I don't remember seeing a green car when we turned around to come back to Mobridge. Of course, I really wasn't looking either," Marlee mumbled, wondering if the

Stones were on their way to Elmwood to talk to Violet and Paula.

The garage was attached to the house and had a side entrance, which also had a window in the door. Hector shielded his eyes from the glare of the early evening sun and peered into the garage. "The car's here."

They must be in the house or away from home without their car," Marlee said. "But wait, the garage was closed when we were here, so they may have had another car inside and that's what they're driving now. Plus, they said something about going to a VFW fundraiser tonight."

"Let's swing by the VFW to see if Connie and Burt are there. If they are, then we can ask them our follow-up questions. If not, then we have to figure out how to find the Stones as soon as possible."

Hector agreed and the two jumped in his car and sped off toward the downtown area where Marlee believed the VFW building stood. Arriving less than two minutes later, they sprang from the car and raced inside the building. Just as the Stones had said, a fundraiser was in full swing. A poster at the front of the door announced that donations were being collected for two young children whose father was stationed in Afghanistan. A husky woman in her sixties sat at a table inside the door. She looked at Marlee and Hector as they raced in.

"Hi, ma'am," Hector said, pulling out his identification. "We're looking for Burt and Connie Stone. We talked to them earlier and they said they were coming here tonight. Have you seen them?"

"*Nooooo...*" The lady thought about her answer as she looked around the room. "I know they planned on attending, but I haven't seen them yet and I've been here taking donations, so I'd have noticed."

Hector thanked the woman for her time as he and Marlee jumped back in the car. After starting the vehicle, they realized that although they were in a hurry to find the Stones, they didn't know which way to go.

"Let's go back to their house. Maybe we can see something else if we peep in the windows," Marlee suggested.

"I'm an officer of the law. I don't peep in windows," Hector said indignantly. He picked up his cell and made contact with his office, asking them to have an officer from the Mobridge Police Department meet them at the Stone residence. Since Hector was out of his jurisdiction, he needed to contact the local law enforcement and apprise them of the situation.

As Marlee and the detective circled around the small town of Mobridge, they kept a watchful eye, hoping they would spot one or both of the Stones out for a walk, entering a business, or riding in a car. They had no luck and by the time they returned to the Stone residence, an officer was exiting his patrol SUV. The tall, slim officer walked with the confidence of a man who had nearly twenty years of law enforcement experience. His thin, black hair ruffled in the breeze. As he approached them, he took off his aviator sunglasses and looped one of the bows into the pocket on his blue uniform shirt.

Introductions were made and Officer Schwartz assured Hector and Marlee that the Stones were good, upstanding citizens and had never been involved in any criminal activity. "Burt and Connie have lived here for over twelve years. Just because they didn't tell their daughter that she was adopted doesn't make them criminals," he said.

"No, it doesn't," Marlee agreed. "But we just talked to them and when we came back to fill in some gaps from their story, they were gone and the house looks like they left in a hurry."

Hector filled Officer Schwartz in on Roxie Harper's murder and how that tied into the sudden disappearance of Burt and Connie Stone. "They told us they were going to a fundraiser at the VFW and when we checked, no one had seen them. That, plus the house in disarray, plus the adoption of Roxie Harper's birth child all adds up to something."

"Yeah, I see what you're saying." Schwartz ran his hand through his sparse hair as he thought. "I guess we should call in an APB."

"Any idea where the Stones might have gone?" Marlee asked. "The only place we could think of was over to Elmwood to make sure no one told Violet she was adopted. Other than that, we're at a loss."

Officer Schwartz chewed on his bottom lip as he thought. "Nope. No clue where they might be, other than on their way to Elmwood."

The officer advised that the Stones were probably driving a newer model, purple mini-van.

"No wonder we didn't see the Stones when we came back to Mobridge." Hector ran to his car and called in an All-Points Bulletin on Burt and Connie Stone, giving a description of them and their vehicle. Hector and Marlee decided that in lieu of any other ideas, they would head back to Elmwood. On the way back to Elmwood, Hector activated his police lights on his dash and drove in record speed. The only things slowing them down were cars, pickups, farm implements, and an occasional small town. "Jesus, everybody's out for a Sunday drive today and it's only Saturday," Hector grumbled as he maneuvered around a slow moving tractor pulling a plow.

By the time they flew into Elmwood, Marlee was rattled. Hector was a horrible driver and nearly ran them off the road numerous times as he veered around other vehicles and made calls on his cell. She added his reckless driving to the negative column in her ongoing assessment of the detective. Although, she had to admit, she was never a good passenger. Marlee liked being in control and that meant being in the driver's seat; both literally and figuratively.

Arriving back at the Stone sisters' apartment, Marlee and Hector bolted out of the vehicle and ran to their apartment door. They knocked repeatedly, but there was no answer and no sounds coming from within the home. As they went back to their car, Hector surveyed the other cars in the parking lot and nearby streets. "Shit, I don't see any purple vans here!"

"Let's go back to Pizza Ranch. Maybe they went there. Violet said she had to work there later and we know Paula was working there a few hours ago," Marlee suggested.

"Good idea." Hector spun out of the parking lot and zoomed over to Pizza Ranch. Before stopping the vehicle, he circled the lot looking for a purple mini-van. An older burgundy van with Manitoba license plates was the vehicle most closely matching the description the sheriff gave them. They went inside Pizza Ranch and looked around for the Stones, even though they knew the search would be fruitless.

Hector asked to speak with the store manager. Moments later a frazzled woman in her late twenties appeared before them. By the looks of the apron she was wearing, it appeared she did more than just supervise others at the restaurant. Bits of fried food and grease stains covered her apron, leaving a not-too-appetizing appearance.

"Yeah?" asked the manager, ready to get back to her duties since it was still the supper rush.

"We're looking for either Violet or Paula Stone. Are they working now?" Marlee asked.

"Paula worked earlier today, but left before her shift was over. Said something about a family emergency. Then Violet called in and said she was sick. Seems a little fishy to me. They've been good workers, but both of them taking off today makes me think they wanted to party with their friends since it's Saturday night. Both of them work tomorrow and I'll have a talk with them. If they don't have a good excuse for missing work then they'll get a write-up," the manager stated. "Is that all? I really need to get back to work. We have a couple school busses coming here shortly and those kids can eat!"

After getting the work hours for Paula and Violet the following day, Marlee and Hector left the restaurant. "We have about two hours before we need to meet Ira Green at Easy Street," Marlee said.

Hector nodded. "Now I'm hungry for chicken. Should we go back in and eat? Then we can drive around a bit more looking for the Stones. And then we can swing over to Johnny Marble's apartment again to see if he knows anything else. He might know where Paula and Violet went."

Marlee was completely down with Hector's plan and made the decision to throw her low carb diet out the window...as she had been doing regularly the past few days. After being seated in a well-worn booth, they made their way to the buffet. Marlee heaped piles of potatoes and gravy on her plate and threw a giant piece of chicken atop it. She and Hector were separated during their quest for food and met up back at the booth. Glancing at Hector's plates, she observed a green salad with a side of cottage cheese, a cup of vegetable beef soup, and two chicken legs.

"Aren't you hungry?" Marlee asked, concerned that the case had thrown off his appetite.

"Yeah, but I can't eat a lot of heavy food at night or else I get heartburn." Hector looked at Marlee's plate and grinned. "Looks like you don't have that problem."

"Nope. Not yet, anyway," Marlee mumbled, shoveling the creamy potatoes and the succulent gravy into her mouth. She limited herself to one plate of food, which was not a usual occurrence at a buffet.

They left the restaurant within an hour of arriving and drove back to Paula and Violet's apartment. Just as before, there was no answer when they knocked and no sounds came from behind the closed door. Hector had run a check on the car the two girls shared and it sat in the parking lot.

Johnny Marble answered his door after the second round of knocking. He was now wearing jeans, a light colored Oxford shirt, and black sports sandals. His face was tanned and he smelled of cologne. It appeared that the young man had been in a tanning booth since they saw him that afternoon. Now he looked as if he were ready to hit a party. Johnny motioned his guests inside and they sat down in the same places they sat earlier that day.

"Johnny, we're looking for Paula and Violet. Paula left work early and Violet called in sick. We think they might be in some sort of trouble and we just want to talk with them. Where are they?" Hector asked, not allowing the possibility that Johnny didn't know the whereabouts of the Stone girls.

"I don't know for sure. Violet called me a few hours ago and said her parents were coming to get her and Paula and they had to leave right away. It was something about a family crisis they needed to take care of," Johnny reported.

"Where is it?" Marlee was on the edge of her seat, hoping this conversation would finally lead to the whereabouts of the whole Stone family and finally clear up several unanswered questions.

"I don't know. Violet didn't say. She just said they had to leave right away. I don't know if she even knew where they were going."

"We need you to call Violet now and find out where they are. Don't tell her we're here," Hector said.

Johnny nodded and reached for his cellphone and selected Violet's name and number from the drop down menu. "Violet, it's Johnny. Call me back as soon as you can."

"Voicemail," Johnny said, looking at Hector and Marlee. "You want me to try Paula too?"

The call to Paula's cellphone yielded the same situation and Johnny left a similar message on Paula's voicemail. At the end of his message he said, "Abracadabra." Looking at Hector and Marlee, Johnny smiled. "It's just a goofy saying Paula and I have. When we leave messages we end it with Abracadabra. We started doing that back in fourth grade after a magician came to our school and showed us a bunch of tricks."

"Johnny, was there any place that the Stones liked to go? Did they take family vacations or have friends they visited?" Hector asked.

Johnny shook his head from side to side. "No, they never really went anywhere other than just a day trip to Elmwood or Bismarck to do some shopping. Otherwise, they were always at home."

Satisfied that they had exhausted Johnny's knowledge of the Stones' whereabouts, Marlee and Hector left the apartment. Hector shrugged. "It's still an hour before we meet with Ira Green, but we could go to Easy Street and wait for him. Marlee nodded. She didn't have any better ideas on how to locate the Stones.

Easy Street was a little hideaway on the east end of Elmwood. It was a sports bar frequented mostly by farmers and blue-collar workers. Marlee was only there once before, and hadn't recognized a single person in the establishment. She assumed Ira Green selected this bar knowing there would be little chance of running into anyone from Midwestern State University. The gravel parking lot was filled with a variety of pickups and motorcycles, all in various stages of their life expectancy. Hector parked near a decrepit white pickup with a blue door and a tan hood. Rust had eaten away the bottom of the passenger side door. The windows were rolled down and Marlee observed the keys still in the ignition. The owner was probably hoping someone would steal it.

The detective and the professor walked into Easy Street and found a booth near the back of the establishment with full view of the door. They weren't in an overly-conspicuous location in the bar and they could easily see who came and left. Marlee and Hector both glanced around, checking to see if Ira Green was already there or if they knew anyone. Green wasn't in the bar yet, unless he was in the restroom. Marlee was glad to see she didn't know anyone. Even though Elmwood had over twenty-five thousand people, it still had the small town feel. Acquaintances and curious strangers would all approach others out in public, just to be friendly.

Hector and Marlee both ordered ice tea when the waitress came by. Marlee was full from her carb blowout supper at Pizza Ranch, so she wouldn't be drinking any beer that night, which was probably a good thing since they needed to have a serious talk with Mean Dean Green. Hector received a phone call from another detective at his office and stepped outside to speak in private. Just then, the door swung open. Marlee's jaw dropped and her heart sank.

Don't let appearances fool you. Unless you like being a fool.

Chapter 21

Standing in the doorway wearing tan and green striped shorts, an aqua blue T-shirt with a bright yellow light bulb, and orange clogs was none other than Marlee's colleague, Della Halter. She spied Marlee in the back booth and hurried over, her breasts jiggling since she was braless as usual.

"Hey, *girrrrl*. What the hell are you doing here?" Della chirped as she slid into the booth.

"Um, just hanging out." Marlee was panicked. Ira Green would be there to meet them in less than an hour. She couldn't have Della there or she would wreck everything with her tactless questions and outright accusations. Della was an intelligent woman, but not very polished in the ways of eliciting information. She normally used the confrontational bullying approach, which wouldn't work with Ira Green, since he was loud and brash. *Ira Green and Della are actually quite a bit alike*, Marlee thought.

Della flagged down the waitress and ordered a beer, oblivious to the fact that she had not been invited to join Marlee. "So, you usually come here on Saturday nights?"

"No, this is only my second time here. What are you doing here?" Marlee was getting fidgety and it wasn't because of the caffeine in the ice tea. She needed to get rid of Della and fast.

"I was supposed to play darts tonight downtown but my friend stood me up so I thought I'd come out here and check this place out," Della said slurping her beer as soon as it was placed in front of her.

Hector walked back inside and came over to the booth. "Ah, I see we have company," he said as he squeezed in beside Marlee.

"Oh, I didn't know you were on a date," Della said. "I'll leave you guys alone as soon as I finish my beer. If that's okay." Marlee and Hector both nodded, but not enthusiastically. "I heard you two were quite an item. Isn't it against the rules to date someone involved in a murder investigation?" Della asked Hector, staring him straight in the eye. How Della knew Marlee and Hector had been spending time together was a mystery. She seemed to know everything connected to MSU.

"If the person is a suspect then it's frowned upon," Hector said. "Luckily, Marlee isn't a suspect any more. I crossed her off the list." Marlee glared at him and elbowed him in the side.

Della brought up the topic of dogs and delivered a monologue for another half hour before she took her leave of Easy Street. "I better leave you two love-birds alone now," she said with an exaggerated wink. They said their goodbyes and just as Della was ready to walk out the door, she yelled, "Don't forget to use protection!"

Marlee turned red as a radish when everyone in the bar turned to look at her and Hector sitting together on the same side of the booth. *Goddamned Della! I'm gonna kill her!* Marlee's face was still burning and she was afraid to look at Hector. Then she heard him laugh. "That Della is quite the character isn't she?"

"*Character* is not the word I would use," Marlee said. "Sorry about that. She likes to be crude to throw people off balance."

"That's fine. I don't mind being a bit off balance," he said with a sly smile.

Turning the topic back to the murder investigation, Marlee asked, "Did you find out anything important from your department?"

"Yeah, I sure did. Turns out Burt and Connie Stone did not adopt Violet. They kidnapped her from Roxie," Hector reported.

"What? Is Connie really Roxie's sister?"

"They're sisters. That's one thing they told us which was true. My department found out that Roxie and the baby were living with Roxie's parents. Connie and Burt lived somewhere nearby and had asked about adopting Violet but Roxie wouldn't agree. Roxie and Connie's parents, Jack and Viva Harper, insisted that the baby would stay with them if Roxie decided not to keep it. That way, Violet would always have contact with Roxie even if Roxie couldn't or wouldn't take care of her."

"Wow!" Marlee exclaimed. "How did the Stones get Violet away from Roxie and the grandparents?"

"Connie was babysitting one night when Jack and Viva went to a retirement party for one of their co-workers. Roxie was supposed to be watching Violet, but wanted to go out and party so she called Connie to come over. Connie knew this would go on for the rest of Violet's childhood and she decided to take matters into her own hands. She took Violet back to her house where she and Burt devised a plan. They packed up as much of their apartment as they could, grabbed both girls, and left the state," Hector said.

"How were the Stones able to adopt Violet without Roxie's permission?" Marlee asked.

"It seems Connie found Violet's birth certificate in the Harpers' home and took it. The father was listed as unknown, so Roxie was the only parent who needed to give consent. Connie also grabbed Roxie's driver's license, Social Security card, and some other ID. Turns out it really wasn't that hard for Connie to pass herself off as Roxie when she needed to."

"All this time, Roxie was looking for Violet? That's so sad," Marlee felt a pang of sadness for what Roxie must have experienced over the past eighteen years. "Have the Stones been hiding out from Roxie and the Harpers all this time?"

"Yes, they have. That's why they moved a few times before finally settling in Mobridge twelve years ago. They figured Roxie and the Harpers would never be able to track them down in the middle of South Dakota. They remained well hidden until it became so easy to find anyone on the Internet."

"She tracked Violet down to Mobridge and MSU? But why did she refer to the baby as 'it' and 'X', I wonder?" Marlee asked.

Hector shrugged. "She clearly knew the baby was a girl. Maybe she thought the baby's name had been changed."

"So the story Paula told us about Violet's adoption was all false," Marlee said. "I bet it's what her parents told her and she thinks the story is true."

"Sounds about right. There's something else." Ramos took a hearty drink from his ice tea. "According to our records, Roxie's never been in prison. The Stones lied about that too."

"What?" Marlee couldn't believe her ears.

"I don't think they've told anyone the real story because it shows what they really are: kidnappers and liars," Hector replied.

"And maybe murderers!" Marlee said, contemplating that the well-groomed, smartly-dressed couple could have poisoned Roxie Harper.

If there's one thing I've learned about people it's this; everyone's working toward their own self-interest. To accomplish that, some people cause damage. A lot of damage. The kind of damage that can't be fixed.

Chapter 22

Reuben Ira Green walked into Easy Street at exactly 9:00 p.m., dressed in what he thought was a disguise. He was a large man, noticeable under any circumstances. The oversized straw hat and dark glasses did nothing to hide his features. Anyone who knew Green without the disguise would surely recognize him with it. He spied Marlee and Hector in the back and quickly strode over to their booth. Green nodded toward the detective as he removed his sunglasses and slid into the opposite side of the booth. The waitress was at their table immediately and he ordered a tap beer.

"You didn't tell anybody else about meeting me here, did you?" Green asked with an accusing tone.

"No, I didn't tell anyone other than Detective Ramos," Marlee said, motioning toward Hector.

"And I have your word you won't try to arrest me after we talk?" Green asked giving Ramos the stare down.

"Sure," Hector lied. The law didn't prevent law enforcement officers from lying to suspects in order to obtain information.

"First thing I want to make sure you understand," Green said leaning on the table and pointing a finger directly at the detective, "is that I had nothing to do with Roxie's death. Got it? I didn't kill her and I don't know who did." Marlee and Hector both nodded as if in agreement that Green was innocent. This was an active listening technique indicating that the speaker was being heard rather than the listeners were in agreement. Green however, seemed to take the nodding as an affirmation of his innocence.

"Why don't you tell me how you met Roxie and about your relationship over the years?" suggested Ramos.

Ira Green repeated the same story he told Marlee a few days earlier. "We met when she was in one of the classes I taught at Keystone State University. We had a brief fling and then I never saw Roxie again until I came to Elmwood. I recognized her and we got together a couple times to talk. The old spark was back and I realized I was in love with her. She played hard to get, like women do." Ira Green shot a knowing look at Detective Ramos before continuing. "One night we went out for coffee and she told me she'd had a baby in college and it was mine. Well, of course I didn't believe her at first, but then she told me the story of how the baby was kidnapped by her own sister and she hadn't seen her in 17 years." Green slugged down half of his beer and set the glass down on the table top with a thud.

"You didn't know Roxie or your child were here at MSU when you took the job? That seems a little far-fetched," Marlee said. Hector kicked her under the table, not wanting Green to become defensive and leave before they gathered all the information they could from the ousted dean.

"I was here in Elmwood before Roxie enrolled. And I had no idea about the child until Roxie told me. She wanted me to help her talk to Violet. To tell her we were her real parents."

"Were you going to help Roxie?" Hector jotted down notes in his pocket sized notebook.

"Well, yeah. I mean, I knew we weren't going to be one big happy family, but I loved Roxie and knew she wanted to be reunited with Violet. I didn't have any huge desire to take on a father role, but Roxie really wanted to be involved in Violet's life now that she'd found her."

"How did Roxie track down Violet?" Hector asked.

"She spent a lot of time on the Internet searching chat rooms, social media sites, and the like. Roxie had named the baby Violet but didn't know if the Stones had renamed her when they kidnapped her. Roxie didn't have anything else to go on, so she kept searching using the name Violet. Since Violet isn't a popular name, like Ashley or Amber, Roxie was able to finally track her down through a MySpace profile. She recognized Violet right away from her profile picture because she looked just like Roxie did when she was a teenager."

"Had either of you made any contact with Violet yet?" Marlee inquired.

"No. Roxie wanted to arrange something after finishing Criminal Justice To Go. She took the class because she knew Violet was in it. She overheard Violet and Paula talking about it and decided it would be a good way to find out more about Violet. Basically, Roxie just wanted to be around her," Green relayed.

"Did Roxie make contact with her sister and brother in-law?" Hector asked.

"No. She was afraid they'd grab Violet and take off again. Anytime she's gotten close to finding them, they'd leave the state and change their last name. Roxie wanted to establish a connection with Violet first before she confronted her sister about the kidnapping. She told me she wanted them arrested for ruining her life and keeping her away from her child all these years."

"How do we know this is true and you're not just throwing suspicion on Burt and Connie Stone?" Marlee asked. She was rewarded with another kick from Hector.

"I didn't kill Roxie! I loved her!" Green wailed. Marlee had never seen him in such a state. He was acting the way a normal, grieving person would act. His usual bluster and bravado were gone.

"Why were you arguing with Roxie at the motel in Chamberlain the night before she died?" Hector asked.

"I wanted her to retract her sexual harassment claim against me and help me get my job back at MSU. I'd called her cell earlier and she agreed to meet with me at her motel room. Roxie sounded like her usual self, but when I went to her room, she was in one of her fits again. She was talking nonsense and we argued and I left. That's it," Green stated.

"What about Mrs. Dean Green?" Marlee asked. "How does she fit into all of this?"

"Her name is Petra," Green said pointedly. "I was going to ask her for a divorce so I could be with Roxie. But then everything fell apart when Roxie accused me of sexually harassing her and got me fired."

"Why would Roxie report you for sexual harassment if she wanted your help in talking to Violet?" Hector inquired.

"I don't know. One minute she's friendly and needs my help and the next minute she's screaming at me to stay away from her. It's like she had multiple personalities."

"Was she always like that?" Marlee wondered if the unstable moods were a new development or if Roxie had acted in this manner throughout her life.

"No, she was really calm back when I knew her as a student at Keystone State. She was very mild mannered here in Elmwood too until the last couple of weeks before she died. A couple times that last week she just flew off the handle and started talking nonsense. I asked her if she was on drugs and she just laughed at me."

"When did you first have contact with Roxie in Elmwood?" Hector busily jotted down facts in his notebook as quickly as Green relayed them.

"It was right before Thanksgiving. I knew it was her the minute I saw her. She knew me too. We talked for a few minutes and then I sought her out a few days later. We started meeting and talking. That's when she told me about Violet."

"Who do you think killed Roxie?" Marlee asked.

"Her sister and brother in-law. They're the ones with the most to lose. If Roxie reported them to the police, they'd be in prison for a long time. And Violet would reject them for taking her away from Roxie."

Marlee nodded. A kidnapping in which the victim was taken over state borders constituted a federal offense. Burt and Connie Stone were facing several years in federal prison if their actions came to light.

"You told me before that your wife was in Florida with her sister. When did she leave?" Ramos asked.

"She flew out the day after I was fired at MSU. Petra was in a rage. She was mad about the damage to my career, but mostly she was upset about my feelings for Roxie. Even though Roxie reported me for sexual harassment, I knew she'd come to her senses and retract her claims. I loved her and she loved me too. She just had a way of overreacting to things." Green continued on with his usual lack of insight.

"Petra said she was leaving you? Leaving the marriage?" asked Marlee.

"That's what she said, but she's done that before. Gets mad and leaves then comes back after a week or so. She just needs some time to cool off. Women!" Green shook his head in disgust, looking at Hector again.

"So you want to get back together with Petra?" Marlee was repulsed by Green before she found out the details of his womanizing, but now it was just getting worse.

"Sure, why wouldn't I want to keep my marriage together? Roxie's dead, so nothing can happen there." The old Mean Dean Green was back in full force. Just because the woman he claimed to love was dead, didn't mean he'd be leaving his wife as he previously intended. Apparently he believed his second choice, Petra, was better than nothing at all when it came to relationships.

Marlee felt like throwing up all over Ira Green. He was a disgusting creature and she'd had enough of his callous treatment of Petra Green, the long suffering wife who had put up with countless indiscretions by her pig of a husband.

"How long have you and Petra been married? How did you meet?" Hector asked, sensing that Marlee was ready to hammer Green with her judgments about his behavior toward women.

"We met at Keystone State. She was a graduate assistant. Petra and I've been together fourteen years this July. Mostly happy times," Green stated, unaware that his wife could have a very different account of their marriage.

"And she was okay with your dalliances with other women?" Marlee asked, moving her leg to avoid another kick from Hector.

"It used to be that the wife looked the other way when her husband needed a little something on the side. Then, with all this women's lib and feminism bullshit...." Green's voice trailed off as he shook his head in disbelief.

"So Petra wasn't willing to look the other way?" Marlee inquired.

"No, she wasn't."

"At what point did Petra find out about you and Roxie?" Hector's pen was poised above his notebook, ready to jot down Green's response.

"It all came out when I was let go at MSU. I had to tell her about getting fired. I tried to leave out the part about Roxie, but she just kept questioning me until I told her. That's when she left Elmwood."

"Are you sure she left?" Marlee asked.

"Of course. I've talked to her a couple times since she's been in Florida at her sister's condo. She's still mad, but I think she'll come around soon," Green said.

"Did she know you were planning to leave her for Roxie?" Hector asked.

"No! Petra never knew about that. As far as she knows, I just had a flirtation with Roxie. She doesn't know about my past with Roxie or our child," Green said.

"So what are your plans? What do you intend to do now?" Marlee asked.

"I decided to appeal my termination at MSU and hope I can get my dean position back. And I want to make sure the cops know I didn't hurt Roxie. That's all I want; to get my good name back and be reinstated at MSU," Green replied.

Ira Green provided no further information on the Roxie Harper murder investigation and the conversation between the former dean, the professor, and the detective ended. Before Green left, Hector obtained Petra Green's cell number and her sister's home number in Florida. The former dean hoisted his large body out of the booth, donned his enormous hat and sunglasses, and departed Easy Street.

Hector and Marlee looked at each other for a full thirty seconds before they broke out in a fit of laughter.

A recipe for disaster: a glass of Coke, a splash of vodka, and a few drops of anti-freeze.

Chapter 23

"Is that guy delusional, or what?" Hector asked, after he and Marlee composed themselves from their laugh riot. "He thinks he's getting his job back and he believes this little talk we just had is enough to clear him from suspicion of murder."

"He has no doubt that Petra will come back to him with arms wide open. And what about that disguise?" Marlee giggled again as she envisioned Ira Green in the oversized hat and jumbo sunglasses, both of which might be appropriate for a day in the hot sun but not for a meeting at 9:00 p.m. inside a dimly-lit bar.

"He's clueless, that's for sure, but I still think he's the one who poisoned Roxie. I just don't have enough to arrest him yet," Hector said, not swayed by anything Ira Green just relayed to them. Before Green left, he divulged his current whereabouts. He spent the first few days sleeping in his car. After he returned to Elmwood, he realized he still had a key to Scobey Hall. He couldn't get into his old office, but he was able to sleep on an old sofa in a never-used faculty lounge in the basement and freshen up in the adjoining restroom. Hector let Green leave on the promise that he would answer his cell phone immediately whenever Hector called him. Ira Green agreed, but it was a gamble that he would keep his word.

"Now what?" asked Marlee.

"I want to run into the Elmwood PD and talk to one of the detectives there. I called them when I was outside earlier and updated them on the investigation. Didn't want to step on anyone's toes since I've been interviewing more suspects and witnesses in their jurisdiction."

"Ah, you have to go play nice with the local cops." Marlee was amused at the level of territorial bullshit that had to be hammered out between law enforcement officers from differing jurisdictions. *Seems as though we should be working together rather than having a war over whose area it is and who gets credit.* "It's nearly ten o'clock and I'm tired. Can you drop me off at home before you go to the PD?"

As Hector and Marlee left Easy Street, she glanced around and still didn't see anyone she knew. The bar was filled with men and women who worked long hard days using their hands and their backs. Most of the patrons were in their twenties and thirties. They were on their feet conversing with each other, playing darts, and drinking Bud Light. A few older customers sat together in the booths and were more sedate that their younger counterparts. One old duffer was dressed in well-worn bib overalls and a green John Deere baseball cap. His greasy gray hair stuck out around his ears and the base of his neck. He sat hunched over a table in the back taking an occasional swig of beer from the amber bottle. His long, slim fingers with neatly clipped nails drummed on the bar, keeping time to the beat of the country music playing on the jukebox.

Hector dropped Marlee off at her house and sped away before she even reached the front door. As she fumbled for her keys, she cursed herself for not turning on the outside light before she left earlier. There weren't many street-lights in Marlee's neighborhood and the one across the street had burned out last week. Marlee tried to find the correct key for the front door just by the feel of it since she couldn't see to distinguish her front door key from the keys to the back door, the garage, her car, Scobey Hall, her office, and her file drawer at work. She tried to fit one key in the lock and had no luck. Marlee was so intent on searching for the correct key to open the front door that she didn't even hear the person sneak up behind her.

Do you have to be hit over the head to get the message? I guess some people do. Literally.

Chapter 24

Darkness. Piercing light. Screams. Someone touching her shoulders. Marlee's senses were dulled and she didn't know what was going on. "Stop touching me," she mumbled, not sure if anyone was even near her.

"Marlee, it's me. It's Hector. Are you okay?" asked the familiar deep voice in a serious tone. The hands that were touching her gently pulled her into a sitting position.

She became more fully aware of her surroundings as she sat upright. She was on her front step and Hector stood over her with a flashlight. His expression was worried but calm. The only thing Marlee could comprehend was that her head hurt like hell. "My head hurts so much," she said, her tongue tripping over the words as if she were intoxicated.

"Hang on. The ambulance is on the way.

Somebody hit you in the back of the head and knocked you out. You might have a concussion," Hector explained as he rubbed Marlee's arm to soothe her.

"Who hit me? Why?" It was incomprehensible to Marlee that someone would be mad enough at her to knock her out.

"I don't know. I just got back here and saw you unconscious on the step. Your head's bleeding and it looks serious." The drone of the ambulance could be heard in the background. Within seconds, it rounded the corner and screeched to a halt in front of Marlee's little Spanish style home. Two police cars, lights flashing and sirens blaring, followed the ambulance and parked behind it.

As Marlee was loaded into the ambulance, a young male officer asked her questions about her attack. The questioning was brief when he realized she recalled nothing of the attack or her assailant. She was then taken to the hospital emergency room. Hector talked with the police officers for a few moments before leaving for the hospital. An examination revealed that Marlee had a severe concussion resulting from a blow to the back of the head. A CT scan didn't show any neurological problems or skull fractures. She was released when Hector volunteered to stay with her until she could be reexamined by her own physician on Monday.

"Sonofabitch! My head really hurts!" Marlee whined on the drive back to her house. "They didn't give me any pain meds. I shoulda asked for morphine." She gingerly touched the back of her head where she'd been hit by a blunt object.

"I don't think they give morphine for concussions." Hector parked his car in front of Marlee's house and helped her inside. "The doctor said you need bed rest, plenty of fluids, and Tylenol for the pain."

"Do I have to stay awake?" Marlee recalled that on television a concussed patient could not fall asleep for fear they would never awaken.

"No, I asked about that specifically. You can sleep. I just have to wake you up every few hours. If you're really hard to wake up or you're incoherent, then I have to take you back to the ER. Otherwise, you should be okay."

"Good, because I'm really tired. I'll take some Tylenol and go to bed."

"Before you do, I just need to ask what you remember about the attack." Hector had his notebook and pen at the ready.

"Nothing. I remember getting out of your car and walking toward my door. That's it," Marlee recalled. "I really wish I knew who did this and why."

"Me too. I think it's related to the Roxie Harper investigation. Somebody is trying to scare you away from asking questions."

"I don't know who it would be. Unless... maybe the Stones are here in town and one of them did it." Marlee was feeling a little better since discussing the Harper case took her mind off her pain and injuries.

"Maybe. But it could also be Ira Green. We know he's here in Elmwood," Hector replied.

"It doesn't seem like a very well thought-out plan. How is knocking me out supposed to discourage me from helping investigate this case? If anything, it makes me want to dig deeper. I think whoever hit me did it as a reaction to something specific," Marlee said.

"Is anyone mad at you? A student? Someone in your department?" Hector inquired.

"No! Actually, I can't think of anyone who's mad at me at all. Some students might get upset about their final grades, but not mad enough to do this," Marlee said pointing at her head. "It has to be someone related to this case."

"Go rest. I'll sleep here on the couch and wake you up a couple times in the night to make sure you're okay," Hector ordered. "On Monday I'll take you to your regular doctor for a check-up."

Marlee nodded, too tired to argue about being bossed around. She kicked off her shoes and tumbled into bed fully clothed and pulled the sheet and quilt up to her chin. Hector woke her twice during the night by calling her name. Satisfied that she wasn't unusually groggy, he let her sleep and returned to the bed he fashioned for himself on the living room couch.

The morning sun was shining on the foot of her bed when Marlee awoke the next morning. Her head was tender where she'd been struck and a mild headache had settled in around the base of her skull. She got up to take a couple Tylenol and planned to return to bed for another hour or two of rest. Her head wound, which the ER doctor thought was the result of being struck with a blunt object, was slightly oozing, but not enough to warrant a bandage.

After chasing two pain relievers with a glass of tap water, Marlee was on her way back to her bedroom when she heard a commotion in the kitchen. Peeking around the corner she was dismayed to see most of her cookware on the counters or in the sink. Egg shells, coffee grounds, and bits of other unidentifiable objects were strewn throughout the kitchen. Hector stood, leaning over the counter. His eyes were focused on a small card and he didn't hear Marlee enter the room.

"Hey, whatcha doing?" Marlee stood behind the detective, looking over his shoulder.

Hector jumped, sloshing coffee from the mug he held onto the counter. "Don't sneak up on me like that!" He squinted his eyes and his lips were pursed until he realized it was Marlee. "You're lucky I didn't have my gun on me or I would've shot you."

"Oh, please. You and I both know you're not going to shoot someone just because they scared you." Marlee wasn't falling for his macho-cop bullshit. "So, are you making something or just seeing how much you can dirty up my kitchen?"

Hector smiled, now relaxed. "I was attempting to cook this breakfast casserole recipe I found in one of your magazines on the coffee table. I'm a good cook, just not so good at following new recipes."

"What have you done so far?" Marlee looked at the complex recipe and realized she didn't have half the ingredients needed.

"I cracked the eggs. And I made a pot of coffee."

Hector reached for a mug and poured Marlee a cup of steaming brew.

"Are you set on making this recipe or would you be satisfied with scrambled eggs?" Marlee was hoping for a quick resolution to Hector's cooking debacle.

"Yeah, that would be okay with me. I just thought I'd try to make something nice for you since you were beaten up last night." The relief was visible in Hector's face and posture. His intentions were good, but he was out of his comfort zone in making anything involving more than two ingredients. As a bachelor for the past ten years, he lived on meat he could grill, frozen dinners, and fast food.

"I wasn't beaten up! I was attacked. There's a huge difference. Beaten up implies that I participated in the fight and lost. Attacked means I didn't see it coming." After two sips of coffee, Marlee was already feeling like her old self.

During breakfast, Marlee and Hector again turned to her assault the previous night. "You know, I didn't see who hit me, but there was something familiar about them."

"Familiar how?" Hector finished the last of the eggs and pushed his plate away from him.

"That's the weird part. I don't know how they seemed familiar. I just have the sense that I know the person who hit me." Marlee knew she wasn't making much sense. She hadn't seen her attacker and couldn't remember him saying any words. Still, she felt she was familiar with the person who assaulted her.

"I hope you're not telling me you have ESP or some sort of psychic powers." Hector looked at Marlee with skepticism.

"No, it's not that. There was something familiar. I just need to think on it for a while." Marlee finished off her first cup of coffee and poured another. While she showered, she put Hector to work cleaning up the mess he made in her kitchen. By the time she was showered and dressed, he was washing the last of the dishes.

"Now I remember why I don't cook very often." Hector pulled the plug on the dirty dishwater and dried his hands.

It was mid-morning and Marlee and Hector planned the rest of their day over another cup of coffee. "I think we should put together a crime chart," suggested Marlee, recalling how helpful that had been last year when a janitor was murdered on campus. It had been the idea of her cousin, Bridget McCabe, who became involved in the investigation when she visited Marlee.

Within minutes, Marlee assembled all the tools necessary to construct the crime chart. A large poster board took up the majority of the table and several markers of different colors were spread out atop it. Marlee picked up the black marker and wrote Roxie's name in the center in large capital letters.

"Now, we write down the other people involved in the case and their connections to Roxie and to each other," Marlee explained.

"Yes, I'm familiar with this process. I watch TV too. Plus, I've actually done this. You know, since I'm a detective." Hector smiled, grabbing a red marker. He wrote down the name of Reuben Ira Green and also Violet Stone and drew direct lines between the two of them and Roxie.

Marlee wrote in the names of Connie and Burt Stone and after considering it for a second, she also scrawled Paula Stone's name on the chart. "I don't think Paula killed Roxie, but she has a connection to the case." Hector nodded in agreement.

"I think we need to include everyone in the class, including you." Hector looked down at the table, not daring to look Marlee in the eye.

"Well, you've just solved the case. I did it!" Marlee threw her hands in the air as if surrendering.

"Very funny. I know you didn't kill her, but we need to include everyone who has a link to Roxie even if we know they didn't do it. It might help us make some connections we hadn't realized."

"Yeah, I know." Marlee wrote her name along the bottom of the chart plus that of her student assistant and the other nine students in Criminal Justice To Go. Hector took the red marker and drew a small heart around her name.

"Knock it off, Hector! We need to concentrate." Marlee's attempt at dismay was futile, as she realized she was smiling. Hector smiled too and put his hand on hers.

"Maybe we need a break from the chart."

"We've only been working on it for ten minutes. I don't think a break is needed just yet. We don't want to lose our momentum," Marlee chastised.

Marlee's cell phone rang just as she and Hector turned their attention back to the crime chart. It was Bethanny Hayes, the student who Donnie Stacks thought might have been harassed by Ira Green. During the short conversation, Bethanny said Green never sexually harassed her, but she thought he was really creepy and had told several people so. "I've never heard of him trying anything with any of the students, but he always made me feel creeped out, you know?" Bethanny asked.

After relaying the conversation to Hector, they again turned their attention to the crime chart. They both sat with markers poised to write down names of other suspects or people connected to the case but weren't able to think of any more. Marlee drew a large question mark and under it wrote Unknown.

"Hey, what about Pete?" Hector shouted. "You know, the guy she mentioned in her diary?" The detective jotted down the new name and nodded with satisfaction.

"Yeah. That's the only person we don't know much about. We have at least some information on everyone else on the chart. Did you print off the diary from Roxie's computer?" Marlee asked.

"I did and it's in my vehicle," Hector said as he sprang out of his chair to retrieve the documents. "I should've thought of that before."

When he returned with the pages of Roxie's diary, Marlee read each page, passing it on to Hector when she was finished. In the diary, Roxie detailed several meetings with Pete at restaurants and cafes in Elmwood. Roxie's writing consisted of only short phrases, not complete sentences. Reading her diary became tedious, as she bounced from one thought to another. Piecing together

Roxie's writing was difficult, but Marlee was able to discern that each of the meetings took place within the three weeks before her death. Prior to that time, there was no mention of Pete.

"There's not much in here about Pete. He came into the picture less than a month before Roxie was poisoned and she was seeing him a few times a week. I can't believe we haven't been able to locate this guy." Marlee jotted down some notes from Roxie's diary and then crumpled up the page and threw it away. "We're missing something and I think it's important."

"Okay, let's brainstorm. We know Pete just came into her life and they were meeting frequently. It could have been a new boyfriend. Maybe somebody she already knew from work or classes?"

"What if it was somebody who knew she was trying to re-establish contact with Violet? What if Pete was trying to help her or even trying to prevent it?" Marlee asked.

"Possible, but how would Pete know about Violet unless Roxie told him? It seems kind of far-fetched that she would just meet someone and confide everything. From what we know about Roxie, I don't think she was very trusting of others. And for good reason," Hector said.

"Maybe Pete was a counselor or a doctor." Marlee said then shook her head. "A doctor isn't going to meet someone at a restaurant a few times a week. They would meet in the doctor's office. A therapist, maybe, but I think that would be in an office setting too."

"What about a sponsor? Like for Alcoholics Anonymous or Narcotics Anonymous? There were a lot of empty alcohol bottles in Roxie's motel room when she died," Hector recalled.

"Hey, I think you may be on to something!" Marlee thumbed through the pages printed from Roxie's online diary. "It was always in the evenings when she met with

Pete. It could've been after an AA meeting. Or maybe Pete was her sponsor and that's the only time he could meet with her."

"Do you know anyone in Elmwood who goes to AA?" Hector asked.

"No, but I know several who should," Marlee said. "Even if I did, it's anonymous. They aren't supposed to reveal the identity of any of the participants or anything said there. Even if we went to all the AA meetings in town, I doubt we'd be able to get any information."

"Here's another angle," Hector said excitedly. "Roxie and Pete were at various restaurants around town so let's go show Roxie's picture around and see if the wait staff remembers her."

"Yes! And then they can give us a description of this Pete guy!"

Hector searched his files for a picture of Roxie and found one. The detective and the professor rushed to his car and set off for Apollo's, one of the eateries mentioned in Roxie's diary.

-

When in doubt, head North.

Chapter 25

Apollo's was the fanciest restaurant in Elmwood and generally saved for special occasions like anniversaries or graduations. The dark interior consisted of forest green, burgundy, and brown. Since it was lunch time, Marlee suggested they eat at Apollo's as a way of covering their investigation. Hector readily agreed. They had already stopped at two other restaurants and staff at both places couldn't recall seeing Roxie.

The hostess led them to the back room and Marlee asked if they could sit in the area secluded from most other diners. Their server was a college-aged male dressed in black pants, a black shirt, and a patterned necktie. His blond hair was short in the back and long in the front. "Hey, my name's Derek and I'll be serving you today."

Marlee ordered unsweetened ice tea and Hector followed suit. While waiting for their drinks, Hector surveyed the atmosphere. "This is a swanky place. How would Roxie have the money to come here regularly?"

"I was thinking the same thing. It's not really a place to come and just have coffee. If she was drinking again by then, there are cheaper places to go get drunk. Maybe Pete was well off."

When Derek delivered the glasses of ice tea, Hector placed the picture of Roxie on the table and pointed to it. "I'm investigating this lady's death. Do you remember seeing her in here?"

"Um, yeah. A few times. Usually at night," Derek stammered. "She's the student who died during the class, isn't she?"

Hector nodded. "Was she with someone when she came in?"

Derek nodded. "I never saw her by herself."

"Who was the other person? What did he look like?" Marlee interjected.

"I don't know who it was, but it wasn't a guy. She was with a lady, a little older than she was," Derek stated.

"Did you ever see her with a man?"

"No. Always the same lady." Derek looked confused as he took their orders and left the table.

"She must have been meeting more than one person at various restaurants," Hector said. "This complicates things even more."

Hector and Marlee enjoyed their gourmet soup and artisan sandwiches and were agonizing over whether or not to order dessert when Hector's phone rang. He excused himself and went outside to take the call. Moments later he jogged back to their table. "Come on! Burt and Connie Stone and the two girls were apprehended this morning and they'll be at the Elmwood Police Department in a few minutes." Marlee grabbed her purse, throwing cash on the table to cover the meal and the tip.

On the short ride to the PD, Hector relayed the information he received from his office. "The Stones were stopped at the border when they attempted to cross into Canada. Their passports were phony and the Canadian officials were aware of the APB out on Burt and Connie. They were taken into custody and questioned but none of them are talking. My guess is that they'll ask for lawyers as soon as I try to talk to them. My office didn't have any other details when they called."

Marlee and Hector made their way to the Elmwood Police Department and were shown into a back room. An older man in a uniform opened the door a crack and motioned for Hector to follow. Marlee was left waiting to ponder the details of the investigation. Moments later, the same older officer appeared and summoned her to follow him. Marlee joined Hector, and Burt and Connie Stone in a room with a two way mirror and audio and visual recording devices.

"I've already explained to the Stones that you wanted to be here for their interviews and they agreed," Hector said nodding at Marlee. She had to keep herself from grinning. Normally when an investigation got to this stage, the police treated her like a dog turd stuck to a shoe.

Connie and Burt Stone were clad in the same clothes Marlee previously saw them wearing when visiting their home in Mobridge. Their once ironed and well-tailored clothing looked like the items had been slept in and then put through a wind tunnel. Burt even had a tear in the sleeve of his Oxford shirt and both had underarm perspiration stains. Besides their clothes being disheveled, the Stones were a wreck. Connie's eyes were red and tear stains streaked down her face. Burt's eyes were sunken and looked ten years older. Both wore the look of despair as they stared at the table with unseeing eyes.

Hector started the interview by activating the visual and audio recording equipment, identifying himself and the others in the room, stating the date, time, and location. After he read the Stones their rights and both agreed that they understood, the questioning began.

Hector took an informal approach when initially dealing with the Stones. A gentler approach often resulted in more cooperation with some suspects. A heavy handed approach could be used later on during the interrogation, if necessary.

"Burt, Connie, I think we all know you're in quite a bit of trouble here." The Stones both nodded glumly, yet neither spoke. "First, I just want to let you know that Paula and Violet are fine. We have them in another room and they've been given some food and drinks."

That seemed to appease Burt and Connie and they both looked up from the table. "Why don't we start from the beginning?" Hector quietly asked.

Connie, although appearing the most distraught, was the first to speak. "I suppose you know everything by now. That we didn't adopt Violet legally and that we've been hiding from Roxie and my parents for nearly eighteen years."

Hector nodded, urging Connie to continue. "I know what you must think of us, but we did it all for Violet. We couldn't let her grow up with Roxie as a mother. Roxie didn't want Violet at first and even thought about an abortion. After Violet was born, Roxie was more concerned with partying and hanging out with her friends. That was no kind of life for Violet. We knew it would be a cycle of Roxie partying, then getting her act together, then drinking over and over again. My parents enabled Roxie, so they were no help in the situation." Connie looked at Hector, pleading for him to understand the plight she and Burt were in those many years ago.

Again, Hector nodded, urging her to tell the story. "So when I had an opportunity, I grabbed Roxie's identification, Violet's birth certificate, and Violet, and we took off. I was able to pose as Roxie since we looked alike. Nobody ever questioned my documents. But then we heard from Roxie and she wanted us to bring Violet back. We just couldn't allow that, so we moved again. And again. When we reached Mobridge we never heard from her any more. We thought she gave up."

Marlee saw a hole in Connie's story and spoke up. "You told us before that Roxie sent a letter from a prison. We know Roxie was never in prison."

Connie and Burt gave each other a quick look. This time, Burt spoke. "We thought you'd find our story more believable if you thought Roxie was an ex-con. Honestly, though, the way she drank and carried on, I wouldn't have been surprised if she had a prison record."

"But she didn't. As near as we can tell, Roxie battled alcoholism off and on, but was never imprisoned or even arrested." Hector jotted down some notes on a legal pad, using his left hand to shield what he was writing. "Now tell me what you were planning to do when you got Paula and Violet into Canada? When you were stopped at the border you all had passports under different names."

"We thought we'd settle in and start over. Maybe in Winnipeg. We could all get jobs and assume our new identities. It's a big enough city that we could get lost and go undetected. Plus, Canada doesn't extradite people to the United States because Canada opposes the U.S.'s use of the death penalty," said Burt.

"That's only when the offense is punishable by the death penalty. Like murder," Hector said, looking Burt straight in the eye. "Let's hear about your meeting with Roxie at the motel in Chamberlain. How did you get her to drink the poison?" Hector had switched interview tactics from gentle questioning to flat out accusations.

"No! Neither one of us had anything to do with that!" Connie shouted as she attempted to stand up before realizing she was handcuffed to the table. She flopped back onto the chair, her eyes swirling madly as she shifted her gaze from Hector, to Marlee, to Burt, and then back again.

"Look, we already know you did it. You poisoned Roxie because she'd finally found Violet and was going to tell her that she was her real mother," Hector growled, the nice guy demeanor long gone. "We already have you on kidnapping and a bunch of other charges. If you confess to poisoning Roxie, we might be able to get the prosecutor to drop the other charges."

"But we didn't do it!" Burt shouted. "We didn't!"

"Look, I understand how it could happen." Hector was back to his gentle approach. "Roxie was an unfit mother and you gave Violet a good life. You didn't want Roxie interfering, so you did what you had to do to protect your family. Most parents will do whatever it takes to keep their kids safe. I think anybody could see how this might happen."

"We didn't poison Roxie!" Connie maintained. "We didn't want her or anyone dead. We just wanted her to leave us alone. We were going to disappear into Canada and hopefully we'd never hear from her again."

"But with the Internet the world has become much, much smaller. It's easy to track down people, even when they change their names. And Roxie was persistent. She'd tracked you down before and you knew she would again," Hector replied.

"We didn't poison Roxie! And that's all we're going to say. We want a lawyer!" Connie shouted.

"Okay, this concludes the interview," Hector stood up and turned off all the recording equipment.

As Marlee and Hector proceeded to leave the interview room, Connie yelled, "And we want a lawyer for Paula and Violet too! Don't talk to them without a lawyer!"

"Both girls are legally adults, so if they want lawyers they can ask for them. It's up to them to decide if they want to talk to us," Hector said matter-of-factly as he closed the door. Connie's wailing could still be heard as they walked down the hallway to the room where Violet and Paula were being held.

Hector repeated the same spiel to Violet and Paula Stone about the interview and their rights. When both girls nodded, he continued. "Right now you're both being held for possession of phony passports and attempting to illegally enter Canada. Since you're both adults, you're being charged as such." The girls, with their light brown curly hair now frizzy and out of control, looked at each other. They too were wearing the same clothes Marlee had seen them in during their last visits.

Paula broke down and began to cry. "All we wanted was to be left alone! We just wanted things to go back to normal like they were."

Violet stared blankly at Paula, then the others in the room, as if struggling to comprehend the situation.

"Violet, do you know what's going on? Do you know why you were going to Canada?" Marlee asked her student who was still in shock.

"We had to leave South Dakota," Violet squeaked.

Paula interrupted, "We didn't want to upset Violet!"

"So she doesn't know the truth?" asked Marlee.

Paula shook her head from side to side. She was deflated, knowing the big secret kept by their family was about to be spilled.

"Violet, Connie Stone isn't your mother. She's your aunt. Connie and Roxie Harper were sisters. Roxie is your birth mother. Connie and Burt stole you away from Roxie when you were just a baby," Hector said with a gentle tone.

After a long pause, Violet looked Hector straight in the eye and said, "I know."

I knew people who believed their own lies. That's the sign of a pathological liar and they're the ones who tend to be the most successful.

Chapter 26

"What?" Paula shrieked. "Mom and Dad didn't kidnap Violet. They adopted her so she would have a better life since Roxie was such a mess."

"No, they kidnapped her." Hector looked up at Violet. "But you already knew?"

Violet nodded. "Roxie told me everything. How my Mom and Dad had taken me away and hid me. How they kept the secret all these years."

"When did Roxie tell you?" Marlee asked.

"On Monday night," Violet said.

"Were you in her room?" Marlee asked

"No, I talked to her outside. It was late and Johnny and Paula were asleep. I couldn't sleep so I slipped outside to walk around a bit. Roxie was drunk and standing outside her room. She was talking nonsense and I tried to get away from her. Then she started talking about being my real mother. I didn't know what to think. I thought she was just drunk and crazy, but she showed me some pictures of me as a baby and she was holding me. I didn't know what to think, so I just went back to my room. I didn't sleep all night."

"Did you poison Roxie?" Hector interjected.

"No! I would never..."

"Why would she do that? It doesn't make any sense!" Paula shouted.

"Maybe to make sure your family wasn't disrupted. So that Connie and Burt wouldn't get into trouble for kidnapping you," Hector suggested, nodding toward Violet.

"No, I didn't poison Roxie. I didn't have any reason to. I wasn't even sure if she really was my mother. I wanted to talk to mom, uh Connie, first to see what she had to say."

"Did you talk to Connie that night?" Marlee asked.

"No, but I talked to dad. I told him what Roxie said and he called her a liar," Violet stated.

"How did you know for sure that you were the baby in the picture Roxie showed you of her holding a baby?" Hector asked.

"Because I was wearing a pink bunny suit, with ears. We have several baby pictures of me wearing that same outfit," Violet said.

"So you were fairly certain that Roxie was telling the truth after she showed you the picture?" Hector inquired.

"I was shocked and at first I didn't believe it, but the more I thought about it that night, I started to believe it. Then I called dad and he said it wasn't true," Violet said.

"How much of this did you know?" Hector asked Paula.

"I didn't know Roxie talked to Violet. I didn't know Violet already found out she was Roxie's child," Paula said.

"Maybe you overheard this conversation between Roxie and Violet and you decided to get rid of Roxie so she wouldn't wreck your family," Hector said accusingly to Paula.

"No, I swear I didn't. I didn't even know Violet left the room. I'm a sound sleeper," Paula insisted.

"Violet, why didn't you tell the officers about this on Monday morning when you learned Roxie was dead?" Hector asked. "You've been lying to me from the beginning."

"I didn't want to get anyone in trouble," Violet mumbled, tears now streaming down her face.

"Who did you think you'd get in trouble?" Hector asked.

"Mom and Dad," Violet whispered.

"You think your Mom and Dad killed Roxie?" Hector leaned in closer toward Violet.

"I don't think they did, but... it would make sense..." Violet was sobbing again and choking her words out between gasps.

"Did your parents tell you they met with Roxie on Monday night?" Marlee asked.

"No. They never said anything about meeting with her." Violet was regaining her composure and was able to talk in complete sentences without crying.

"When you met with Roxie, did she say anything about being scared of someone or worried about something?" Marlee asked.

"No. She just showed me the picture and told me I was her real daughter. Then I ran off."

"Did you say anything to Roxie that would upset her?" Hector asked.

"No. Why?"

"I know why. You think Roxie was upset when Violet didn't immediately accept her as her real mother.

Then that pushed her over the edge and caused her to poison herself." Paula glared at the detective. "Violet isn't responsible for Roxie's death in any way. None of us are! Why aren't you looking for the real killer instead of harassing our family?"

"You're right," Hector conceded. "We still don't know for sure that Roxie's death was a murder and not a suicide. We're still waiting on testing from the lab for a final determination."

Paula nodded, still shooting daggers at Hector as he asked additional questions. When it became clear that Paula and Violet either could not or would not offer up any additional information, the questioning came to a close.

As Marlee stood, she thought of one non-related detail that could be put into place right now. "Which one of you is seeing Johnny Marble? Romantically."

Paula and Violet both looked at each other, deciding whether to lie or come clean.

"I am," said Violet, hesitantly.

"Why did you lie about it?" Marlee asked in her best non-accusatory tone.

"I don't know. It didn't seem like anybody's business but ours," Violet said.

"Did you know?" Marlee raised her eyebrows as she looked at Paula.

"Yeah, I knew."

"And Johnny knew you two and your parents were fleeing to Canada didn't he?" Hector asked.

The Stone girls both nodded, neither looking at Marlee or the detective.

"When he left voicemail messages for you he sent you a hint that the cops were after you, right?" Marlee asked. Hector raised his eyebrows, wondering how Marlee knew this.

"Yeah. Our code word was abracadabra, and he was supposed to say it if the cops were questioning him about us," Paula said.

"So Johnny knew you were going to Canada. Did he know about Burt and Connie taking Violet from Roxie when she was a baby?" Hector asked.

"I told him everything that night when I got back to the room. I couldn't sleep and I finally woke him up and told him what Roxie told me," Violet mumbled.

"And were you in on the conversation too?" Hector asked Paula.

"No, I was asleep in the other bed. I took an allergy pill after drinking alcohol and was out like a light," Paula said. "I didn't hear anything from the time I went to bed until I woke up the next morning."

"One last thing," Hector said before he walked out the door. "Do you know a guy that hung around with Roxie? His name is Pete." Both girls indicated that they did not.

After Marlee and Hector left Violet and Paula Stone, Hector asked, "How did you know one of the Stone girls was seeing Johnny?"

"I didn't know for sure, but suspected it and then when Violet confirmed it, I knew he was helping them get away," Marlee said. "I think we need to talk to Johnny again to see what he can tell us."

"Yeah, I already had one of the patrol units pick him up. He's in another interview room waiting. I don't know how much we'll get from him. One thing I've learned about these so-called nice kids is that they're all very sophisticated liars!"

If it looks like a duck and quacks like a duck and smells like a duck, then most likely it's a duck.

Chapter 27

Johnny Marble sat slouched in the interview room. He tried to appear nonchalant, but his tapping foot betrayed his true feelings. He was dressed in jeans shorts, a plain blue t-shirt, and brown sandals. The hickies on his neck were now a sickly green color as they faded. He wore a heavy splash of cologne that overtook the jailhouse stench.

Hector took a different approach in interviewing Johnny than he had with the Stone girls. He pulled his chair up right next to Johnny, so close that they were almost touching. Hector leaned in toward Johnny, who sat up straight in an attempt to regain some personal space. "Look here, you little punk. You've been lying to me from the start. I know all about you and Violet being lovey-dovey. She told us you knew about Roxie being her mother and that you tried to help the Stones escape to Canada. Right now you're looking at several different criminal charges and a long time in prison, so you need to tell us everything you know right now!"

Johnny paused, looking from Hector to Marlee. After what seemed an eternity he said, "I want a lawyer." The student then folded his arms across his chest and looked away, a small, smug smile creeping to his lips.

Hector stormed out of the interview room and Marlee followed behind. "Damn it! I was hoping we could get something from this kid!" Hector's frustration was contagious as Marlee also thought Johnny could reveal new information or at least poke holes in the stories the Stones were telling.

"Me too. He has a lot to say. We just need to figure out how to get him to talk."

Hector found a quiet place in the police station for the two of them to discuss the case. "Let's talk about what we know now."

"Burt and Connie both have a motive for killing Roxie, but now Violet, Paula, and Johnny all have motives too. Plus, each of them have lied to us on more than one occasion," Marlee summarized.

"True and they might all be in on it. Or one of them killed Roxie and the others are all covering for them," Hector said.

"There's something about Johnny that keeps bothering me. I don't know what it is. It's like my subconscious knows but I can't access it," Marlee said.

"Sounds like a Psychology 101 topic," Hector teased.

"It does, doesn't it?" Marlee laughed, thinking back to the class she took her freshman year of college.

"Burt and Connie asked for a lawyer, so we can't talk to them anymore right now. Same for Johnny. Violet and Paula didn't ask for a lawyer, so we can keep talking to them, but I'd like to let them sit for a while. Waiting and not knowing what's going on will turn up the pressure on them to talk even more," Hector said. "Let's go back to your house and look at the crime chart again."

As they were getting in the car to leave, Marlee shouted, "Wait! Johnny's the one who hit me on the head! I'm one hundred percent positive!"

"How do you know?" Hector quizzed.

"I remember the smell of his cologne. The person who hit me was wearing the same type of cologne Johnny wears. That can't be a coincidence!"

The pair strode back into the interview room where Johnny sat, awaiting his legal representation to arrive. "Johnny, I know you asked for a lawyer and we're not going to ask you any more questions. Dr. McCabe just had something she wanted to say to you," Hector said.

"Johnny, I know you hit me in the back of the head when I was outside my house on Saturday night. I know it was you because I remember the smell of your cologne. The same cologne you're wearing now." Marlee looked at Johnny and he looked away.

Hector and Marlee paused, waiting for Johnny to speak. When they'd given up hope and moved toward the door, Johnny said, "Wait. I'll talk."

When the bird begins to sing, all will hear his tune.

Chapter 28

"You agree to talk to us without your lawyer present?" Hector asked after he'd activated the recording equipment in the room. Johnny nodded his assent.

When Johnny began to speak, his voice wavered and his eyes were teary. "You're right. It was me. I'm so sorry, Dr. M. I didn't mean to hurt you. I just wanted you to stop chasing Violet and her family. Knocking you out was the only way I could get you to stop investigating them for a bit. They just needed to get to Canada and they'd be fine."

Even though Marlee felt Johnny's words were sincere, she thought the tears and the unsteady voice were staged. "You realize you could've seriously hurt me or even killed me?" She stared the student down, letting him know she was in no mood for any more of his bullshit.

Johnny nodded. "I'm sorry. I don't know what else to say. I was desperate and did the only thing I could think of. I had a bat in my car and I just grabbed it and hid alongside your house."

"Did you assault Dr. McCabe because you poisoned Roxie?" Hector was straight forward, eschewing the good cop role altogether.

"No! I never spent any time alone with Roxie!" Johnny howled.

"We know it was either you, Paula, Violet, or their parents who killed Roxie. Who was it?" Hector growled.

"I don't know who did it. I don't think any of them did," Johnny mumbled.

"You're an accessory to murder, Johnny-Boy. By helping the Stones escape to Canada, you helped them avoid prosecution for murder. You'll be looking at almost as much time as they are unless you tell us everything right now!" Hector shouted, bits of spittle flying in Johnny's face.

"I don't know anything about Roxie's murder. No one told me anything! That's the truth!" Johnny yelled, jumping out of the chair.

The door to the interrogation room opened and in walked a short, rotund woman in a red dress. "I'm representing Mr. Marble and I'd like a moment with my client," she said. "And I don't want anyone talking to him without me present."

Hector and Marlee left the room. "What do you think about Johnny?" Hector asked.

"I think he was overacting about how bad he felt about hurting me. I believe some of what he said, though. I really don't think he poisoned Roxie, but he might know which of the Stones did."

"I think he's in this up to his ears," Hector said. "If one of the Stones killed Roxie, and I think they did, then Johnny knows who it was."

The remainder of the afternoon was spent talking to the attorneys representing Burt and Connie Stone and Johnny Marble. None of them would allow Hector to talk to their clients without them present. Neither Paula nor Violet had asked for a lawyer, so Marlee and Hector met with them again. Both young women stuck to their stories, maintaining they knew nothing of Roxie's death. Since they were at an impasse, Marlee suggested they go back to her house to relax a bit and talk about the case.

Once back at Marlee's house, she found the message light blinking on her home phone. The first message was from Weight Watchers, reminding her that her winter flab wouldn't go away unless she joined their program. "Frickin' Weight Watchers!" Marlee yelled at her phone to Hector's amusement.

The second message was from Ira Green. "McCabe! Call me back!"

Marlee rolled her eyes as she dialed Green's number. "It's me. What do you want?" Marlee asked in a clipped tone. She wasn't in the mood to put up with him and his antics today.

"I called for a status report," Green stated.

"What? A status report? As in you want to know what I've found out?" Marlee was stunned. The former dean was still acting like her boss. Just as she was about to explode, she heard a woman's voice in the background. "Who's there with you, Ira? Marlee asked.

"Petra came back from Florida. She called me and we talked. We're getting back together," Green stated.

Then to his wife he said, "Isn't that right, Pete?"

You can't unring a bell
You can't uncast a spell
You can't unfart a smell
My AA group liked my poem. My poetry professor, not
so much.

Chapter 29

"Oh. My. God," Marlee whispered.

"What's that, McCabe? I didn't hear you," Green said.

"Um, you said you and Pete were going to get back together? You call your wife Pete?"

"Yeah, it's her nickname. She's had it since childhood. Guess her dad wanted a boy," the former dean said with a chuckle.

"Look, I can't talk right now. Where are you at?" Marlee asked.

"Pete and I are in the basement of Scobey Hall. In the lounge where I've been hiding out for the last week. Why?"

"No reason. I'll call you back shortly, okay?" Marlee said before hanging up the phone.

She turned and faced Hector. "Pete is Petra Green, Ira's wife. Pete is her nickname. She's the person Roxie referenced in her online diary. That's why the waiter at

Apollo's said he only saw Roxie with a woman. It was Petra." Marlee relayed the Greens' location to Hector and they took off for the MSU campus.

Marlee had a key to Scobey Hall since her office was once housed in that building. She'd neglected to return the key when her department moved to a new location, an oversight she now appreciated. The recently-vacant Scobey Hall was the ideal hiding place for the displaced dean and his wife, Petra. Since the building was no longer in use and would be demolished shortly, no one set foot in the rickety old structure anymore.

After arriving on campus, Marlee used her key to gain entry to Scobey Hall. Although the building was vacant, the electricity was still on. The lights in the stairwells and hallways remained on permanently, so finding their way to the basement lounge was easy. They approached the lounge, taking care to be as quiet as they could. Whoever had the element of surprise held the upper hand. As they neared the lounge, the voices of Ira Green and his wife could be overheard. Marlee and Hector hung back to listen.

"Never in a million years would I have thought you'd do something like this!" barked Ira Green.

"I never in a million years thought I'd have to. Don't put this all on me. You're the one that brought it on," Petra Green shot back.

"You knew I loved Roxie and was going to leave you. That's why you killed her!"

"We had a deal," Petra said with an eerie calmness. "You were free to see whomever you liked as long as you didn't parade them in front of me and it didn't get serious. You broke our agreement and that's why the rules of the game changed."

"But to kill her? Nothing Roxie or I ever did justifies that! We're done! I'm calling the police and then filing for divorce!" Ira's voice was still booming, but it held a level of sadness which was rare for the crass and grumpy former dean.

Marlee and Hector looked at each other from their hiding spots outside the lounge. Their mouths were agape as they made sense of the conversation they were overhearing. Petra killed Roxie because she knew Ira was in love with Roxie and wanted to be with her, thus leaving Petra cast aside.

TING TINKLE TING! At this inopportune time, Marlee's key slipped from her hand and bounced twice before landing on the hard surfaced floor.

"What's that? Who's there?" Petra shouted with suspicion.

"Probably just the pipes. It's an old building. It'll be torn down soon," Green said.

Hector and Marlee looked at each other and nodded. They chose this time to confront Ira and Petra to determine what really happened to Roxie. Taking a deep breath, they entered the lounge and came face to face with Roxie's killer.

"It's us," Marlee said. "You told me where you were and we came over to talk."

"Why? I hope nobody sees you here," Ira spat, worried that the professor and the detective had advertised his hiding spot.

Hector, with his gun at his side was the first to speak to Petra. "We heard your conversation. We know you killed Roxie because you thought Ira was leaving you."

Petra looked at the floor, then at Hector, deciding whether to lie or come clean. She gave a loud sigh and recounted the events surrounding Roxie's murder. "I'll tell you everything. My life is over anyway. I overheard a phone conversation between Ira and someone who I later found out was Roxie. He was telling her how much he loved her and that he wanted to get rid of me so they could be together. He was laughing when he said it. Like I didn't matter anymore. I followed him around campus and figured out who Roxie was and then I followed her around until I was able to meet with her."

"Didn't Ira see you on campus?" Marlee asked, incredulous that the former dean wouldn't notice his wife following him around the small university.

"I wore a disguise. I minored in theater in college and worked with costumes and makeup," Petra said.

"It's true," Ira said nodding. "She can completely transform herself."

"Are her disguises better than the one you wore to Easy Street on Saturday night?" Marlee asked Ira, recalling his ridiculous getup.

"That wasn't really a disguise," Ira said.

"I was there. At Easy Street when you met," Petra said. "I was sitting at a table in the back dressed like an old farmer. None of you even noticed."

Marlee's jaw dropped. She remembered seeing an old farmer dressed in overalls and a John Deere baseball cap that night at the bar. "That was you?"

"It was me. And I overheard everything you said," Petra said in a crisp tone.

"Getting back to Roxie, how did you meet up with her and gain her confidence?" Hector asked.

"I followed her to an AA meeting in the Methodist Church basement and went in. Over the next two weeks I made it a point to sit next to Roxie and then began chatting her up. She was lonely and opened up to me when she found out I had a history of alcohol abuse too. I really don't, but I guess I put on a good enough act that she believed it. That theater minor has paid for itself over the years. Then we started getting together after the meetings to chat. She'd been sober for nearly twelve years and was proud of it. Roxie loved Coke and I'm a coffee drinker, so we'd go out for non-alcoholic drinks and pie. We always had pie after the AA meetings," Petra recalled.

"What did Roxie tell you about Ira?" Marlee asked.

"She told me how she met Ira back when she was a student and had a fling with him. She also told me about their baby that was stolen by a relative and how she had tracked the child down and needed Ira's help to talk to their child. Roxie always denied that she had romantic intentions toward Ira, but I knew better. She seemed like the scheming type to go after any guy she wanted. I knew I had to put a stop to things," Petra said.

"What did you do?" Hector asked, relaxing his hold on the gun at his side.

"First, I started spiking Roxie's Coke with small amounts of vodka. When she went to the restroom I took a syringe I filled with vodka and emptied it into her Coke. It was such a small amount that she didn't even notice it. But her body knew it was alcohol. After spiking her drink a few times that week, Roxie was off the wagon and binge drinking again," Petra recounted.

"But just getting her to drink again wasn't enough was it?" Marlee asked.

"I thought it would be at first, but I just knew she would try to steal my husband. She still denied having feelings for him, but I knew better. We went to her apartment one night after the AA meeting and talked. I broke in the day before the prison tour class started and put a few drops of anti-freeze in each of the twenty-ounce plastic Coke bottles in her refrigerator. They had twist off caps so I really tightened them up after I put the poison in. Anti-freeze has a sweet taste, so she wouldn't even notice it in her soda. I thought that would take care of her, but she was so busy drinking alcohol that she wasn't drinking as much Coke."

"Did you find any Coke bottles in Roxie's car or room when you searched them?" Marlee asked Hector.

"Yeah. There was a half empty bottle in the cup holder in her car and an overturned Coke bottle in the motel room. There was a small cooler filled with Cokes in the motel room. She could've brought them from home or bought them while on the road," Hector said.

"I'm guessing Roxie ingested some of the poisoned Coke while driving to Pierre on Monday. That would account for her irrational behavior at the Women's Prison and then later on at the pool in Chamberlain," Marlee surmised.

Hector nodded in agreement. "She was drinking again by then, so she may have had some alcohol in her system too. If she was drinking vodka, you wouldn't be able to smell it on her breath."

Hector turned again to Petra. "Tell us about meeting Roxie on Monday night at the motel in Chamberlain."

"Roxie called me on my cell. I was honestly surprised she was still alive. She was drunk and said she'd met with her daughter and told her everything and then the daughter ran off. She didn't know what to do. Ira had been there to talk to her before that and she told him to go away. It was well after midnight when I met up with Roxie in her motel room. She'd switched from beer to mixed drinks. Jack Daniels and Coke, I think that was what she was drinking. I knew she was drinking one of the poisoned Cokes because she was completely out of her mind, shouting nonsense. I tried to get her to drink more Coke, but she knocked it out of my hand and slapped me. We wrestled around until I got her on the bed and held her down by her neck. She calmed down a bit and I convinced her to drink some Coke without alcohol...to sober up. After she drank most of a bottle of Coke, she passed out and then went into convulsions and then...just drifted off. I felt her pulse later and she was dead. Then I left. I drove my rental car back to the motel where I was staying here in Elmwood. I've been there ever since."

"You weren't in Florida with your sister? Pete, you lied to me!" Ira asked, as if that deception was the worst act Petra committed.

"You needed a little time to think about things. I knew you'd be ready to get back together after Roxie was gone. I'm the one you love. Me!" Petra shouted pointing a long slim finger at her heart.

"Petra, I don't think Roxie loved Ira. I think she just wanted his help in talking to Violet. At most, she wanted friendship from him, but he ruined that. Did Ira tell you that Roxie filed a sexual harassment claim against him at MSU?" Hector said.

"What? No, I didn't... I didn't know. So, she didn't love him? They weren't going to set up house with the little brat they produced?" Petra's eyes darted from Hector to Ira, searching for answers.

"Ira wanted to divorce you and be with Roxie, but Roxie had no interest in him. He told me he would stay with you since Roxie died." Marlee didn't relish breaking Petra's heart, but she needed to know Ira's true intentions or she'd pine away for that old fart for the rest of her life.

Petra collapsed to the floor, one hand over her mouth as she struggled to suppress a scream. Hector hoisted Petra to her feet and placed her in handcuffs as he read her the *Miranda* rights. As the detective escorted her out of the basement lounge, Petra turned to her husband and shouted, "You! You're the poison!"

Tears streamed down her face as Hector led her away.

Just when you think everything is all well and fine... the shit hits the fan.

Chapter 30

Petra signed a full confession and was charged with first degree murder. She was booked into the Elmwood jail for the night but would make her initial court appearance the following day in Chamberlain since that's where Roxie ingested the fatal dose of poison. Since Ira hadn't committed any actual crimes, other than being a complete and total jerk, he was released after further questioning at the police station.

Burt and Connie Stone were booked on charges of kidnapping, using false documents, and numerous other charges relating to their actions seventeen years ago and the recent efforts to keep them buried. They remained in jail pending a court hearing which would be held later on Monday. If Marlee were to hazard a guess, the Stones wouldn't be getting out of jail anytime soon. Paula and Violet Stone were charged with using fake passports since they knowingly tried to enter Canada under false pretenses. They were held overnight in the jail, but Marlee suspected they would be released after making their initial court appearances.

Johnny Marble was charged with aggravated assault for knocking Marlee unconscious. He was also held in the Elmwood jail pending a court appearance. Because of Roxie's death, Violet's kidnapping, and the subsequent steps to cover up both offenses, six people now sat in the local jail awaiting their days in court.

It was into the early hours of Monday morning when Marlee and Hector arrived back at her house. "Wow, I can't believe how that all came together today!" Marlee exclaimed as she flopped down on her overstuffed couch.

"I would've bet money that Ira did it," Hector said as he sat next to her on the couch.

"My money was on Burt and Connie Stone," Marlee said, barely suppressing a yawn. "I have the last day of Criminal Justice To Go in a few hours. Luckily, we'll only be meeting for a bit and then I can come home and take a nap. I'm so tired I can barely stay awake." "Me too," Hector said through a yawn.

BANG BANG BANG!

Marlee jumped from the couch to her feet. She and Hector had fallen asleep on the couch but he was nowhere to be seen. The morning light was shining through the living room windows.

BANG BANG BANG!

What the hell is that noise? Marlee rubbed her eyes and looked around. Then she remembered her doorbell only worked part of the time. Someone was at the door. Marlee smiled. *Probably Hector with some breakfast and coffee for us. I could get used to this...*

Marlee flung open the door, ready with a smart ass comment for Hector. But it wasn't Hector. It was Vince Chipperton, with his brother Spud and a grumpy looking female in her late twenties.

"Uh, Vince. What are you doing here?" Marlee asked.

"This is our cousin, Shari. She's been staying with us while her apartment is being painted. She and Spud have something they want to tell you," Vince said, pushing Spud up closer to the door.

"Uh, hi, Marlee," said Spud with a smarmy grin. "You're never going to believe this. Shari and I decided to play a little trick on you."

"No we didn't," said Shari. "It was Spud's idea and I just went along with it so he wouldn't tell Vince that I smoked marijuana at their house."

"You know I could lose my job for that, don't you?" Vince said, giving Shari the evil eye.

"It was just once. Anyway, when you called, I acted like I was Vince's old girlfriend so you'd think they were back together," Shari said nodding toward Marlee.

"Why in the hell would you do that?" Marlee asked.

"Because Spud wanted you and Vince to break up so he could date you," Shari said with a matter of fact tone.

"Yeah, right! Like that would ever happen," Marlee said with a disgusted look at Spud. "I'd rather kiss a toilet seat than go on a date with him!"

"Hey, now..." Spud sputtered. That was not the reaction he'd expected.

"So I didn't cheat on you with Suzanne or anyone else. It was these two knuckleheads who made you think I'd dumped you," said Vince. "Can we please just get together tonight after work and talk about all of this? I don't want to break up. I wanted to talk to you about moving in together after you came back from your class trip, but then all this happened..."

Hector rounded the corner from the bathroom wearing a towel around his waist, fresh from a shower.

"What's going on?"

Afterword

Petra Green was sentenced to life in prison. She accepted the plea deal offered by the prosecution so she wouldn't face the death penalty. At the sentencing hearing, she never offered any remorse for poisoning Roxie. Petra's statement to the court dealt only with her justification for the murder; to keep her marriage intact. When investigators searched her motel room and car, they found multiple wigs, an array of disguises, and a variety of makeup. She admitted that for the years she lived in Elmwood, she left home every day, usually dressed as someone else.

What puzzled Marlee and Hector was how Ira Green was able to drive all over Elmwood and not be noticed. During the last interview, Ira confessed that he'd stashed his car in Della Halter's garage. Ira suspected he was going to be terminated when he had his final meeting with the MSU President, so he grabbed a few personnel files on the faculty. He approached Della immediately after he left MSU and they struck a deal. He could lodge his car in her garage and also borrow her oversized SUV with tinted windows. In exchange, Ira would hand over Della's personnel file to her. Ira Green stuck to his end of the deal and wouldn't divulge the information in Della's file, no matter how much Marlee pleaded with him. Reuben Ira Green left Elmwood, destination unknown. One thing was for sure; he'd land another job at a

BRENDA DONELAN

university under a variation of his own name. Then he'd be free to resume sexually harassing young women on campus.

Connie and Burt Stone both pled guilty in federal court to kidnapping and in exchange, the other charges against them were dropped. Since the kidnapping had extended for seventeen years and spanned several states, the case fell under federal jurisdiction. Both Stones were sentenced to eight years in prison, a lesser amount than Marlee expected. What worked in Burt and Connie's favor was that Violet testified on their behalf, saying she didn't fault them for what they did all those years ago. Violet believed she had a better life because of Burt and Connie's actions than if she had remained in the care of her birth mother, Roxie Harper.

Violet and Paula Stone were both placed on probation for providing false information to law enforcement. All other charges against them were dropped. Johnny Marble wasn't so lucky. His admission to assaulting Marlee with a baseball bat garnered him sixty days in county jail to be followed by three years of community supervision. The three students returned to MSU to further their education in the fall. Since they all had criminal convictions now, they switched their majors. A conviction was a major stumbling block in getting a job in the criminal justice field, so they changed their majors to other areas in which they could find employment upon graduation.

Marlee, who was usually unattached, found herself in the middle of a love triangle. She started a relationship with Hector when under the assumption that Vince was cheating on her. When that proved untrue, Marlee had some tough decisions to make. Her love life was in turmoil, but for once her career was soaring. Her teaching contract at MSU was renewed, giving her full-time

322

employment until May of 2007. Plus, she was able to apply for tenure during the next year, which would provide her with guaranteed employment at MSU, barring any major violations like bringing a hand grenade to class, or slugging a fellow professor in the gut.

I tracked down Violet about a year before she started classes at MSU. I knew there was no way I could go undetected in a small town like Mobridge, so I rented an apartment and started college at MSU. Paula was already attending college there and I hoped Violet would follow suit. When she did, I was ecstatic! I'd finally found my daughter and would be able to talk to her. To tell her what happened and why I wasn't in her life while she grew up. I wanted to let her know that I'd been sober for nearly twelve years and would have my college degree in another two years. Mostly, I just wanted to talk to her and find out everything about her. Her favorite color, her favorite foods, all the things a mother should know about her child.

As soon as I talked to Violet I was going to report everything I knew about Burt and Connie to the police. Over the years I'd enlisted law enforcement, social services, and anyone else I could to help me find Violet. No one was of any help at all. I had to do it all on my own because no one cared. By the time I tracked them to Mobridge, I knew I'd handle it my own way. Burt and Connie were going to pay for all my missed years with Violet.

When I met up with Reuben Ira Green on campus, I was shocked. He didn't know about Violet, but agreed to help me talk to her. At first, I enjoyed his friendship since

I didn't know anyone else on campus. Then he came on really strong; touching me, and trying to kiss me. I told him fifty times that I didn't want to have a romantic relationship with him of any type, but he wouldn't listen. When he grabbed me at the library, that was the last straw. I filed a sexual harassment complaint against him so he would leave me alone. Then he threatened not to help me talk to Violet. Unless I recanted the sexual harassment claim and helped him get his job back at MSU.

Meeting Pete at AA was a godsend. Finally, someone I could talk to and confide in. I had no idea she was playing me for a fool. And I never suspected she would kill me. If I were still alive, I'd like to think that Violet and I would have reconnected and were able to have a real mother-daughter bond.

But now that can never happen...

Did You Enjoy This Book?

Reviews are the most important way to get my books noticed by other mystery lovers. If you've enjoyed this book I would love for you to leave a review on the book's Amazon page. The review can be as brief or as detailed as you like.

Without reviews from readers like you, my books will be less visible on Amazon. Honest reviews of my books help bring them to the attention of other mystery lovers.

Thank you so much!

Acknowledgements

Many thanks to everyone who supported me during the writing of Murder To Go. I appreciate the pep talks and wise suggestions from what I call "The Four Fs"; family, friends, fans, and fellow writers. A special word of thanks goes to my beta reader, Stacy Jundt. Her careful reading of my manuscript and thoughtful critiques helped me to improve my writing. Alastair Stephens is also to be credited for his patience and diligence in editing my book.

Murder To Go would be without a name were it not for Rhoda Smith. She suggested the title, which I think fits perfectly with the theme of the book. Thanks, Rhoda!

A big thank you goes out to my mother, Patty Donelan. She is the best salesperson I know. Mom has been instrumental in selling my paperbacks to family, friends, people at the Senior Citizen Center, the men and women in her coffee group, the doctor who performed her cataract surgery, the car salesman where my parents bought their new vehicle, and a whole host of other unsuspecting victims.

Samantha Lund Hillmer and I met in the fall of 1986 when we became roommates in Young Hall at South Dakota State University. Fast forward almost thirty years and my longtime friend is now the designer of my book covers and my website. I also want to recognize Aimintang for the cover photography, courtesy of iStock.

I appreciate the help provided by one of my former students, Marissa Mickelson. She was kind enough to give me information about her home town of Mobridge, SD, which is featured in this book.

Finally, I am ever grateful for National Novel Writing Month (NaNoWriMo). A portion of Murder To Go was written during the Fall 2014 Nanowrimo program.

About The Author

Brenda Donelan is a life-long resident of South Dakota. She grew up on a cattle ranch in Stanley County, attended college in Brookings, and worked in Aberdeen as a probation officer and later as a college professor. Currently, she resides in Sioux Falls.

Murder To Go is the third book in the University Mystery Series. Brenda is currently working on the fourth book, Art of Deception.

The author can be reached by email at brendadonelanauthor@gmail.com. For more information on Brenda Donelan, books in the University Mystery Series, and tour dates, check out her website at brendadonelan.com or find her on Facebook at Brenda Donelan–Author.

Also by Brenda Donelan

Day Of The Dead

When a college professor is found dead on campus, rumors and innuendo begin to swirl at Midwestern State University. The police department and the university are mysteriously secretive about the professor's background and the ongoing investigation. Marlee McCabe, a professor of Criminology, is unwittingly pulled into the investigation leading her to question the integrity of the police department and her university. Despite warnings, Marlee uncovers information on the professor's death, making her the next target of someone who has nothing left to lose.

Holiday Homicide

Criminology professor Marlee McCabe is thrust into a criminal investigation when a janitor is murdered at Midwestern State University. Marlee's sleuthing leads her to the Lake Traverse Indian Reservation and into the dangerous underworld of trafficking Native American artifacts and sacred cultural items. Those involved are not afraid to use threats, violence, and even murder to keep their secrets buried. What will they do to keep Marlee from exposing the truth?

Art Of Deception

A million-dollar antique is stolen from an art show in Elmwood and Professor Marlee McCabe jumps into the investigation when her cousin, Bridget, is arrested and thrown in jail. Marlee steadfastly defends her cousin until secret details of Bridget's life call that loyalty into question. As Marlee struggles between dedication to family and the pursuit of justice, she is forced to make decisions which may destroy the rest of her life.

Fatal Footsteps

Get ready for a wild ride as Criminology Professor Marlee McCabe looks back to her earliest adventure as an amateur detective. It's 1987, the time of acid wash jeans and big, permed hair. When a college dorm mate is found dead in the snow outside a party house, Marlee puts her newly-learned Criminology knowledge to use as she strives to find out who killed the co-ed and why. The more involved Marlee and her roommate become in the investigation, the more deadly it becomes for them and their friends. As the body count rises, Marlee fears she's next on the killer's hit list.

Made in the USA
Monee, IL
20 October 2023

44900335R00184